PLANETARY FEEDLOT

E. R. Cook

To David: for showing me how to dream again

AUTHOR'S NOTE

This is a complete work of fiction, so any relation to actual people, places, actions or anything is pure coincidence. But the greatest fiction also makes you wonder if there isn't just a little truth in it.

This book was born from a question as I listened to a song with an audio clip. It was born from countless B movies and monster movies that I've devoured throughout my lifetime. It was born from all the fantasy books and science fiction I've dived into, the stories that took me so far beyond my little farm in Iowa as a child and taught me to dream bigger and ask questions. It was born from a dream of having a story that someone else wanted to read and putting that story down on paper.

This story might be pretty dark for some people. It's a dive not only into a conspiracy, it's a dive into humanity and asks the question: is darkness just a human thing?

So sit back, grab some popcorn and prepare for the ride.

1

***

Captain Heather Smith's heels clicked sharply against the concrete floor as she rushed to keep up with Colonel Holloway as he strode down the hallway. "Another summons?"

Colonel Eugene R. Holloway was a hard-bitten survivor of the military machine. His chiseled face, gray hair and deeply lined face spoke of the wars he had fought throughout his long career, both literally and politically. On the surface, he was a strict master who demanded the highest standards from his subordinates. Underneath, he loathed the restrictions. Rumor spoke that his constant coloring outside of the lines had cost him a promotion to General.

He did not turn, but looked at her out of the corner of his eye. "His Majesty is unhappy."

Heather had met "His Majesty" six months ago after being transferred from the Pentagon to D69, the code name for this facility. She had come in as one of the Army's top facilitators, meaning she handled everything from shipping logistics to media blackouts. Heather had earned her reputation as a flawless cleaner, but after that meeting, she wasn't sure she was up to this job. Still, she had never been one to back down from a fight, and this was not the time to start.

Heather's nervous anticipation grew as they walked down the long, narrow hallway to a secure door. The

Colonel punched a code into the keypad, scanning his palm and then his retina, the keypad beeping and turning green. As it did, the door slid open, revealing darkness. He stepped forward without hesitation.

Heather drew in a breath, stepping into the darkened interior. Humid, fetid air slapped her in the face. The door closed behind her; the click echoing through the room like the locks in a prison.

The room was completely dark save for a single brilliant light that shone down on an occupied golden throne on top of a stage, a multitude of steps leading down to the ground. A single runner of red carpet stretched from the stage towards the door. She knew 'he' liked dramatics, wanting to intimidate any who approached him. It didn't work on her; she had seen enough royalty in her day. What did work was the creature that sat upon the throne. She watched as the Colonel strode down the runner, bending his knee before the throne. Heather stayed in the darkness by the door, trying to make herself as small as possible.

"You are late." An eel-slick voice hissed across the open air, the creature's English accented sharply as alien lips formed the words.

Heather instinctively froze, like a rabbit before a fox.

The Colonel stood there, bowed and frozen before the throne. "Forgive me, my Lord."

Avar glared down at him. A reptilian hide covered his enormous body, the scales changing color from blue to black as the creature shifted in the light. Red eyes blazed as a forked tongue flicked out to taste the air. Muscles flexed and clenched as he moved, every gesture normal yet radiating his coiled power and strength. He grinned at the Colonel, exposing a row of silver teeth that glinted in the artificial light like silver daggers.

He growled, "Delays can be dangerous to one's health. Right, Beren?"

Another creature stepped out of the shadows. Heather could see this one stood over ten feet tall. He wore leather armor strapped to his shoulders and forearms, with a belt with a large double-headed war ax, the handle made to fit his razor clawed hands. His hands did not move, but she could hear his clawed feet scraping on the concrete as the muscles flexed in anticipation of movement.

Beren's eye roved over to the Colonel. "Yes, my Lord. Especially when one is so small and helpless."

Absently, Heather wondered why creatures who had such massive teeth and claws even needed weapons. *I guess in a world where everyone has the same weapons, you still need to invoke fear.*

Her body shivered involuntarily at the thought of an alien world full of these beings. An ancient and primal fear of being in the presence of a powerful predator bubbled up from deep inside her core. She struggled to contain it, but it burst out of her lips as a small gasp. Beren's head snapped up, his eyes scanning the darkness.

"A Breeder? In our presence? Explain!" Beren snarled, stepping forward.

The Colonel swallowed nervously. "She is important, my Lord. Other than some soldiers, she is one of the few officers I can trust with your secret."

"You keep telling me that. But she is a Breeder! How important can she be?" Avar growled, the sound rolling through the spacious hall like thunder.

"She is the one who helps keep you safe, my Lord." The Colonel's voice was strained.

"Then what is it you do? Remind me again why I tolerate your presence?"

The Colonel rose, his voice firm, "It takes work to assure the peace between our people holds, my Lord. The world is a large place, and it is hard to keep secrets. There are many who would not understand and would seek your destruction."

"Politics. You should settle them as we do. Bite off the traitors' heads."

"If only things were so simple, my Lord." The Colonel tried for a bit of lighter tone, but quieted under Avar's glare.

Avar grinned. "Perhaps someday they will be. Come

forward, Breeder. I will tolerate your presence."

Heather's knees shook as she walked forward. Her rational mind bristled at being called a Breeder. She had spent too many years in the military machine facing sexism and patriarchy as she strode to excel at her career; in the public mind, her promotions and awards were always her sleeping her way to the top or simply because the department needed a token woman when the fact was she refused to take a job just because she had *breasts. If she took a job, it was because she had earned it.* Yet the fear bubbled up within her, her senses picking up the faint scent as she approached; the scent of a predator. These two minds warred between wanting to tell the creature where he could stuff his patriarchal brain and wanting to collapse in a puddle. *She stopped shakily before the throne, trying to draw on some scant fleck of courage.*

"Thank you, my Lord." Her voice sounded calmer than she felt.

"Do not speak. I will tolerate your presence but not your voice." Avar turned back to the Colonel. "Enough of the distractions. You have yet to bring me the traitor."

"Our intel tells us that the one called Reven is planning an attack, my Lord."

"Of course he is. The fool will not rest until I and my kind are dead. What I want to know is why you have not captured him yet?"

Beren spoke, "You should let me hunt him, my Lord. I can sniff him out. His blood will be on my claws before sunset."

Avar held up a hand to quiet him. "You will remain in the chamber. We have given our word to these people and we will not break it. But Colonel…"

Avar stood for the first time, towering even over Beren. His ember eyes blazed to life as he glared at them. "I am displeased with your incompetency. Bring him to me before the moon becomes full, or I will end our peace."

"My Lord, you can't do that. The war that would follow would not benefit you."

Avar screamed, the sound vibrating through the air like a physical force. The Colonel and Heather shied away from the sound, falling to their knees and covering their ears to protect them from the primal rage. Beren bared his ax, snarling. Avar fell to silence, his mouth breaking into a wide grin as he saw his prey cowering.

He growled, "Who are you to say what I can and can't do? You humans with your superiority; thinking that just because you can think philosophically that you can decide what is right and wrong for the entire universe. My people would wipe this earth clean in mere moments. It is only out of the benefits that we keep this peace."

"Forgive me, my Lord. I spoke out of turn. You will have

the traitor at once."

Avar slowly sat back down on the throne, every inch of his body giving them the impression that they were not worth his notice now that he had proven his point of who was in charge. "See that I do. Dismissed, as you say."

The pair slowly backed away towards the door, their natural instincts telling them not to turn away from the predators. The door opened with a hiss and they exited, both holding their breath as the door closed. As soon as it clicked, Heather collapsed.

"What the hell." She exhaled.

The Colonel stood there, jaw clenched and fists balled up tight. He stared at the door whispering, "Appear weak when you are strong and strong when you are weak."

"Sir?" Heather asked, confused.

The Colonel shook his head, as if suddenly realizing she was there.

"Sun Tzu." He said, as if that explained everything. He reached out a hand to help her.

She reached for the hand and stood up as he assisted her. "There's only two. Why do we tolerate-"

He held up a hand. "Walk."

They started down the hallway.

The Colonel whispered, "You have to be careful what you say. They have incredible hearing, even through the walls."

She nodded.

He continued. "You weren't here during the first days of the gate when those two came through; just the two of them wiped out an entire division by themselves."

Heather stumbled. Could she have heard that right? An entire division? "Sir?"

"I'm not exaggerating. I saw it."

Silence fell between them for a second before Heather dared speak. "Then what good is this peace if they can just wipe us out at any moment? What do we have against them?"

The Colonel reached the elevator, pressing the up button. "Nothing other than keeping us alive benefits them more than conquering us. Even though they're incredibly strong, we still have ways of hurting them and any smart predator takes the path of least injury. In reality, we're more slaves than partners; forced to give them whatever they want in exchange for not being eradicated. But the advantage isn't all one-sided. They had to give us something very important in order to get what they wanted and that thing may be our key to making sure that no one, not even these beasts, ever threatens our country, our world again."

"You're talking about the gateway tech?" Heather had never seen the gate but had heard enough stories that it made her skin crawl just letting the words pass over her lips.

"Yes. The gate energy is unstable, prone to explosions. Without a way to control the energy, you do not know how or where you will end up if you live through it at all. With what they've given us, no one will ever threaten us again. Imagine, all this time lost trying to travel through space in ships when the key lay in something as simple as a doorway through the dimensions."

The doors of the elevator dinged and slid open, revealing the cool comfort of their temporary escape from this nightmare. The Colonel and Heather marched inside. Heather sighed in relief as the doors closed and the car slipped upwards. The more distance she could put between herself and that room, the better.

"You said no one would threaten us. Even them?" She asked.

The Colonel cracked a small smile. "Let's just say we are figuring out how to renegotiate the peace."

2

***

Amy stretched backward, the office chair tilting backward to the dangerous tipping point, her adrenalin spiking slightly as the fear of falling over rushed through her brain. Sitting up, she sighed and rubbed at her temples. *Definitely not enough caffeine.*

Lines of code flashed before her on a screen of black. The nonsensical lines were all green, which she ignored. She was waiting for the algorithms to flash up something that they either didn't understand or that lay within the parameters of a hit. Her eyes flicked to the list of trigger words the algorithms were looking for within the mountains of data compiled from every computer and cell phone within the entire nation. She used to shiver when she realized they had recruited her to spy on the United States citizenry for the government. But the word lists always seemed harmless.

"Too early for a headache. You just started your shift." Jeff, dressed in his Army uniform, smiled at her from the next station over.

Amy looked down momentarily at her own sweatshirt over jeans. Sometimes she felt like a slob next to Jeff and the other military personnel in their uniforms, even next to some of the other civilians in their dress clothes. But then she shrugged. If they wanted a professional dresser, they shouldn't have come knocking on my van.

"I swear Becker hates me and that's why I keep getting stuck with the early shift. I mean, who has ever heard of a hacker being up at four in the morning?" Amy twirled in her chair.

"Especially since you stayed awake until 3 playing video games." He teased her.

She stuck her tongue out at him. "I entered the new list yesterday. Now all I have to do is let Rover run and see if he brings me anything back. Saying I'm bored is an understatement."

"Oh poor baby, having to sit there and do nothing. They got me on videos today. Do you know how mind-numbing it is watching kids eat Tide Pods over and over because there might be some secret encryption or message hidden in the video? Then feeling like a soulless monster when you silently cheer them on because you know it's one less idiot in the world?" Jeff grimaced.

"Well, we all had souls and morals once upon a time." Amy looked up at the ceiling of the gray concrete room. "I swear Becker is really Satan, stealing our souls for junk food."

"Speak of the Devil." Jeff muttered and turned back to his screens.

A small thin man walked into the room, dressed in an immaculate uniform festooned with bright medals. He stood at the doorway for a moment, scanning the round room filled with circles of computer terminals, all surrounding a central tower filled with large computer screens. His eyes focused and sharpened, laser targeting on Amy, his face morphing into a sneer. He stalked over. "Taggart! Status."

Amy swallowed the exasperated sigh that always rose in her throat when dealing with Becker. She spoke up, "List entered, sir. Rover is running. All is well."

"We're not paying you to sit here and spin." He sniffed and looked down his nose at her.

"You're not paying me at all, Becker. None of us get paid. All the free junk food and video games I can play, as long as I play nice and work for Secret Uncle Sam. Just like the rest of us. If you have a problem with how I spend my time, take it up with Addison. Unless you're afraid to tell him why you pissed off one of the highest level hackers in the Western Hemisphere?"

"You just watch your tongue, young lady. Addison can't protect you forever!" He stamped his foot and flounced out of the room.

Jeff whistled once he was out the door. "You live dangerously."

Amy allowed the sigh to escape.

"Becker is just a glorified accountant who thinks he has power. If they weren't monitoring me, I'd hack his life and wreck it just to bring him down a notch."

"So, you really were some high-level hacker?" Jeff asked.

"What do you mean 'were'?" She twirled in her chair, stopping to point at her screen. "Who do you think wrote Rover? Ever heard of the tag "TabbyKat"?"

Jeff said, "Wow. Feel like I should bow down prostrating myself or something before the Queen."

Amy punched his arm. "Quit. I wasn't that good or they wouldn't have caught me."

"So what is this? Punishment?"

"A choice. Come to work for them or get tossed in some hellhole no one knows exists. At least this way I still get to play with computers."

"What if Becker reports you?"

"I'm not scared. Addison is the team leader, not him. Becker's just day-to-day supervision. Addison doesn't give a shit about anything but finding what the bosses want. If Becker tries going over his head, Addison will rip him from head to toe, and Becker knows it. As much as the government has a hold over me, they also know they're better with me than without me. Besides, Rover is my baby. No one knows how to get him to heel but me."

"I wondered why we all had to rotate jobs except you."

"What can I say? I have a skill set. I know how to make myself essential." Amy grinned mischievously, then spun her chair again. She stopped suddenly, noticing a slightly nauseous feeling.

"Ever wonder about the list?" She asked to take her mind off the momentary feeling of wanting to throw up.

"It doesn't pay to wonder around here." Jeff turned back to his screen, knowing where this conversation was going and wanting to cut it off.

"Oh c'mon, Jeff. Aren't you just a little curious about what we're doing here and all the secret hush-hush stuff? Look at all the rules we have: no going off campus, no communication with anyone on the outside, and anything else we do online goes through five levels of security scanning and delays. We don't even have phones for crying out loud. We should at least talk to each other!"

"You would think. But remember David? He started talking about getting out, getting us to organize, and asking questions. Now, no one's seen him in a while."

"Aw, David was just fired. He was never that good."

"You forget I've been in the Army for a while and I know their myopic way of thinking. Fired in a place like this? It's code for permanently disappearing."

"Dramatic much?" She ripped down the list. "You're as bad as some of those conspiracy nuts we have to monitor. Look at these latest additions. 'Avar, Beren, Reven, Tark' I mean, they don't come up in any language database I try."

Jeff shook his head. "Let it go Amy. You may be valuable, but no one is non-replaceable."

She sighed, "You're no fun."

"Yup. I enjoy breathing too much not to be."

Amy was about to respond when her console beeped. She glanced over. The screen had stopped scrolling, a line of code flashing red. She clicked on it and whistled. Jeff looked over her shoulder.

"What?" He asked.

She didn't respond, but hit a button. A page of paper flashed out of the printer underneath the desk. She said, "Probably nothing. But looks like a legitimate hit to one word on the new list."

"Say no more." He turned back to his console.

"You're not curious? You?"

Jeff just waved, clicking on a new video to watch. Amy shook her head and walked out of the viewing room.

The doorway led to a concrete hallway lit by LED bulbs. The hallway ran in a circle around the spherical room that she had just exited that the techs had affectionately named the Eyeball. In a ring around the Eye, on the opposite side of the hallway, were the offices of the senior officials. At intervals around the ring were elevators, all leading up to the Hub where the dormitories, cafeteria, hospital and other units were located. Below lay the things that peons like her didn't get to know about. She walked down the hallway to a gray door that looked like all the other gray doors except for the name plate placed outside. She buzzed the console.

"Come in." A crackly voice barked.

She pushed a button, and the door slid aside.

Captain Mark Addison sat typing on his computer, surrounded by stacks of computer printouts and manila file folders. More papers sat stacked haphazardly on chairs. All the techs in the Eyeball secretly had a bet on how many paper avalanches he had in a day. The man in question had his tie half loosened and his shirt collar undone. A forgotten suit jacket lay sprawled over a nearby chair back, his shirt sleeves rolled up. Unlike most of the other officials in here, he acted more like a civilian, which was nice for her because he was one of the few officers she felt comfortable with. Addison gazed at the paper he held intently for a moment, then sighed and pushed his glasses up to perch on top of his head and rubbed the bridge of his nose. "Hey Amy. What you got?"

She handed over the printout. "Hit on one word."

Addison stared at her with a stoney expression on his face and reached for the paper. A knot formed in her gut as she felt his reaction. He scanned the paper for a moment, grimacing. "Thanks. You're excused."

Amy startled at the harsh demeanor. Addison had a very blunt and to the point personality, but he usually was friendly with her. "What's wrong?"

He shook his head. "Nothing I can tell you. Same old bullshit. Now go on. I have calls to make."

Her nerves riled at the dismissal, but she obediently turned. She paused just long enough on the threshold to hear him pick up the phone.

Addison spoke, "Colonel? We got him."

The door closed behind her with a click.

We got him.

He. Reven was a person. A living being that she was tracking.

Amy closed her eyes and took a deep breath, steadying herself. *Obviously, this guy did something bad; otherwise, we wouldn't be tracking him, right?*

That other part of her mind, the one that usually sent her down a path of trouble, spoke up. *You really trust our government to only go after bad people?*

It's fine. I don't have a choice. This is my job.

Sure. Keep telling yourself that. Ignorance being bliss and all of that.

It's not my problem. I have to take care of myself. I can't cause trouble. There is no place to go. There's nothing wrong with looking out for myself, right?

Amy ignored the niggling in the back of her brain that wanted to say no, that wanted to have a problem with this.

She heard a clanking sound and a muffled alarm far overhead. She knew the sound and her stomach dropped. The troops being assembled. A wave of fear washed over her, flashbacks of when they came for her racing into the forefront of her mind. She shook her head, dismissing the troubling thoughts. *We all have to sell our soul for something.*

3

* * *

"Beta Team to Alpha One."

Emerson hit the button on his headset. He whispered, "Go for Alpha."

"Building surrounded, sir. Theta and Zeta have snipers set. Helicopters ETA 5 min within the call."

"Keep the copters back. Don't want to give it away. Prepare for my count."

"Yes sir. Beta out."

Emerson used a special scope to peer around the corner of the alley at the building across the street. Their target was a large, blocky warehouse sitting on the edge of a polluted river, an abandoned relic with broken windows and peeling paint on an old sign announcing it had once been a furniture store. Through the night vision of the scope, the place flickered with green and black static. Nothing moved on the street; there might not have been enough life down here for even the strays to survive. Or perhaps they just knew that tonight was a good night to stay away. He clicked his headset again.

"Benson, report."

"Heat signatures show five, although one is abnormal."

"Abnormal?"

"It's showing too cool. Like he's covered in ice or something. But it's definitely a living signature."

"10-4. Alpha out."

Emerson steadied his breath, thinking. *Now or never.* "All teams. Move in on my count. 3, 2, 1 Go!"

Inky shadows silently separated themselves from the darker shadows of the night. The shadows converged like ants on the target building, all noise muffled except for the slap of combat boots and the jangling of metal. Some threw silent hand signals, directing others to flow around them or stay behind, the ants flowing in well-coordinated, practiced movements. If one looked closely, they would see the moonlight glinting off of gun tips. The ants paused as they reached the doorways on the exterior of the building. One second passed, then two, then everyone was in position.

Emerson keyed a special button on his headset.

The world exploded as four of the teams threw concussion grenades inside the broken windows. The soldiers ripped off their night vision goggles, the world suddenly glaring with a thousand burning suns inside the building. Men started screaming and yelling orders, and the flood of ants entered the building. More chaos as surprised yells ripped through the air, and bullets ripped into the night.

Five chaotic minutes later, a group of people huddled on the first floor with their hands bound behind their backs with black zipties, a ring of soldiers standing around them. Emerson walked up to one, an average sized man with black hair and blue eyes. The man looked up at him, staring with intense hatred and revulsion. Emerson allowed a smirk to cross his stony face.

"Sergeant." He barked out.

A young man came up to his shoulder.

"Sir?"

"Call in the copters. Get them loaded on the transport. I want this one," he pointed to the black-haired man, "in special containment by dawn. Activate the cleansing teams. No screwups, you understand?"

"Yes, sir." The man saluted.

The sergeant scurried off, barking orders over his headset. Emerson turned back to the group of prisoners. He knelt down by the black-haired man.

"Nice to meet you, Reven. We've got some friends who are eager to meet you."

The man just glared at him, his jaw muscles tight.

Emerson chuckled. "Nothing to say? Doesn't matter. You'll talk soon enough."

He stood back up and walked to the door.

Another soldier dropped in beside him. "Job well done, sir."

"Not done yet Lieutenant. Got to get him back to base."

"Think someone will try a rescue?"

Emerson shrugged. "Anything's possible in this reality. I'm paid to solve problems. Solved the first, catching the bastard. Now we just have to solve the second, getting him to the base. Once he's secure there, then I'll celebrate."

"What did he do, sir?"

"I'm not paid to think, soldier. Neither are you. Safer that way. Boss said grab him, that's what we did."

4

***

Amy toyed with her omelet. She had propped a book up behind her bowl to read, but her mind couldn't seem to focus. It kept drifting off into the atmosphere, while her eyes kept rereading the same page over and over. It was in the middle of one of these drifts that a sharp clatter sounded near to her and she jumped, her adrenalin spiking from a jolt of fear. Her cheeks felt warm as a blush worked its way up her body at being spooked. Amy looked up to see Jeff standing on the other side of the table with his own tray, and she dipped her head for a moment, hoping he wouldn't tease her too much about being scared. Then, realizing that she was falling back into that bad old habit, she straightened up and looked him in the eye.

"Hey." He sat down. "Good book?"

"Enthralling. Want it?" She tossed it over.

He picked it up, gave her an odd look, and set it aside. "Been a while since you've been in the Hub for a meal."

The Hub was the name given to the central area of the base. It was an enormous open space surrounded by elevators that went from level to level. Each level led to different areas: the personnel quarters, the medical wing, the entertainment zones, and so on. The bottom level of the space was a cafeteria with a food court. While all the personnel quarters had a stocked kitchen, a lot of the base's personnel ate in the Hub for the social aspect.

"What's up with you? You went to talk to Addison, then you didn't come back to the Eyeball." Jeff said.

"Needed some air."

"Air. Huh. That's funny. The last time any of us saw the sun was when we came into this place."

"Maybe that's it. I realized I don't do confinement well."

"But the hit brought it on?" Jeff wasn't dumb.

Amy glanced around her to see if anyone was close enough to hear. She leaned in, whispering. "I saw the word that hit. It was 'Reven'. When I took it to Addison, I overheard him talking to the Colonel. He said 'we got him'. Him. Reven is a guy."

"So? Amy, you've been here for two years. Surely you knew what we were doing. We spy on the American public."

"I know. It's just. . . When I was on my own, I never went after innocent people."

"You were a white hat before they grabbed you."

She shrugged. "I never really cared for labels. Mainly I was just trying to get enough money to support myself. But I never went after innocent people: corporations, greedy rich assholes, scammers, that sort of thing. But most regular people are just trying to survive, like I was. Why make their lives any harder?"

"So, you suddenly realized today that what we do goes after innocent people?"

Amy said, "I know it sounds stupid. When I first came, I was just happy to not be in prison. You delude yourself into thinking that you're serving a purpose, even if it's a little warped. But that was five years ago. Junk food, video games and safety aren't the incentives they used to be. Now, I'm wondering things."

"What are you going to do with this crisis of conscience?" Jeff said.

"What can I do? It's not like any of us can just walk out of here. Especially me. That was the deal. Work here or go to prison. They'd probably just kill me now." She buried her head in her hands.

"Dramatic much?"

"C'mon Jeff. You're the one hinting at David being axed, literally. Are you telling me this, all of this, on some level, doesn't bother you?"

"Stop right there. You know it does, but you forget I volunteered for this. My life was Army intelligence before I got recruited. I feel like a creep spying on the normal public. But if that's what it takes to do the mission, it's what I have to do. So do you. Rover searches every phone call, every text, every keystroke typed by people that do not know that their secret conversations are being recorded."

"Well. . . it's different when it's an anonymous word. I can lie to myself. Tell myself it doesn't matter. You find out it's a person, and it raises uncomfortable questions within my conscience."

"So, what did this guy do? I mean, if he's a terrorist, that should calm your conscience."

Amy took a bite of food. The warmth sliced through the coldness she felt. "Like Addison would tell me. Maybe that's what's bothering me, not knowing what he did. But it must be big. I mean, to contact the Colonel directly and then send out Whisper."

Jeff's eyes grew wide. "He told you that? That they were sending Whisper?"

"No, but I can read between the lines. The second he called the Colonel, the alarms went off and there were noises overhead in the bay. I guess they don't need to be subtle with it. Who are we going to tell?"

"Still. It's been a while since they've activated Whisper. Normally they just contact the CIA or whomever wanted the search."

"What kind of name do you think Reven is, anyway?"

Jeff shrugged. "Who knows? Doesn't sound like anything I've heard before. Maybe something someone made up. Like one of those cult leaders or something. They like dramatics."

"Maybe." She took another bite of food, listening.

The one fact about the base everyone knew was that it

existed under a vast mountain range. The military had turned the top of the mountain into a secret hangar that helicopters could fly in and out of without being seen. She had seen a brief glimpse of it when they had first brought her in, although it had been at night and poorly lit. It was also the home of Operation Whisper. Whisper was full of ex Navy SEALS, Marines and Rangers along with other select personnel, all chosen for their stealth, speed, discretion and fighting ability. When activated for a mission, the bumps and bangs of the great doors opening and closing would echo down into the Hub. If any member of the Hub belonged to the team, no one knew. They floated in and out of the shadows, as ephemeral as the name they had given themselves. Just whispers.

Her skin itched. Even with the multitude of plants and day lights set to resemble sunlight, she missed the sky and a true breeze. When they had first brought her here, they had said she would get used to it. Yet she counted every day. Every minute. Itching for when she could leave, even as much as she tried to ignore it.

She had left her home at age sixteen, in a rusted out van she'd bought for $500 that she'd save doing odd jobs. That van had been her home for five years, pieced together with duct tape and string. In that van, she had been queen. She had stalked her targets from her computer screen. Her life had been amazing. But she hadn't been good enough. She had gone after the wrong people, people who knew people in Washington, D.C. The next thing she knew, Whisper was at her door with an ultimatum.

Not that it was all bad. A state-of-the-art two-bedroom apartment all to her own. Big screen TV. Access to all the streaming services and entertainment. Video games. Junk food. Fully equipped gym. They even had a rainforest room, complete with birds and reptiles. That was her favorite.

Still, her skin itched.

A loud thunk echoed overhead, followed by a groaning mechanical sound. Both Jeff and Amy looked upwards, along with everyone else in the cafeteria.

Jeff swallowed the food he'd been chewing. "Guess someone's home."

"So, what's the betting pool at for our new guest? Hub or Catacombs?"

Jeff got a wicked grin. "Amy! I'm aghast at the fact that you think we would bet on something so tawdry as someone's imprisonment. Or that I'd have had time to put it together. I just found out we were having a guest."

Amy snorted. "Right. Nobody sneezes around this place without you being the second person to know. But I'm also your friend, which is why I didn't call bullshit about you acting surprised earlier when I told you about Whisper."

"What can I say? I'm a nosy little shit. If you must know, it's leaning towards the Hub right now. Want in?"

She shook her head.

Jeff shrugged. "Spoilsport. You on shift this afternoon?"

"No, I got the early shift again tomorrow. Going to go try to get some sleep." A thought had suddenly leapt into Amy's mind, the same little curious voice that had been with her during her happy hacker days.

"Don't do it, Amy." Jeff's somber voice startled her.

She said. "Don't do what? Sleep? Kind of need that, Jeff."

"You know what I mean. I see that gleam in your eye."

"I don't know what you're talking about." She stared at him as innocently as she could.

"Stop it. You're not Mary Poppins and the spoonful of sugar doesn't make things go down. You think you'd get away with it? Right under their nose?"

"I'm not planning anything." She stood, gathering her food tray, trying to sound indignant at his accusation.

Jeff eyed her warily. "Sure. Just going to go. . . sleep. Well, sleep carefully."

She paused. *If Jeff told...* "You plan on telling anyone about my sleeping, Mr. Army Intelligence?"

"I'm not that big of a dick." He smiled that lopsided smile she almost thought was cute. "Just be careful."

"Thanks." She walked away, but stopped and turned back. "Jeff, I hear you. It's just . . . he's a person."

"They're all people, Amy."

"I know. That's what's bothering me."

5

***

The helicopter hovered in front of the mountain. "Home Base, this is Echo Two. We have the package. Permission to enter. Codes sent."

"Codes accepted Echo Two. Prepare for entry."

The mountainside shifted in the darkness, the projected hologram of rocks and bushes fading to reveal a giant metal door set into the side of the mountain gleaming in the early morning sunlight. As the door slid down, the internal mechanisms moaned through the air. The pilot expertly guided the helicopter into the narrow space, avoiding hitting the massive swirling blade on the roof. Two more helicopters followed him in, being careful as they navigated in the enclosed space of the hangar. As soon as the last crossed the threshold, the door closed.

Soldiers piled out of the helicopters. Emerson stepped out of the lead chopper, watching his team converge on the last helicopter to land. A door on the far side of the hangar opened. Colonel Holloway stepped through with Captain Smith a hair's breadth behind; their eyes took a second to absorb the chaos of soldiers, then focused on Emerson and walked over to greet him.

The Colonel spoke first. "You got him?"

"Affirmative, sir. There is one who matches the description."

"You don't know if it is him?"

"It's not like I can run a DNA test out there, now is it? I got the one who matched the description."

The Colonel stared at Emerson for a moment, his jaw muscles clenching. Emerson didn't flinch; he knew his worth to the Colonel. No one else in the world had the expertise to run a team like Whisper. He wasn't about to bow and scrape before some high-privileged office boy. If they wanted his skills, his attitude went with it.

The Colonel turned his attention back to the helicopter. "Get them unloaded. Take the target down to the Catacombs. The rest can wait in holding. See what they know and start preparing them for transport to Leavenworth."

Emerson saluted. "Yes, sir."

He hurried over to the helicopter.

Heather watched him go. "You're releasing them to Leavenworth? Isn't that kind of dangerous?"

"We can't risk them staying in the same place as Reven, in case they have a plan, otherwise we'd send them with a shipment. Besides, we have an arrangement with Leavenworth. After the Treatment, they won't be any trouble. We have our target. That's what is important."

Emerson arrived at the last helicopter. "All right, folks. Guns up, safeties off. If you have to shoot, aim for a kneecap. Target goes downstairs, all the rest go for Treatment. Got it?"

The semi-circle of soldiers nodded. Their guns raised as one.

Emerson stepped up to grasp the locking handle of the door. "Okay, children. Play nice now."

He opened the door. Two soldiers were inside, their guns trained on the group whose silent faces turned to look at Emerson, blinking in the sudden light.

He motioned with his hand. "C'mon kiddies. Out of the pool."

One by one the people came to the edge of the door, being helped down by the two soldiers who handed them off to others, all under the gaze of the semi-circle of guns. The last one out was the black-haired man. Under the lights, Emerson could see that he looked to be in his thirties, slender but with a muscular build. He grabbed the man's arm and helped him step down from the van. The man looked up as he stood on solid ground, his eyes meeting Emerson's. Emerson's breath caught in his throat. Crystal blue eyes flecked with gold stared into his own. Time froze, a thousand years passing in a second. Emerson saw his own birth, his life, his death. He saw a thousand lives beyond his own.

"Sir?" The voice broke the connection, and the man turned his gaze away.

"Um, yeah." Emerson shivered, shaking the feeling away. *Whatever the fuck that was.* "Get him down below. Double guards. Leave the shackles on."

The soldier saluted. "Yes, sir."

The Colonel stepped up to his shoulder. "That's him?"

"Yes sir. The one you call Reven."

The Colonel nodded. "Good work Captain. There will be some rewards waiting for you in your quarters for this one."

Emerson smiled. "Yes sir. And my men?"

"Oh, they'll get their reward, too."

Emerson saluted. "Thank you, sir."

He motioned towards the elevators where the groups were boarding. The Colonel stepped forward; his ever present shadow Captain Smith falling in beside him. Emerson fell a step behind, enjoying the view of Heather's tight skirt. She glanced behind her for a moment, frowning, and he threw her a bright smile. She snorted in disgust and tried to walk faster, which made the view even more entertaining. Even with the reward waiting for him, he liked a challenge and the Captain certainly was one. But you had to be careful with targets like her. Get on their wrong side and they bit back hard.

6

***

Amy sat, her fingers tapping anxiously on the keyboard. She had retreated to her room, sitting on her bed with her laptop. But that was all she had been doing for the last half an hour, staring at the wallpaper on her desktop, too scared to open up a command window. She stood on top of the diving board, waiting to plunge off. But why couldn't she?

Jeff was right. What was she thinking? The military had arrested her for this very act, and here she was trying to hack them under their noses. Yet the words of her mentor kept ringing in her head: It's easier to steal from inside a bank than outside of it.

She was already inside the systems and had access to a lot of the treasure troves. There would be traps, but maybe not as many as they had on the perimeter. Perhaps they had gotten complacent, even though the Hub was full of top-level hackers and computer scientists the world offered. But the military had trapped them all here within this cage. All contact with the outside world was strictly limited and monitored. Even if they found out any classified information, there was no way to get it to the outside world. With all that security in place, maybe the internal firewalls weren't as dense as it had led them to believe. Maybe it was merely the fear that kept them all in line, kept them from learning the truth. The curious voice kept whispering. *We can do this. We've done it before. Think of all the fun secrets we can find and expose. We love doing that!*

Well, you know what they say. Being timid got no one a prize.

Her fingers started tapping on the keys.

Lines and layers of code started racing past her eyes, her fingers flying faster. In her mind, the lines of code formed a passageway winding back and forth. Periodically along the hall were doors, some locked, some open. She ignored the open doors and concentrated on the locked ones. Most had a simple tracking algorithm that she could have fooled with a few keystrokes. But she ignored them as well. While she was betting on the security being lax, whatever she wanted would have the strongest security. She dove deeper and deeper into the maze.

Then she saw it. The door that wasn't a door. A door that didn't seem to exist in her system. A void in the files that showed as being there, but there was no accessible point. This could be interesting.

She paused, noticing the high levels of security on the non-door. There were things that would get her in, but not without every alarm in the place blaring into life. But there was always another way into a system.

When you can't get in, go under.

She started looking in the surrounding files, seeing if there were any weaknesses. Some of the other files started appearing, but nothing close to the void. The level of security was astounding. These protections weren't chain-link fences. This was foot thick steel with land mines.

She growled in frustration as the root levels defied her attempts. No way in without breaking the password and one wrong try could set off the mousetrap. Amy sighed. Well, at least she could look at some of the other files. Maybe they would give her some clue about what was going on.

She searched for the word "Reven". Five files popped up. The first three were revenue statements from some tech company she had never heard of. The fourth looked like a PDF file. When she opened it, it was a copy of a blog post by some guy calling himself "Omni". Scanning it quickly, it was just a bunch of disjointed ramblings about UFO conspiracies and the government. She saw the name Reven, but it was only in connection with some underground group trying to "find the truth".

Amy snorted. Was that all it was? Trying to keep track of some nut? Then why all the secrecy? Why send out Whisper? Were they planning some terrorist attack or something?

Then the date of the last file caught her eye. Today's date.

She opened it and found a procedural order for Whisper, including a prisoner transfer of 'target subject and incidentals'. Amy grinned. Good old government. Even with their secret missions, they still needed red tape and paperwork.

The form stated the target was to be interred in the Catacombs. The 'incidentals' were to be sent for interrogation and Treatment. *Treatment?* Amy frowned at the unfamiliar word and typed it in the search. She found more files, mostly for orders with names on them and listings of medication used, but one was an old order from twenty years ago. *By application of a certain group of medications along with electrical stimulation, patients will be revert to a permanent state of dementia, remembering nothing but the most basic of essential tasks and rendering the patient's speech to incoherent mumbling and mimicking symptoms of paranoid schizophrenia. Once released, the patient's wild ramblings will alienate the public and get them labeled as mentally unstable if the patients can survive at all.*

Amy's stomach dropped. What the hell was going on here? She returned to the named orders and searched until she saw David's name, and clicked on it. It linked her to a medical file, with a date of Treatment. The date he left. The date he was supposedly 'fired'. She steeled herself against the nausea, her stomach threatening to send what little food she had eaten at lunch back up. *Oh my god, Jeff was right. Is that what happened to everyone who wanted to leave? What is so secret that they would protect it this hard?*

She leaned back against her headboard. Treatment.

Reven. Whisper. Monitoring. All of it, all the little suspicions that she'd ignored, all the red flags started clicking into place. Her rational mind screamed to leave it alone, to remain ignorant. But her mama had never called her smart, especially when someone had something to hide. She was like a cat, searching out that one thing you didn't want her to find and then breaking it. She was curious that way. Just couldn't leave it alone. She had to pick at the scab.

Reven was a terrorist. I did a good thing. I can just leave this alone and go on and live my life.

Maybe if she kept repeating it enough, she would believe it and it would be true.

Maybe cupcakes would start raining down from the ceiling.

But what could she do? She was already flirting with disaster. Most of the staff knew there were top-secret classified levels far below the Hub and Eye. Only a few select staff had access to those levels; mostly top level officers who were so married to the flag there was no way they would spill a secret. It was suicide to go to those levels without permission. Any who tried. . .

Yet there was no way her conscious was going to be quiet about this one. She had spent her young life fighting against secrets and corruption, and now she was helping the most corrupt conspiracy of all. *It's not like this is new,* the voice in her mind purred. *You've known this was bad for a while.*

Not this bad. She argued back.

Lie to yourself all you want. You got him in here. You fed him to the wolves. Now, what are you going to do about it?

What could she do? There would be cameras, keypads, probably retina scans or fingerprint readers. Not to mention that staffing down there was more than likely restricted to a small group; people would know that she didn't belong. Amy wanted to scream. She was good, but there was no way to hack her way into this situation. She sat staring at the screen for a few minutes, her brain running through every trick and scam she knew and coming up empty.

Then a switch flicked in her mind. Maybe it wasn't about hacking the computer, but the people. Quickly, she opened another screen and her fingers started flying over the keyboard.

A few minutes later, she got out of bed, stuffing her laptop into her backpack and swinging it onto her shoulders. She left her quarters and headed to the medical wing. It was a fully stocked hospital, complete with surgeons and specialists. The doors parted and let her in. A nurse at reception looked up as she entered. "Can I help you?"

"Yes, is Dr. Canata on duty?"

"Do you have an appointment?" The receptionist looked at her computer screen.

Amy said, "No, but he wanted me to come in and discuss some test results. Right away."

The receptionist frowned for a moment and tapped a few keys on her computer. "What's your name?"

"Cassidy. Cassidy Tate."

The receptionist tapped a few more keys. "Oh okay. I see the note here."

Of course you do, I just put it there. Amy fought not to fidget. At least hacking the medical records had been easier than the classified ones.

The receptionist said, "You're lucky. He's free for a bit. You can wait in Exam Room 1."

"Thanks." Amy hurried down the hallway.

The Exam Room was just like any other. Simple computer and desk. Sterile elevated padded table with a white sheet of paper pulled over it. Required medical anatomy pictures on the wall. Overwhelming antiseptic smell. She set her bag on the table, pacing the floor in her nervous anxiety as she waited. She could feel her adrenalin rising, that same thrill she had always gotten before when she was working on a target. Only now it shared space with the rising anxiety of who she was trying to hack and the odds she faced. She was walking a tight wire with a thirty mile-an-hour side wind with no idea where the rope anchored or how far she would have to walk.

Just when her nerves had reached the breaking point, and she almost called the whole thing off, the door opened, admitting a man in a white lab coat preoccupied with looking at a chart while he walked into the room. "Hi Cassidy. I'll just need a minute to look over your files. I didn't remember having any tests for you."

He closed the door. Only then did he look up at his patient. His face fell. "Amy."

"Hey Doc. How's it going?"

"Great, until just now. Do I want to know how or why you pulled this little trick?" Dr. Chris Canata glared at her.

"Probably not. Aren't you excited about seeing me?"

"You know I'm not, otherwise you wouldn't have pulled this little stunt."

"Are you still mad about me hacking the medical records? I told you, I was just curious. I didn't think it was a big deal and I'm sorry those records got switched. Harry didn't need his appendix anyway, right? And Tommy lived. But hey, I got you the sweet room upgrade, right? And who was it that made sure Kelly and Katie had access to those cartoons they loved when you weren't able to get through the filters?"

He said, "Yes, you got us that larger space. The girls can't thank you enough for the cartoons. Neither can I, as a matter of fact. I can actually get some naps in now that they're entertained and not bugging me about Pretty Princess Unicorns. But I know you didn't just drop in for a social call. What do you need?"

"I'm calling in my favor. I need to see the new prisoner Whisper brought in."

Only the slightest twitch at the edge of his mouth gave him away. Amy knew she had him. She said, "I know he's in the Catacombs. The only people who can go below besides command are you and your staff."

"Amy..."

She held up a hand. "Stop, Chris. I know it's crazy, stupid, insane, all the bad adjectives. But I need to know something."

"What do you need to know?"

"I need to know that he's a terrorist. That I'm hunting him for a good reason. If he's not, I got an innocent man imprisoned."

"Amy..." Chris repeated.

"Don't Amy me. I know it's crazy. You don't think I can hear myself? But you also don't have to live with me in your head."

Maybe she was crazy, saying something like that. But Chris started nodding, like he understood.

Chris said, "You really want to call your favor in for this?"

She nodded.

Chris sighed. "The Colonel knows my staff. He'll know you aren't one of them."

"Let me worry about that. I'll wear a mask or a disguise or something. Just get me down there."

"How? If this guy is important enough to take to the Catacombs, they will not invite us in."

She thought for a moment, biting her lip. Then an idea made her eyes light up. "Isn't it standard procedure to screen all incoming personnel for viruses or disease that could be contagious to the community? What happens if you find something? Have to quarantine everyone? You can do that, right?"

Chris spoke slowly, mulling over the idea. "Technically, I have that authority, but I've never had to test it. What do you want me to say?"

"I know they sent a bunch of them to Treatment, so it would be logical that you would examine them, make sure they weren't bringing anything into the base. Maybe you could say during your examination you found something. You would need to test the prisoner to see if he's infected because he came in with them. I can help you do that and ask him the questions I need."

"You? You don't have any medical training."

"I know enough to fake it, and that's all I need."

He shook his head. "This is nuts, Amy. You're asking me to put myself and my family in danger. For what?"

"I don't know. I have to trust my gut. It's the only thing I have left."

"What if this blows up? They'll imprison all of us, or worse. This life may not be perfect, but it's safe."

"I only need to talk to him for a minute. I'll be in and out. No one will even know, and you'll be protected. I can put in any fake tests or documentation we need to cover your ass. But I need that way in."

Chris asked, "Why do you need to do this?"

"I told you…"

"No!" He yelled, staring fiercely into her eyes. "Why?"

She stared at him for a moment, then took a deep breath. "I need to do it for me. Because I have been ignoring something since they first brought me here. I ignored it because I was just happy to be alive and not in jail. But today I realized that I'm not alive. I'm as stuck in a jail as any prisoner. One that's probably a lot worse."

"Amy…"

"You can't look me in the eye and tell me they aren't doing some fucked up shit down here. All the secrecy. The Catacombs. Whisper. Why do you need all of that if you're not up to some next level bullshit?"

Chris said, "They're protecting the country."

"No. They're protecting something, and taking out people to do it. I mean, the Treatments? That's inhumane, Chris. You know it."

He hung his head. It hadn't occurred to her that as medical staff, he probably knew about the Treatments. Probably helped administer them. Her stomach roiled, but she pushed it down. *We all do what we have to do to survive.*

She begged. "Chris. Please. He's a normal human being. Just like all of us were before we got swept up into this. I used to be a good person, and yet I've spent the last two years spying on good people because I wanted to save my neck. I need to know what's going on or I'll never have another moment's peace. Don't you want to know you're dedicating your life to a good thing? That you're still a good person?"

"You're still a good person, Amy."

"Am I?" She stood face to face with him. "I'm getting people arrested for things that I don't even know. Working for a government agency that probably doesn't exist. Spying on people who do not know they are being monitored. People who are just trying to live their lives. And I've done it because it saved my ass from going to prison. No Chris. My karma is in the toilet. So is the karma of everyone else who works here."

He stared at her for a moment more, then nodded. "Ok. Let's go get some good karma back."

7

***

Reven strode down the hallway, surrounded by armed soldiers and the officers. As he walked, Colonel Holloway looked over at Emerson, who grinned at him and started gesticulating towards Heather suggestively.

The Colonel grimaced. *Lunatic.*

Just as the group reached the first interrogation room, hurried footsteps got his attention. He glanced over to see Corporal Kune running up, a sheaf of papers in his hand. Colonel Holloway waved at the corporal to wait while he watched the prisoner.

One soldier unlocked the door. Two others escorted the prisoner inside, chaining him to the table. Other than the table and two chairs, the room was bare concrete; the prisoner forced to face a one-way mirror set into the wall.

Colonel Holloway smiled. *Let him stew in there for a while. Then we'll see if he's ready to talk.*

Colonel Holloway watched as the soldiers chained the prisoner to the table. Once the door was closed, he turned to the Corporal. "What do you want?"

Kune startled, tearing his eyes away from where the prisoner had been. His eyes were full of questions, but he knew enough to not to ask them. He gulped nervously and shoved a sheaf of papers at the Colonel. "Reports of a security breech, sir."

"To the base? Why aren't the alarms going off?" The

Colonel grabbed the papers, his eyes scanning the documents even as his mind was whirling with protocols and how to handle the next step.

"It's not an attack from outside. It was internal, to the databases."

The Colonel's mind calmed but methodically started going through the questions about the intrusion. *How in the hell did someone get into the system? The internal databases are completely off the grid.* "Did they get anything?"

"Hard to tell, sir. They were good at covering their tracks. We think they made it to the lower level but weren't able to access any information."

"You think? You think? Why don't you know, goddammit?"

The Corporal shook slightly but stood his ground against the onslaught of the Colonel's temper. "Our tech guys said whoever it was, they were good, sir. They're still trying to uncover all the intrusion tracks. However, we know the hack was internal, and they weren't able to contact the outside world. So, even if they got something, it's still confined to the base."

"Great. Any ideas on specifically who this was?"

"We don't know, sir. All we know is that they were good. The best."

The Colonel consumed and chewed over the

information. "Pick up our red list and bring them to the interrogation rooms. On the double."

"Yes, sir." Kune saluted and scurried off.

Heather had been silent but listening during this time. "Red list, sir?"

"A list of the hackers we've brought in. You know, the 'behave or you'll end up in a hole' hackers."

"You think one stopped playing nice?"

"Has to be. Only one of them could confuse our IT boys and get to that level of the database. Let's just hope they didn't see too much. The wrong information gets out and we could have a riot in the base."

Heather was about to respond when her phone beeped. She answered it, listened for a moment before talking. "Yes. He's right here. I'll tell him."

She hung up and looked at the Colonel. "Our guests have summoned you."

He sighed. "Damn. How did they know?"

"What are you going to do? You know they want him."

"Stall for as long as I can. I want a crack at him first." He walked away but then stopped, turning back to Heather. "I doubt they'll give me long. You interview him."

"Me, sir?"

"Yes. I want everything he knows about our 'friends'. Their weaknesses. Their strengths. They wouldn't want him so bad if he didn't present some sort of threat to them. I'll go down and try to persuade them he's better off in our custody."

"I somehow doubt that will happen. What if Reven won't talk?"

"We need an upper hand and he might give us a better one than we have now." The Colonel said. "If he doesn't give you anything voluntarily, take him down to the science boys. I bet they'll have fun figuring out his secrets."

Heather grimaced inwardly at the thought of going *there,* but schooled her face to be still. She looked through the window in the door at Reven. "It's just so odd. He seems so human. He has to be another alien, right?"

The Colonel said. "That's what you're going to find out, Captain. Now, I better get moving before His Highness gets cranky."

Colonel Holloway left quickly, heading for the elevators. He hoped to god Heather could give him something. He knew better than to believe he could negotiate anything else with the aliens.

The elevator trip seemed quicker than usual, and the room felt colder as he stepped into the darkness. Avar looked up as he entered and snarled. "About time."

"I came as soon as I got the summons, Lord Avar."

"I sense he is here. You captured him?"

Irritation tickled at his spine and he shoved it down. Either these bastards read minds or they had a mole on his team. "It's possible. We intercepted a message that Reven was going to be in a certain place. We surrounded the factory and arrested all inside. There is one we have possibly identified as 'not human'. However, we have yet to confirm anything."

"Bring him to me, and I will tell you all you need to know."

"He's in interrogation right now and getting cleared through intake. Once that's done..."

"Stalling. Are you trying to play me, human? I should have been told immediately, not finding out after the fact. Bring him to me!"

Beren stepped out from behind the shadows of the throne, growling. The Colonel forced himself not to take a step back. "Lord Avar, of course, that will be done. But we must follow protocols."

"Protocols! You humans and your protocols." Avar snarled. "The one called Reven is a matter for my people, not yours. He is our enemy and is to be arrested and taken to the Home World by order of the Queen."

That's why I want to find out why you fear him so much. "You will have him, Lord Avar. All in good time."

"The time is now human. Or do you want to find out what happens when you don't obey us? Like your predecessor did?" He growled, his lips rippling to reveal razor-sharp teeth.

The Colonel shivered, both at the sight and the memory. "No, Lord Avar. We will bring the prisoner to you."

"Good. Dismissed."

The Colonel turned and stalked out of the room. *You better have gotten him talking, Smith!*

8

***

Heather glared dubiously at the man in the hazmat suit in front of her. "What do you mean, quarantine?"

"What I said." Chris' mouth went dry. He wasn't used to trying to deceive command. But he knew how to be authoritative. "One of the other prisoners is exhibiting some strange symptoms. We need to quarantine and test all those who have come into contact with the prisoners. You haven't touched one of them, have you?"

"Heaven's no!" Heather involuntarily stepped back.

Chris stepped forward, pressing his advantage. "Are you feeling any different? Any coughing? Pain? Swelling?"

"What? No! Ugh." She stepped further away from Chris. "I'm fine."

"Good. But you and the others could carry the infection and not be showing symptoms. We'll need to restrict everyone until the tests come back, especially Whisper. My assistant will also need access to the prisoner to run some tests."

"That is out of the question. I have an important interrogation to run."

"Well, I have an outbreak to contain. You really want to see what an infection can do within confined spaces like this? Do you want to answer for that after the fact? Because I will be more than happy to point the finger at you!"

"Stand down, Lieutenant. May I remind you your

appointment is civilian? I will not succumb to threats on military matters!"

Chris straightened up, trying to look as commanding as he could in a giant rubber suit. "I will not watch over half of this station die when every orifice of their body starts leaking liquid guts! Now, will you issue the orders or do I need to contact the General?"

Heather tried not to squirm at the visual image of orifices leaking. "Very well. Don't say later I didn't cooperate in a time of need."

She turned to a soldier and said, "Send word to Whisper. Everyone is to report to Isolation immediately. Everyone else who was near the prisoners will report to the medical department for testing."

The messenger ran off and she turned to Chris. "Satisfied?"

Chris nodded. "Now, we just need access to the prisoner you have in the interrogation room."

"Out of the question. He is to be interrogated..."

"I assure you, Captain. It will only take a moment. Better you know than to go in there and catch something, right? What if he spits on you? Or God forbid he bites you? Humans can carry rabies too, you know."

"Rabies? You were talking about leaking orifices before."

"Frankly, we don't know what we're dealing with, only

that I've never seen its like before. If we don't get a handle on it now, whatever this is, it could sweep through the station like wildfire."

Heather gulped again, hesitating. The Colonel wanted her to interrogate Reven. He wouldn't be able to stall the others for very long, no matter what he thought. But leaking orifices and rabies! Her skin crawled. *He is an alien. Who knows what diseases he's brought in here?* "Alright. Do what you have to do. But make it quick."

Chris turned to Amy, decked out in her own Hazmat suit, keeping her head down in case anyone recognized her. He touched her shoulder. "Go in and test the prisoner. I'll take care of everyone out here."

Amy nodded. Heather unlocked the door and Amy stepped inside, finally releasing the breath she had held, waiting to see if their ploy would work. It was one thing to think about an operation like this, a whole other thing to be in it! Her palms were sweaty, her heart was beating so hard she thought she'd break a rib, and her whole body shook. Carefully, she placed the testing box she carried on the table. Then she turned to the lone occupant of the cell.

He was sitting at the cold metal table, his hands chained to the top, his dark eyes watching her with a bemused grin on his face. "What? Did I accidentally wander onto some movie set, or do you always overreact to newcomers?"

Amy didn't know what she'd been expecting, but it wasn't someone so calm. "What do they want you for?"

"They? Aren't you with them? Or is this some kind of new interrogation technique?"

Amy removed her Hazmat helmet so she could breathe better. Her alarm bells went off that someone could stand on the other side of the one-way mirror and hear her, but she hoped Chris had rounded the rest of them up for 'inspection'. "I'm not with them. Not in the way you'd think. Now tell me, why do they want you?"

"Why do you want to know?"

"Because I'm the one that found you and I need to know why."

"Didn't they tell you?"

"It's the military. They don't tell peons shit."

He looked her up and down with a careful eye, judging her. "So you faked a virus outbreak to sneak down here because...why? Curiosity? Or some sense of morality?"

"Does it matter? Look, I don't have time. We can't stall them forever. What did you do they want you so bad?" Amy was growing frustrated. She was supposed to be getting answers, not giving them! Her palms got even sweatier, worrying about how Chris was doing. She knew he wouldn't hold Captain Smith off forever.

"We?"

"My friend who helped me get down here."

"So, you believed so strongly that you needed to talk to me, that you risked someone else too? What if I've done something completely horrible?"

"Then I'll go back to my prison cell happy that I could extract justice. Is that what you're telling me? That you did something horrible?" She snapped.

He smiled and sat back, apparently satisfied now that he had gotten a rise out of her. "No. I just wondered. You bust in here all alone after someone that you didn't even know because your conscience was nagging at you. Ballsy for a human."

"Yeah, they're so big I have to wear them on my chest. Now, will you please tell me what you did so I can go back? I don't think I'm cut out for this action stuff."

"What if I didn't do something bad? What if they want me for nothing?"

Amy paused. What would she do? All her plans up to this point had just been talking to Reven. If he even was Reven. What would she do if he were innocent? "I don't know. Kind of making this up as I go along. I guess I try to get you out somehow. I found you. It's my responsibility to help you."

"Noble. But that will not work for me. I needed into this place and now I'm here."

"What?" Amy didn't think she was hearing this correctly.

"You wanted to get caught?"

"I've been trying to get into here for years with no success. This was the only way I could think of making it happen. Although now that you're here, if you can get me out of these handcuffs and this room, I would appreciate it."

"Why would you want to break in here?" Amy still couldn't believe what she was hearing.

"I'm looking for someone."

"Someone else they've arrested?"

"Someone they're hiding here. A terrible someone. I need to find them." He lifted his hands, making the handcuffs clank. "So, are you going to help me?"

Amy stared at him for a moment, gave an exasperated sigh, then started stripping off the rest of the bulky suit. Fortunately, it had hidden her backpack of hacker toys. She started pulling things out even as she frowned at him. *Damn my stupid curiosity. Damn my stupid need to be challenged. I should just walk out of here, go back to my life. Yet I keep pulling things out of my bag because why not? Damn it!*

The little voice in her head chortled. *You didn't think we'd actually just stop at asking questions, did you? There's an adventure to be had!*

"Tell me this. Is that why they wanted you? Because you were trying to get in here?" Amy asked as she worked.

"They wanted me because I prove a danger to their guest.

As long as I'm alive, they're not safe here."

"Are you an assassin or something?" Amy peeked out the window. The hallway was clear, amazingly enough. *Thank you Chris. I owe you big time.*

"Nothing like that. I just know about them. As long as I'm out there, they can't hide. A lot of their power comes from being able to hide."

"Seems like you're giving them exactly what they wanted." She tossed a set of handcuff keys she'd stashed in her pack to Reven. Then, she turned to the door and inserted a blank key card into a slot at the bottom, the end of the card connected to a maze of cables running to a small handheld monitor. She toggled a few switches and typed in some codes. Numbers started blazing across the screen too fast to be read.

"Well, I had to give them something to get what I wanted. I need to kill their guests if I can. But if nothing else, find evidence of their existence so that others will listen."

"If they're being protected by the military, that might be a tall order." She thought of the classified files and sighed. He looked at her quizzically. "When I was trying to find information on you, I found a bunch of classified files. They might contain info on your enemies. But there's no way into them without setting off some major alarm bells. Once we do that, our chances of getting out of here go from slim to absolute zero."

"Our?"

"Well, yeah. You're taking me with you. No way I'm staying around here after all of this. You have a plan for getting out, right?"

He hesitated, and she glared at him. Amy said, "That's the only way this works, especially since I still don't know who you are or exactly what you've done. But all of this smells, and I'm done with it. So, I help you, you help me. Deal?"

He nodded slowly. "But you don't know what you're getting yourself into."

"Like that's ever stopped me before." The monitor beeped three times, and she grinned, pushing another button. The door clicked and slid aside. "Bingo."

"Won't they have cameras in the hallway? They'll see us."

"Not for long, they don't." She pulled out her phone and clicked on a program. More lines of code flowed over the screen. Suddenly, the hallway lights went out.

"Here." She handed a flashlight to Reven. "No power. No cameras."

"No way to open doors." Reven said.

"I can remotely activate different areas as we need them."

"You seem awfully prepared for this moment."

Amy laughed. "What can I say? Hackers are curious creatures. I was curious one day how easy it would be to control the environmental conditions of the base. Funny enough, turned out it was pretty easy."

"Well, I'm glad for curiosity then. Let's get moving. This won't confuse them for long."

Amy nodded and tiptoed out into the hallway.

"Which way?" Reven asked.

"Go right. I don't know where they're holding these people you are after, but following super secret government logic, the lower in the base something is, the more secretive it is. There's an elevator I saw in the floor plans over to the right. That should lead us to your mysterious guests."

They walked down the hallway as silently as they could, their bodies and senses tensed for the slightest sound. Amy tried to hush her breathing, but her heartbeat was thumping like a bass drum, blood whooshing in her ears. She was a hacker! What in the world was she doing sneaking around in the basement of a super secret military base?

But she had chosen this the moment she had searched for the files. She had gotten Chris involved, and sent a silent hope that he was okay. *What the hell was I thinking?*

Yet, even as her rational mind was berating her for all of this madness, for the tornado of poor decisions that had swept up Chris, her feet kept walking, driven by the excitement of adventure. The pair continued down the hallway and with every step; she felt her confidence growing.

Maybe she could do this. People did this all the time in movies, right?

"How much further to the elevator?" Reven whispered.

Amy said, "Right around the corner to the left."

"I don't like this."

Amy said, "We'll be fine. The good guys always win, right?"

She turned around the corner just as the lights in the hallway blazed to life. She shielded her eyes, suddenly blinded. But her ears were working fine as she heard a lot of guns clicking the safeties off. Her body froze.

A voice said, "Well, well. I think we found our hacker, gentlemen."

Amy's heart sank. She knew that voice. She lowered her arm, blinking rapidly until her eyes adjusted. The Colonel and several heavily armed soldiers came into focus standing in front of her and Reven, their automatic rifles pointed at her chest. Her breath caught, her muscles freezing, the bag dropping with a thunk from her shoulder.

"Going somewhere, you two?" The Colonel sneered. "Arrest them."

Amy protested as they pulled her arms behind her back. Her skin crawled as they slid the cold metal handcuffs around her wrists, a sob trying to escape as they clicked shut. Out of the corner of her eye, she saw Reven, his body as still and serene as a statue as they cuffed him. He simply stared forward, glaring at the Colonel.

She forced herself to take a deep breath. *If he can be calm, so can I.*

Not that it helped when her brain started helpfully supplying all that would happen now. Maybe they'd contain her in the Catacombs, a prisoner in solitary confinement for the rest of her days. More likely they'd send her to Treatment. That thought made her want to squirm and whimper again. *What the hell have I done? Just had to see, didn't I? Thought I was something special again. Now look at me.*

A soldier said, "What do you want us to do with them, Colonel?"

The Colonel stared at the prisoners, seething. *Damn, I wanted some time. Fuck Heather for falling for this shit. But maybe this could still work to my advantage somehow.* "Since these two seem so excited to meet our guests, let's introduce them. Take them below."

9

***

The entire group filed into the elevator. The car shuddered and descended. Amy shivered, even as the temperature rose within the confined space from the mass of bodies. One soldier prodded her in the back and she stiffened, but didn't complain. She glanced at Reven. He stared at the doors, beads of sweat forming on his brow.

"I guess you get your wish." She whispered.

He said, "Not exactly how I was picturing this moment."

"Quiet!" a soldier barked.

Amy hung her head and forced her tears back. Nothing good ended at this ride. She had thought the worst thing was going to Treatment but now she had gotten herself into this. Whatever this was. She had always thought herself clever before. Maybe there was still a way out of this. *Yeah, because you're so good at that. Every time you try to do something, you end up in a worse place than before.*

The elevator slowed, then settled with a slight groan. The doors opened, and she saw they were in a long hallway with a single door at the end. At an unseen signal, the group moved forward. Amy trudged down the hall, every step making her stomach fall heavier to the floor. The Colonel typed in the code and the door opened to reveal nothing but blackness. Amy cringed for a moment, but the soldier nudged her with the gun again. She stumbled forward, following the others into the abyss.

She stopped in her tracks as she saw the throne. Frozen. Her brain exploded as a million synapses screamed. Her stomach roiled as her world flipped over. There was something *else* there. Something huge, mean and alien. Probabilities rolled through her mind. Everything from the creatures were special effect puppets from Hollywood or some elaborate ruse to scare the prisoners into talking. But then the wheel stopped spinning and landed on the only outcome that made any sense.

THEY. WERE. REAL.

"I see you have brought us prisoners, Colonel." Avar said, his mouth curling into a toothy grin. "You have pleased us. But we only asked for the traitor. Who is this Breeder that you have brought?"

"An ally of the traitor we caught helping him. I thought she would make a welcome addition to the next shipment."

"What was it I told you about thinking? About how you shouldn't?" He snorted. "Well, I suppose she might have some useful information. You have done well, Colonel."

Avar almost purred. "Beren! When is the next shipment?"

"Tomorrow morning, my Lord."

"Good." Avar got up, descending from the throne and walking toward the group. His thick muscular tail swung behind him, his skin shifting colors, rippling across the muscular body.

Amy's stomach dry heaved as the stench of his body rolled ahead of him. She could see the bits of dried flesh and blood on his teeth. It gave her a little comfort that the Colonel quivered as well, struggling to maintain his stone exterior.

As Avar came forward, the ring of soldiers shifted nervously, backing away from Reven.

Reven just stared defiantly at this behemoth that towered over him. He stood his ground, as still as a marble statue. A king looking up at a giant.

Avar snarled and curled a claw under Reven's chin, lifting it up slightly. Reven didn't even flinch. "Yes. We will please the Queen very much with your arrest. After all the trouble you have brought us, I would have thought you would be more substantial. Pathetic."

Beren and Avar both chuckled, a grating sound that made her spine want to separate and run in different directions. Avar returned to his throne. He spoke again to the Colonel. "Take them to the hold to await shipment. Keep the traitor under tight supervision. We wouldn't want to disappoint the Queen with any incompetence, now would we?"

"I can assure there you will be no escape."

"See to it you keep that promise, Colonel. Dismissed."

The soldiers quickly collected Reven and Amy and escorted them out of the door. The quick step continued down the hall. Amy kept quiet, her head bowed.

The group reached the elevator and got in. As the doors closed, the Colonel opened a special panel and flipped a red button. The elevator walls groaned and clanged as gears unlatched and then meshed again. Without warning, the car jerked sideways, forcing Amy to brace herself against Reven to keep her balance.

She looked in alarm at the others, but their faces were stone. Even Reven looked like he had been expecting this, staring straight ahead as if seeing something far away. Amy looked down at her feet, feeling disembodied as they moved sideways through space. She looked overhead, imagining the mountain of steel and stone that existed overhead. Of her room, her once peaceful life that she had apparently thrown away. A life that existed before aliens became real. Now anything was possible, and anything was horrible.

What the hell have I done?

10

***

A few minutes later, the elevator shuddered to a stop. The doors opened, and the group filed out. As Amy stepped out into the artificial light, she gasped in surprise.

They were in a large underground warehouse, much larger than the Hub. She could see steel catwalks and industrial lighting overhead. They stood on another metal walkway suspended between rooms made of a clear plastic material.

The little group marched down the walkway, passing saluting soldiers who were guarding the rooms, each heavily armed. Other humans in white lab coats walked back and forth, consulting clipboards and peering into rooms, checking data on the screens that were placed by the doors. As the group passed one room, Amy saw odd beige shapes huddled in side. At first she shivered, thinking that these were more alien creatures. But the truth smacked her in the face as one of the beige shapes shifted and looked up, its eyes locking on hers. The huddled shapes were people, hundreds of people!

"What in the..." Amy whispered, pausing as she stared in disbelief.

"Quiet!" the soldier barked and shoved her forward with his gun.

Colonel Holloway stopped in front of a metal door set into a concrete wall. Soldiers unlocked their handcuffs, then shoved Amy and Reven into the room, the pair stumbling and trying to regain their balance.

All the Colonel said was, "Welcome to your new home. For now."

Then the metal door slammed shut.

She dropped to her knees. "What . . . the . . . hell."

Reven's eyes hadn't left the door. "Gods. It's worse than I thought."

She rounded on Reven. "What is that out there? Those people!"

"Welcome to the Feedlot." He whispered. He sunk to the floor against the wall, holding his head in his arms.

"I'm sorry. The Feedlot?"

"It's where they store all the humans until it's time to send a shipment. I'd heard about it, of course, but to see it in person . . ." He hung his head, shaking it as if to shake off the memories of what he had seen. She thought she saw a tear fall down his face, but stayed silent.

He raised his head, a sad smile on his face. "Bet you're sorry you got involved now."

"I'll be sorry later. Right now, I'm angry. Tell me right now what is going on. What are those things? What the hell is going on with those people, and who the hell are you?"

"Those things are the Tark."

"The Tark?" Amy rolled the unfamiliar word on her

tongue. "I can't believe it. Aliens on Earth."

Reven chuckled. "Alien. That word's definition in your vocabulary is about to change. You're as alien to them as they are to you. As for the Tark, that is a long, complicated, horrible story."

Amy tried to steady herself by taking a deep breath. Panicking wouldn't serve her any good. She walked over to Reven and sank down to sit beside him. "I don't think we're going anywhere right now. So, it would probably be a good time to chat."

He eyed her. "You sure? It is a lot for some people to take. The truth."

"I'm not sure about anything. But I've always been able to survive because I had information. So, spill it."

She took a deep breath. A niggling thought was blossoming in her mind. "Besides, who better to tell me about aliens than an alien?"

His eyes widened. "You know?"

Amy shivered. "I didn't until just now. But I was wondering why those Tark wanted you so bad. What would they have to fear from humans? But another alien . . . that thought crossed my mind. Although knowing it's true doesn't make that easier. But you've not tried to eat me yet, so you can't be that bad. Just promise me you won't lie anymore. Especially with the form. The human likeness is weird."

He said, "I didn't lie before. My name is Reven. It means 'avenger' in my language. Guess my parents knew about my future. As for being an alien, I am a member of the Ra'shek. This is my true form."

Amy said, "But . . . you look like a normal human."

"Yes. Modern television and all their ideas about other life forms. Hollywood did a horrible job of preparing humanity for other beings. But there is a wide universe out there, and a lot of life has found interesting ways of developing. Like our 'friends' the Tark back there. As far as why you look like us, it's simple. You are the ancestors of Ra'shek travelers who became stranded here."

"You . . .you mean I'm. . ."

"You are not Ra'shek. You are human. After they became stranded here, your ancestors developed into their own race. Humanity."

I'm descended from aliens. What the hell? Amy closed her eyes and leaned her head against the cool wall, trying to will away the headache that was forming behind her eyes.

Aliens were real. Other life forms were real. She was talking to one. "So, tell me the story."

"You still want to know?"

"No. But I'm here and I'm a prisoner. Might as well know what I'm going to die for."

"You think you're going to die?"

She stared at him. "Seems a reasonable assumption, judging from your friend's claws and teeth. So tell me. What is going on?"

He said, "I don't even know how to start. I guess I'd start with the Tark. They're powerful, vicious, intelligent beings. At least, intelligent with war and destroying things."

"Huh. Well, they're not all that different from humans then."

"No, they're not. Only you've not figured out how to get off your planet. Not really, anyway. The Tark though, they mastered interspace travel long ago."

A lightbulb clicked in Amy's mind. She whispered. "Roswell. I knew it."

"Roswell?"

"The ship that crashed."

An explosive laugh ripped out of Reven. She stared at him with a sour expression on her face. He looked at her and shook his head. "Sorry, it's just. . .No. That was a hoax. Perpetrated by the government to mask the actual story."

"You mean they wanted us to believe it was a spaceship? They weren't trying to cover it up?"

"Oh, there was a coverup. They just wanted everyone looking the wrong way. Get the wrong idea."

"I don't get any of this." Amy closed her eyes again,

wondering if she went to sleep she'd wake up to find this had just been a nightmare. *Too much junk food and video games. That has to be it.*

Reven said, "There's a lot to take in. A lot of history. But if we're going to survive, which is a slim possibility, it might help if you get a crash course."

"Did you have to say crash?" She winced. "Doesn't exactly inspire confidence."

That brought out another smile. "Well, you still haven't lost your sense of humor. That's good. I know this is a lot. But forget the idea of UFOs. The Tark don't move by ships. There is no way to cover the vast distances of the universe in a ship, at least not and get somewhere else before everyone on board has aged and died. No, they discovered a way to travel planet to planet that had nothing to do with ships. Interdimensional travel."

"I don't understand. I thought physics said that was impossible."

"Physics. You humans and your need for rules and order. Yes, the rules of physics apply. Yet there are things out there that your science doesn't understand. Things made of energy and dark matter that you can't quantify with a number or a term. Shadows that lie between the rules. It's in these shadows that the Tark play. Hopping and skipping from planet to planet. That's what happened in your Roswell. It wasn't a ship crashing. It was a blast of energy from the Tarks, creating a gateway."

"Why did they come?"

He took a deep breath. "Tarks only come to a planet for one of two reasons. To annihilate the dominant life form and strip it of its resources, or to subjugate the locals and use them as an ongoing food source."

"Food?" Amy felt her face go pale as the blood drained out. *The people out there...*

"Tarks are carnivores. You get the picture."

Amy felt her stomach plummeted through the floor. "So those people out there. . ."

"All part of the Feedlot. In exchange for not ruining your planet and extinguishing humanity, your leaders agree to send a certain amount of food to the Home World for the Tark's consumption."

"Is that what happened to your people?"

His voice became tight. "No. My people would not bow. The Tark slaughtered them. They razed the cities, carrying off what they could and destroying what they could not. They burned the forests, tore down our fields. My planet died."

"I'm sorry."

His voice grew somber. "It was a long time ago. It doesn't matter now."

Amy was silent, letting the storm pass from his face. *Grief never ends, no matter what we want to lie and tell ourselves. I can't imagine...*

Time to change the train of conversation. "They called me a Breeder."

Reven's eyes were still unfocused, lost in the past, but he pulled himself back at her question. "They call the female of any species Breeder. Their way to signify that you are not just food, you create more food. Unfortunately for you, they consider any Breeder the lowest of the low in rank."

"God." *Even aliens are sexist, great.* "So that's it. I'm food now? Or a food creation system? Those are my choices?"

"Maybe for you, but I'm not giving up yet."

Amy glared daggers at him. "You seem awfully confident for someone locked in a concrete room. I don't have my hacker toys anymore, remember? They sent your people to Treatment. The lizards know you're here, and we're going to be shipped. Unless you've suddenly sprouted the ability to shoot laser beams out of your eyes, I don't really see any other solution to this scenario than both of us dying."

"Well, yeah. Got me there. But there's always a way." His head snapped up as the bolt on the door clicked. "Maybe here's one now."

He said the last part so quietly Amy wasn't sure she heard

it. But before she could ask him to repeat it, the door swung open. She stiffened, expecting the hoard of soldiers that would carry her to her doom. But it was only Colonel Holloway. He strode in, closing the door behind him. He waited, listening for something, then nodded in satisfaction at some unseen signal.

"I'll make this brief." He ignored Amy and locked eyes with Reven. "We have little time before the next scheduled shipment. I've just received word that Beren himself is coming to oversee it. They sure hate you, Mr. Reven."

"We have a long history." Reven's lips curled into a smile as he glared at the Colonel.

"Pity that I don't have time to hear all about it. But perhaps we can still assist each other."

"Assist you?" Amy spat out. "You're sending us off to be lunch."

"Shut up, you nosy bitch. If you hadn't involved yourself, I wouldn't have to be doing this."

"Hey! She's not a part of this. Leave her alone." Reven jumped to his feet.

Colonel Holloway chuckled. "Coming to the aid of the damsel already? How noble. Now sit down. I'm here to present you with an alternative to your current situation."

"Aren't you afraid your overlords will figure out you're conspiring with us?" Reven asked with a smirk.

"If this room works like its supposed to, they won't even know." The Colonel answered.

Reven looked around the thick metal walls. "You put us in here on purpose?"

"Didn't you think it was odd we didn't just put you in an empty cell with the others? Well, have to say I'm a little disappointed. I thought you would be more astute considering how scared of you our friends are. I built this room to block out every heightened physical sense we could think of. Unless your friends can read minds." The Colonel stared intensely at Reven. "Can they?"

Reven shook his head. "No. I don't think so. They are very good guessers and know how to manipulate people's emotions. But I've not seen any of them read a mind. They do have a connected hive mind, though. They can talk to each other over great distances."

"Drat. So if we ambushed one…"

"The other would know about it. I'm not sure how far the range extends, but I know the queen can command her troops from great distances on the same planet."

"You've been to their home planet?"

Reven shook his head. "No. But I have friends."

Colonel Holloway smiled that predatory smile. "I knew it."

Why is Reven giving anything to this eel? Amy wanted to

scream, but held her tongue. Her mouth had already gotten her in enough trouble. Besides, Reven had a look in his eye that told her he knew what he was doing.

Reven leaned back against the wall. "Don't tell me you want to join the Resistance. Somehow, I don't see you as a team player."

"Your kind can't win, and you know it. I play to win, simple as that." Colonel Holloway took a deep breath. "But these pests threaten my world. I want them gone. I think you know how."

Reven said, "Perhaps I do. But I wonder how willing you are to pay the price."

"What price? Your freedom?"

Reven laughed. "We both know that will not happen. No, I'm talking about how much of a price are you willing to pay in blood because that's what it's going to take to destroy the Tark."

The Colonel grew solemn. "Try me."

Reven bowed his head for a moment, then raised it, holding the Colonel with his gaze. "The two sent here are scouts. They send scouts ahead to assess a planet: finding its weak points, seeing what resources it provides, what resistance they might find, and so on. Killing the scouts will get you nothing except being put on the annihilate list."

Colonel Holloway nodded his head. "And?"

"The Tarks' greatest strength is also their weakness. The queen. Take her out, and it will be thrown into chaos."

"They will die?"

Reven shrugged. "We don't know. No one has been able to get close enough to test the theory. They may be so closely linked that the queen's death would kill them all, but that's a very slim chance. We have been able to figure out that because of their hive mind, a death of a commander causes great pain and disorientation to the ones who hear them. The queen is connected to every single Tark when she wishes. Imagine the pain radiating from her death."

Silence ensued as the Colonel digested Reven's words. Then he snorted. "How are we to get to the Queen?"

"Especially as two scouts were enough to cow your army and you're talking about a planet of thousands if not millions? How indeed." A smirk crept across Reven's face. *Big bad army man and his puffed up ego. I've been fighting these monsters longer than anyone. Fool doesn't even know an ally when he sees one. He thinks I'm just a tool.*

The Colonel snarled, suddenly leaping at Reven, pinning him to the wall. "Worthless. You're worthless!"

"You wanted a way." Reven choked out. "I gave it to you. It's the only one I know of."

The Colonel snarled again, but released Reven who slumped to the ground. He glared down at the man.

"Useless."

The Colonel stormed out, the door slamming and locking behind him. Amy turned to Reven, angry. "Why did you tell him? You didn't even bargain for our release! What if he tells the Tark?"

Reven shook his head "The Colonel doesn't have the power to release us, so I didn't bother asking. Beren himself is coming to oversee the shipment. He'd know if we weren't in it. The Colonel isn't going to risk that. As to him telling the Tark, he might if it gets him a better deal, but it won't. All it does is tell the Tark he knows their secret, and so is a threat to them."

"So, you played him. If he tells, he's dead. If he doesn't, the Tark are still unaware that others know their secret."

"Right. We can't be released, but if he's pushed enough he might become an ally, even if an unwilling one. With the army's firepower, an invasion against the Tark could be worked out. If he doesn't, we have a secret we can hold over him, one that would prove his death if we revealed it to the Tark. They don't take kindly to traitors."

"So, what happens now? The shipment?"

Reven sighed. "We'll be sent to the Tark Home World. Hopefully, my friends will get us out before we become dinner."

Amy wanted to ask more questions, then stopped. She

eyed the walls. "They could be listening."

"The Tark know about the Resistance. That's why they wanted me. They think by taking me out, the Resistance will fall."

"Will it?"

Reven looked at her and smiled. "No way."

Amy sighed and leaned back against the wall. "So, why do you do it? Put yourself in danger?"

"Well, my people had a saying. 'Ta a'no shen' It means 'Our hearts are bound together'."

"That's beautiful. But I don't understand?"

"I didn't for the longest time either." He sighed. "My people were some of the first to fall to the Tark. We were a convergence point, a point in the universe where the energies are greater making it easier for gateways to emerge. Gateways just happen naturally on our worlds, although my people created technologies that allowed us to control and direct the gateways. The Tark planet is another convergence point. When the Tarks found their gates, they blundered onto our world. My people were not natural warriors, but we were fierce. We did not bow. We fought, but lost to the Tark onslaught. The Tarks tortured and enslaved some of my people, enough to understand the use of the gates."

His breath caught in his throat, and his eyes roved to the ceiling while he gathered his thoughts. "I escaped. I used the gateway to try to reach the Tark Home World, but ended up on anther world instead."

He looked down at his hands, a warm smile on his face. "The people of that world were nice. Even though I was different, they took me in. They were a simple people, hunters and farmers. But I grew to love that world. My heart started healing. Only, the Tark came. They destroyed the world. Enslaved the people. Their cries are etched into my brain, just like the ones of my people. I managed to avoid the Tark once more, but that attack taught me something."

"What was that?"

"That every creature, every breathing thing on every planet is bound together. All of our hearts are bound together, whether we feel them or not. When death comes for one heart, it comes for every single one of them. And the Tarks, this death, would never stop coming for those hearts. Not unless someone stood up against them."

"So, you decided to stand up to them?"

Reven nodded. "As time passed, others stood up with me. Even on the Tark Home World, some escaped and worked to free others. That was the start of the true Resistance. We fight together to protect the universe."

"Wow." Amy shook her head. "That's why you came here? To save the humans."

Reven nodded. "I was trying."

Amy smiled a sad smile. "Well, A for effort I guess. Although, the whole me getting eaten thing feels like a failure."

"You're not eaten yet."

"You're arrested. Ever been this trapped before?"

He sighed. "Nothing this...dire. But one thing I've learned, never give up hope. Giving up hope lets them win before the battle has even been fought. We always hold out hope for luck to side with us."

She knew it was meant to be comforting, but all it did was turn her insides numb. *Luck and I have never been friends. Guess curiosity is finally going to kill this TabbyKat.*

Reven watched as Amy slumped against the wall, closing her eyes. She looked so small and helpless. For the first time since he had hatched this plan weeks ago, he shivered. He looked upwards, wondering what was happening to his friends. Kevin. Tosh. Sophia. That certainly hadn't been in the plan, them getting arrested with him. But Whisper moved faster than he thought. And Amy...

He watched her, wondering if she was asleep or just resigned to her fate. The hard, rational part of his brain dismissed her as another casualty of war. There had been enough of them over the years. But looking at her now, he knew how she felt. Her whole world view had just been shattered. She was here because she had tried to help him, a human sacrificing herself for someone she didn't even know, for a situation that she hadn't understood. Trapped. As brave as he felt, he didn't think he could get out of this, let alone get her out with him.

He had been so focused on getting in and getting to the scouts. *Can I finally admit it? The thing I've known all along. I never had a plan. I got mad. I got frustrated. I rushed in here, determined to get at them. I got nothing. I know better, but I rushed in anyway because I didn't care what happened to me. Because I was so determined to be the Avenger, so tired of running and not being able to take the fight to them. I didn't care if my life ended. Maybe...maybe I even welcomed the thought of it all ending.*

He looked over at Amy again. *But it's not just my life at stake, is it?*

11

***

A group of soldiers came into the room the next morning, waking them. One of them barked, "Get up."

Once handcuffed, the soldiers led them from the room. All the clear prisons had opened, and a flood of people flowed down the walkways of the Feedlot. The soldiers shoved Reven and Amy into that flood. People staggered and stumbled along, mostly silent except for the shuffling of feet, the silence punctuated randomly with a sob or whimper. Any eye Amy caught quickly looked away, fearful of reprisal from the soldiers. It shocked Amy to see that although the prisoners wore clean beige smocks, many had bruises and scars that spoke of a rough life.

"The homeless. The throwaways." Reven whispered to her.

"What?"

"That is who your government sends. The ones that people will not miss. Have you ever wondered at all the people that go missing every year?"

"Well..." No. She had never worried. She hadn't even given it a thought. But looking at the flood now... "So many."

"Too many." Reven's face was grim. "Brace yourself."

"For what?" Her eyes found the answer as they drifted forward. The flood had brought them to what appeared to be the end of the facility. Gray rock towered above them, the facility carved out of the ground like a man-made cave. But that is not what chilled her to the core.

A ring of metal towered three stories above the crowd. It sat perched on a dais, stairs leading from the floor up to the base of the ring. In the middle of this metal ring, lightning cracked. Not the quick crack of lightning from a storm, the one that is gone in a blinding flash, but a continuous bolt that writhed and snaked from two points in space. The center burned white like flaring magnesium. From this, blue and purple lightning snaked out, searching and reaching for victims. As she watched, soldiers pushed a pair of people up the stairs.

The pair paused at the foot of the ring, crying out. One screamed as a tendril touched him, a red mark searing across his arm. Tears flowed, and they tried to scramble backward. The soldiers growled and shoved them roughly. The couple staggered forward into the central beam.

A sharp snap cracked through the air. A flash of blinding light. When Amy's vision cleared, the people were gone. The dais was empty of everything except that crackling bolt of energy within the ring.

A thousand things happened at once. Amy's body lost control and her boneless legs folded to the floor. The flood screamed as one and started pushing and shoving, wanting to be anywhere but where that light touched. The roar of a thousand voices screaming and crying filled the cavern. Whips and rifles cracked in the air, trying to be heard above the noise and calm the crowd, but only serving to further increase the panic.

Reven crouched beside her as the flood panicked, trying to shield her with his body. He was saying something, screaming it to her over the noise. Her eyes followed that his mouth was moving. But all she heard was that crack of the beam enveloping those people, again and again. After what seemed like an hour, her mind snapped into focus again.

"Amy!" Reven yelled. "Amy, do you hear me?"

"I . . . I hear you."

"Listen. Listen to me."

"I'm listening." She shrank against him as the crowd bucked again. The soldiers formed a ring around the two, protecting them from the worst as others worked to control the panicked beasts.

"Your only chance to survive going through the beam is to focus. Focus on something or you'll lose your mind."

"What?"

"That beam is the gateway, the same one the Tarks used to reach this world. I don't have time to explain it, but it pulls apart your atoms and transfers it through space to the gateway on the Tark world. If you don't focus on something, it will pull your essence apart. You won't survive."

Science fiction. It was like every science fiction movie or game she had ever played. Only it was real. Too real. "I can't do it."

"Yes, you can. Focus. If you don't, the gateway will destroy your mind."

Amy wanted to respond, but suddenly a voice bellowed into the air, a menacing, predatory growl that echoed through her bones. "Enough!"

The group quieted on cue, all staring at the dais. Beren walked out of the shadows, towering over the people. Some whimpered and cried, but most stayed as silent as they could. Amy could almost feel their minds breaking at the sight, as hers had when she had seen the Tark. Now she glared up at their captor.

Beren looked down at the mass of people and growled. "Be good beasts and go through."

He glared down at the soldiers. "Make them move."

Amy saw with just a little satisfaction that the soldiers closest to Beren jumped. For a second, she wondered how they could send their own kind to death. But putting herself in their place, she understood. Better the missing than them. She watched as more soldiers poured in, pushing the crowd back into a line. Slowly, the line started moving. The beam snapped and crackled with great urgency now as the soldiers sent pair after pair through the gate.

Their own escort pulled Reven and Amy to their feet, shoving them forward. They reached the dais, and it took every ounce of strength to make her sluggish feet move and climb. Tears fell silently down her cheeks. She hated the fact that everyone could see her fear. But she didn't know how to make the tears stop.

Their escort stopped short of the top, and Beren came over, smiling. "Avar wants me to escort these two personally. The Queen will be pleased to see them."

The Colonel appeared and nodded. "Will you be staying on the Home World long?"

Beren chuckled, a horrible grating sound. "You would like that, wouldn't you human? Thinking about catching us napping? No, I will stay only long enough to hand them over."

The Colonel struggled not to look disappointed and almost managed. "Very well."

Beren turned and strode confidently into the light. It enveloped him with a snap.

The Colonel turned to face Reven. "Any last words? You could still help us."

"Help yourself, you mean. Nothing I say will get me out of these cuffs now."

The Colonel sneered. "You put yourself in those cuffs when you were stupid enough to fight them head on.

Enough. Beren is waiting."

The Colonel nodded at their escort. "Get going."

Their group moved forward. Reven turned his head to Amy. "Grab my hands."

"How? They cuffed us behind our backs."

"Stand back to back. Grab my hands."

"Why?"

They were within a few steps now. She could smell the ozone burning as they approached, the heat crawling on her skin. Once more her legs tried to buckle, but the pressure of the soldier kept them moving.

Reven's voice became desperate. "Grab my hands. Focus on something. Or your mind will snap."

She didn't really hear the words. But knew she had seconds to do something. Anything was better than facing that unknown alone. She swirled to face away, grabbing for his hands. They were warm and solid. His fingers interlocked with hers.

"Remember." The wind crackled and roared, threatening to overcome his voice. Yet, she heard it as if he leaned into her ear. "I am here. Ta a'no shen."

Light enveloped her, and her ears burst with a sound that wasn't a sound. The ground dropped out beneath her feet and she felt herself hurling through nothing. The only connection she had was his hands, strong and warm. She focused on them, anchoring her thoughts as her body burst apart in a million points of light, swirling away, caught in a whirlpool.

His touch was everything. Blazing hot winds lashed at her body. Lightning crackled over her eyes, her retinas exploding in a burst of color. Still, she clung to him. Him and the last words he had said. *Ta a'no shen. Our hearts are bound.*

Then she was standing on solid ground again. A dais matching the one they had left. But even as her senses focused, a world of horror presented itself to her.

Her stomach retched, the contents joining the flood of sick that rolled down the stairs. They were in another chamber, this one made of black stone that shone like glass. A gaping black mouth opened on one end of the chamber, through which a stumbling torrent of people walked. Tarks, masses of them, stood on either side, pushing the humans along. The people stared straight ahead, no emotions at all. Some couldn't even walk and had slumped to the ground at the foot of the dais. Or were dead. It was hard to tell. A pair of Tarks picked them up and slung them into a wagon.

Reven pressed his body into hers, his warmth and strength flowing into her body, steadying her and driving back the searing cold that had chilled her to the core. She looked up at him, her voice wavering. "What?"

It was one word, but Reven understood it covered a flood of questions. He gave her a wan smile. "Welcome to the Terminal on Kalluk. The Tark Home World."

She glanced up just as two Tarks came from out of the shadows, pushing them down the dais. Behind her, she heard a snap and two more humans appeared. They both vomited like her, one collapsing and rolling down the stairs. They pushed the other forward to join the massive line out of the chamber.

They led Reven and Amy to where Beren stood talking to two other Tarks. They were different, with red crests on their heads decorated with jewels. Amy noted with a little satisfaction that the once mighty Beren was acting subordinate to these new ones.

"Sirs, Avar sends the Queen a gift, the rebel called Reven." Beren swept his hand to show Reven and Amy.

The two turned lazily toward them. One's lips curled in distaste. "Sorry excuse for a rebel. What is with the Breeder? It's been all sick over itself."

The other chuckled. "Weak human. Can't even handle a little travel."

"Sirs, if I may..." Beren tried to speak up, but the first one backhanded him hard.

"Silence, scout! I did not give you permission to speak."

The first glared at Reven, cupping his chin with a claw.

"Do you know who I am, rebel? No? Well, let me introduce you. I am Quantar of the Queen's Own. You are lucky enough to get a personal escort to the palace where your death awaits."

"Sir, Avar asked if..." Beren tried again.

"Avar asks nothing!" Quantar growled. "If I want to listen to the nattering of a lowly off-world scout who has become too full of himself watching over a mudhole, I'll go through the gate myself."

"Yes, sir." Beren shrank back.

"What about the Breeder?" The other one asked, amused by the interplay between Quantar and Beren. "Is she somehow important to this interchange?"

Beren looked up at Quantar fearfully. Quantar nodded ever so slightly and Beren rushed his words out. "She was helping the rebel. Avar thought it best..."

"Avar never could think or he wouldn't be a scout." Quantar snorted. His gaze turned to Amy, whose knees turned to jelly. "Still, she could have information. We will bring her before the Queen as well. I think she will be quite pleased with what Tobas and I have brought her."

Beren looked confused. "Sir? But Avar and I?"

Quantar growled and lashed out at Beren, swiftly kicking him across the floor where he crashed into the line, knocking ten humans down beneath his bulk. Quantar watched him struggle to get up and laughed. "You have done nothing. Now, get back to your little mud world before I decide to bite your head off."

Amy could see Beren's body tense as he death-stared Quantar. For a moment, his hand flexed by the axe on his belt. The air between the two hummed with tension. Then Beren snorted, bowed his head, and turned back to the dais. With a snap of energy, he was gone.

Quantar snorted. "Imbecile."

He glared at the second one. "Tobas, what are you still doing here? Raise an escort and take them to the castle."

Tobas shrugged and gave a brief grin. "As you wish, sir."

Tobas sauntered off. Two of the other Tark soldiers took Amy and Reven and pushed them to the ground on the side of the dais. Amy sighed and shivered. Her head ached, and all she wanted to do was lay down and sleep, not have to think about dealing with this nightmarish place and her survival.

"You okay?" Reven whispered.

"Well, other than the obvious, my head is killing me."

"Transport sickness. You were lucky to just get a mild case, then. Good."

"Good?" She wanted to be angry, but didn't have the energy. "Transport sickness. Is that what happened to them?"

She pointed at the growing pile with her chin. Reven sighed. "I didn't know it was this bad. But I guess you don't care if your meat arrives dead or alive, or with a brain."

Amy gulped as her stomach threatened to come up again. "Would that have happened to me?"

"That's why I told you to concentrate and hold on to me. Transporting through a gate causes major stress to your brain, and can cause serious damage. After a time, a species grows to deal with the strain. But your people have no immunity. Focusing can help. You'll still have a horrible headache for a while, even with a mild case."

Amy leaned back against the cold stone of the dais. *Maybe it would have been better to lose my brain.* "I didn't think the Tark here would speak English."

Reven gave her an odd look. "What are you talking about?"

"I can understand them. They're speaking English, right? Like the scouts back at the base. That I kind of understood, but why would they speak English here?"

Reven looked confused for a moment, but then his eyes opened up in wonder. "The gate gave you its gift."

"Gift?"

"I told you the gates affect your mind. In some, they destroy it. In others, they give it a gift. Like me, it gave you the ability to hear and speak other languages, but you think it's your own."

"So, you think you're speaking the language of the

Ra'shek even though I hear you in English?" She stared at him in wonder. *The gates messed with my brain and now I hear other languages.*

"No. I learned English. But that's what's happening. They are speaking their native tongue, but you hear their words in yours."

"Oh goody. My brain short-circuited, and now I can hear them talking about eating me. Yippee."

Reven stared off into the distance, but a smile grew on his face. "It could come in handy. Especially if everyone believes you don't understand them."

Before she could ask more questions, Tobas and a group of guards all with red crests showed up. "Looks like our escort is here."

Reven nodded with a grim look on his face. "We need to be careful. I've heard of the Queen's Own. The best of the best and the worst of the worst. They're manipulative and cunning. They won't think twice about slitting your throat."

"Oh, joy." Amy sarcastically replied.

"Just stay close to me and say nothing. If an opportunity to escape presents itself, we can't miss it."

The group approached and pulled them to their feet. Quantar sneered as she stumbled and she looked up into his eyes. Her knees threatened to fold again, but she held them stiff. He wanted her to be afraid, off-balance. He was a predator who wanted to see his prey squirm, like a cat playing with a mouse.

"Ready to go, sir." Tobas drawled.

Quantar nodded, and the group set off out of the chamber through the exit. As the darkness of the tunnel descended around her, the thought that had been sniping at Amy since they had first stepped through the gate blossomed in her mind.

She was no longer on earth. She was the alien here.

12

***

Amy wasn't sure what she expected as their group emerged from the Terminal, but nothing prepared her for what she saw. She blinked, blinded by the blazing sun overhead. Wait, suns. Twin suns blazed in the bright blue sky. Heat blasted her as her eyes blinked against the harsh light.

They were standing at the side of a mountain, the peak towering far above them. Red stone houses stretched away out into the distance, the houses simple but sized for the Tark's massive bulk. At the edge of the city, an enormous palace of red stone loomed over the city, its massive red spires twisted and reaching into the sky like claws.

"Welcome to Cahatch." Reven whispered. "The one and only city of the Tark and home to both their grand army and Queen."

A massive two-wheeled cart stood nearby, harnessed to a tall, gaunt four-legged creature that reminded her of a horse. Amy gasped as one soldier picked her up, his claws pinning her arms to her side, and tossed her unceremoniously into the back of the cart. Reven landed with a thump beside her. The driver looked down at them for a moment before turning back to the front. With a click and a harsh word, the horse creature bellowed, and the cart lurched forward.

When she finally struggled to sit upright, her only view was of the high cart walls and what was directly behind them. Two of the soldiers trotted behind the cart. The rest of the soldiers were probably encircling the cart, Amy surmissed. Once in a while she heard a shout to 'Make Way' or 'Clear the Road'. She caught glimpses of a crowd of Tarks staring in bewildered expressions at the cart as they passed. They were all about six feet tall, dressed in an array of robes in white, gray, and brown. Some carried baskets.

Reven pulled himself up to a sitting position, balancing himself against the jolting of the cart. "Civilians."

"Civilians?"

"It's what the Tark call them, or at least what it translates to. The lower class of the Tark people. Makers, those who produce goods, are all male. The Breeders are all female and give birth to the soldiers and Makers. The soldiers all think themselves above the Makers, and especially the Breeders, but begrudgingly respect them as essential for existence."

"I was expecting something more…advanced. Stone walls and wooden carts. I don't…"

"Understand how they mastered intergalactic travel? Don't let the appearances fool you. They're not as backward as you might think. They worked with what the land gave them. But they got lucky with the interdimensional travel. They stumbled onto it. One accident saved their civilization and doomed dozens more."

"Saved them?"

Reven nodded. "The Tark are a brave and strong people,

but their ruling class is just as stupid as any other. There are tales it was once a lush land, filled with different tribes. The tribes would have small skirmishes and wars, but nothing large-scale. Then the ruling classes got it in their heads that they needed to own everything. So every one of them set out to destroy everyone else. Soon, they destroyed the entire planet. The entire world is a desert, filled with dry lakes, broken mountains and dead trees."

"Which is why they have to go after other worlds and races."

"Yup. One day, someone got smart and created an army to destroy all the other tribes and brought them under one ruler. Their first Queen. It stopped the wars, at least with each other, but the damage was done. There was nothing left in this world. Without the gates, they would have starved and died out."

"Why don't they leave this world?"

"Because transporting your people to another world is a monumental task. Besides, no one would dare attack them, not openly."

"Why not?"

"Think about it. The gates open up right into the principal city, full of their entire fighting force. Maybe you could get out of the Terminal and into the city, providing your soldiers were even fit to fight after transporting from wherever. But it would be suicide."

"But you want to take them down, right?"

Reven grinned, whispering low. "There are multiple ways to win a war. Not everyone needs an army."

Amy sighed. "My head hurts."

Reven's eyes softened. "It's been a lot. I'm sorry."

"What do you think will happen when we get there? Taken to the Queen, I mean."

Reven did not speak, but that silence spoke volumes. Amy sighed again and closed her eyes. "Yeah. That's what I thought."

She heard a shuffling, then felt Reven sitting beside her, so close she could feel the heat from his body. He did not speak, and she relished in his closeness. The tangible touch of another being, the one person in the universe who didn't want to see her dead and on a dinner platter.

Finally, Reven spoke. "Don't give up hope yet."

Amy opened her mouth to unleash a sarcastic response, but shut it quickly as the air suddenly exploded with a loud crash of thunder. The cart jumped and bounced sideways, spilling Reven and Amy to the ground. She cried out as splintered wood cut through her skin, her body jolting as it hit the ground. A choking fit cut off her cries as smoke and dust filled the air.

Suddenly, out of the cloud of chaos, a dark figure far too

small to be a Tark and dressed in a hooded cloak loomed over her. Before she could react, the figure had snatched her up and thrown her over its shoulder. She saw a similar figure grabbing Reven. A second later, the foursome was bounding off into the darkness. She heard the yells and growls of the Tark interspersed with the clanging of weapons. But the sounds faded as they turned a corner and the figure carried Amy down a narrow alleyway.

The dust soon cleared, but her only viewpoint was the ground as her captor ran through the twisting and turning alleyways. Bells rang out, soldiers yelled, but the stone walls that towered over them muffled all. Finally, her transport stopped, and they lowered her to the ground.

"There. That should confuse them for a while." Her captor's voice was young and strong, with a hint of a British accent. She looked up to see shining blue eyes smiling at her over a mask. "You ok, miss?"

The second person had arrived with Reven in tow. Reven already had his wrist restraints off, and he knelt behind Amy to undo hers. "You okay?"

"Yes, sorry for the rough ride, miss. Needed a bit of distraction to pull that off in broad daylight."

Amy rubbed her wrists, unsure who to answer first, then decided she could answer both with a simple. "I'm alright."

Reven stood up and reached out a hand. "Well done

Tam. And quickly put together."

The man pulled back his hood, revealing black spiky hair and a youthful face that put him in his twenties. "Save the thank you, sir, until we're free. We need to get off the street."

Reven nodded and the other unidentified man walked over to a grate set into a wall, pulling it aside. Reven looked back the way they had come. "What about the others?"

Tam was already walking over to the hole revealed by the grate. "They'll be along shortly, sir. Taking their own routes. Can't have anyone following us."

"Right." Reven knelt down beside Amy. "You okay to walk?"

Amy felt touched by his concern, but just nodded. Her body ached with a deep bruising pain and experience told her tomorrow would not be fun, but she could move without too much pain. Right now, she would do anything to be away from the dust and alarms. "I can make it."

Reven helped her up, and she hobbled to the hole. She gasped as she saw it was a tube leading down beneath the earth, a ladder set into the side. The unidentified man was already down and Tam crouched at the entrance. "In you go, miss. I'll take the back guard, just in case."

Right. No stranger than anything else I've done today. Amy lowered her body down into the tube, tentatively testing the strength of the rungs. She stepped down until she was grasping the first rail, looking up at Reven, fear in her eyes. What if she slipped? What if her arms weren't strong enough, or her legs gave out?

He smiled down at her. "Don't worry. You can do this. I'll be right behind you."

She nodded hesitantly and took a deep breath. No going back now.

The tunnel went straight down for about fifty feet. Just when she felt as if her legs were going to give out, she felt powerful hands grab her and pull her off. The first man had lowered his hood. He was tall and muscular, with short cropped blond hair that was turning gray. A scar ran across one eye, although the eye seemed to still work. "I'm Tyler."

"Hi Tyler." Amy took a breath, looking around. There was no light except for a torch Tyler held. It bounced off rough rock over their heads. "I'm Amy."

"Nice to meet you, Amy. Welcome to the Underground."

"Tunnels. You built tunnels. And sized them small enough so that the Tark can't get in."

"Yes ma'am. It has taken our people a while, but the Resistance has routes going everywhere under the city. Of course, the beasts know about it. Even tried to breed some smaller ones so that they could get down here and flush us out. But didn't work."

Reven came into view and she stepped aside. He looked around and whistled. "Nice."

"Tyler."

Reven shook his head. "Reven."

"Oh, we all know who you are, sir. The One has been waiting to speak to you. We weren't expecting you to have a companion."

Reven nodded. "Amy tried to help rescue me on Earth before she understood any of this."

Like the fact that you got captured on purpose. Amy thought wryly.

Just then, Tam alighted and looked around the group with a smile, lighting another torch. "All together then? Good. We should get going. Just because the beasts can't fit down here won't mean they won't send some slaves down."

The group started walking and Amy turned to Tam. "Slaves?"

Tam had an uneasy look. "I don't know how much you know already miss but..."

"She knows about the Feedlot." Reven supplied.

"Well then. Not all the humans go to food. Some others, the ones who come through sane, get taken as slaves. Help for the upper classes. Clean up and cook and stuff. But we've heard rumors that some of the Tark soldiers got the idea to train their slaves as fighters so they could send them down here after us.”

“I don’t believe it.” Tyler huffed. “Lizards would be too scared they’d come to our side.”

“Maybe.” Reven said. “But if it’s true, it worries me. What does the One say?”

“That they are rumors, but we should always be vigilant against attack. The usual.” Tam shrugged. “C’mon. The One will be waiting.”

Reven and Tam continued talking about the latest developments on the planet. Tyler walked up front, his torch cutting into the darkness and searching for ambushes. Amy stumbled along at the back, concentrating on not stubbing a toe or tripping on the uneven floor. Her mind swirled with emotions. This morning she had been a simple hacker, happy in her uncomplicated if confining life. Now, she was tripping through a tunnel beneath an alien civilization running for her life. Her body ached. Blood dripped down her leg from a scrape. Her head beat at her like a drum, like it was trying to break out of her skull. All she wanted to do was lie down, curl up and sleep forever. Maybe never wake up, if it meant not facing this nightmare. But still she tripped on, numbly following Reven’s back. Her world condensed to that few feet of fabric in front of her. Mile after mile. The pain and confusion receded, replaced by the thoughts of the tired: just keep walking, just keep following.

She was so deep in her trance, she almost slammed into Reven when he stopped. Peeking around him, she blinked as light lit the tunnel and she realized she was at an entrance into an enormous cavern. Odd colored lights dangled from the ceiling high overhead. As her eyes adjusted, she saw there was a city. A huge underground city built underneath the one above. A sturdy stone wall interspersed with towers encircled the city as protection, leaving a fifty yard perimeter circle of bared stone to the walls of the cavern.

This space was now filled with people, all of whom turned at their entrance. A raucous cheer went up, the sound booming off the stone.

Finally, a man dressed in fatigues stepped forward, the crowd falling silent. He glared at the group with a critical eye before breaking into a wide smile. "About time."

He raised his sword, and everyone cheered. Reven looked down at Amy's stunned face as Tyler and Tam went forward to greet their compatriots. "Welcome to the Resistance."

13

***

They descended into the crowd. Reven, Tam and Tyler smiled as they received their hero's welcome. Amy didn't feel like a hero, though. She felt like a panic attack was coming on. There were way too many people all looking at her. She huddled behind Reven, trying to hide as much as possible.

"Oi there, you two!"

The procession stopped, and the crowd quieted as a tall, broad-shouldered woman with a thick braid of flaming red hair approached them. She wore a simple cotton tunic and breeches, but her manner made them seem like the richest silk dress. She glared at Tam and Tyler for a moment, and the crowd held its breath. Then she broke into a wide grin, her green eyes sparkling as she wrapped the two in a hug. "Well-done, you two."

Tyler and Tam looked slightly ashamed but hugged the woman back. Tam spoke up. "Course we got 'em. Think we'd take a chance on failing and facin' your wrath, Maven?"

The crowd cheered as Maven laughed, releasing the two and turning to face Reven. A rapt expression crossed her face. "As I live and breath. You're finally here."

Reven stepped forward, offering her a hand. "Mistress Maven. I've heard quite a lot about you."

She eyed his hand for a moment, then barked a laugh and swept him up into a hug. "You don't know how long we have all waited for you."

Maven looked over his shoulder, spotting Amy hiding behind him. "Oh. And who is this wee thing?"

Reven looked shocked, as if he just remembered Amy. "This is Amy. She tried to help me escape. Then we got caught, and I'm sorry to say she got dragged into all of this."

Maven waved him away. "Enough, enough. I get it. Poor lass looks like a mouse the cats have been playing with. Let's get you tended to, love."

She wrapped an arm around Amy. Amy wanted to push away just as Reven opened his mouth to say something, but Maven's personality was like a tidal wave. There was no fighting it, only going with the flow. Maven turned to Reven. "The One will want to see you. As for the rest of you, we have work to do. Now git!"

The others scrambled to obey. Reven walked away, following Tyler and Tam, looking over his shoulder back at Amy. She wanted to beg him to stay. It was like watching her lifeline float off into the distance; the rope connecting them stretching thinner and thinner until she was sure it would snap, leaving her to drift out into the deep ocean to drown.

Maven looked down at her with a pitying smile. "Let's get you tended to. You must have had quite a shock today."

More than you know. She wanted to say something, even thank you, but her tongue was numb. Her head was still pounding, the drumbeats echoing through her skull. Every muscle screamed, every bone vibrated with exhaustion. Amy was pretty sure she could sleep for a thousand years and still feel tired.

Maven led her through the streets. They had made the buildings of the same black stone as the cave. Some were large, others small and squat. Maven led her to a ring of long, low buildings filled with windows. "Welcome to the dormitories. It ain't much, but it's home."

Maven led her to a single small building that sat amidst the circle. "I'm sort of the overseer of this community, at least from the non-military standpoint. That's handled by Rail and his cohort. Because of my job, I get my very own place. It's a bugger having the responsibility of dealing with everything and trying to keep everyone safe. But it has its advantages."

Amy had expected more cold and damp, but stepped into a room full of warmth and cheer. A fire crackled in the fireplace, although it produced little smoke. Wave of heat flooded the room, absorbed by the stone walls and floor and reflected into the room. As Amy gazed, Maven pushed her down into a plush chair by the fire. The fabric was threadbare, and the stuffing was coming out, but it was comfortable.

Amy looked around in amazement. "Your place is beautiful. How did you get all of this stuff?"

Maven smiled. "Humans aren't the only things Earth

sends the lizards. They send them many offerings, fruits, cloth, furniture, and so on. Other things are Tark made that we either steal or barter for with the few that will. Not all the Tark civilians are bad, just trying to survive. It's the soldiers who you have to avoid at all costs."

Maven walked over to the fireplace and ladled something into a cup. She handed it to Amy, who cradled it thankfully. She gave it a sniff. The aroma of herbs and sweetness filtered through her mind.

Maven sat down opposite her. "A little chamomile tea to help soothe your nerves. Normally we don't have such niceties, but the patrol hit a shipment not too long ago that had some. Go on, take a sip. The warmth will do your insides good."

Amy obeyed, taking a small sip, and winced a little as the scalding liquid burned her tongue. But Maven was right. She could feel something release as the liquid burned down her throat. Amy traced it all the way down into her stomach, the warmth seeming to radiate within her. She took another sip, and another, the spiced water leeching into her veins and breaking down the block of ice that had been sitting within her since the soldiers had arrested her back at the base.

Maven had watched all this silently and when the mug was gone, got up and refilled it without a word. She sat again, watching Amy silently. After the second cup was half-gone,

Amy looked up. "Thank you."

It was just a whisper, but it felt like she had given a speech. It felt good. She was warm. She was safe, at least she thought so. Maven smiled.

"You're welcome. I know how trying the crossing can be. Not to mention being rescued and dragged halfway across the city." She got up and walked over to a small kitchen area, pulling out some hard cheese and a loaf of bread and placing them on a platter. She handed them to Amy. "Here, love. Eat up. You need something on your stomach besides tea after the gates."

"Where am I?" Amy took the platter. At first she wanted to refuse, her stomach still a roiling mess. But as the smell of the bread and cheese made it to her nose, her hunger took over. She took a bite of the bread, surprised at how soft and warm it was.

"This place doesn't really have a name, although most of us call it the Refuge. It's a home the Resistance has built over the generations, trying to keep people safe from the Tark." She pulled a chair over by Amy, then got a small jar out of a cabinet. As she opened it, Amy caught the scents of mint and honey.

Maven smiled, dipping a finger in the jar. "We don't get a lot of Band-Aids in the shipments, so we had to come up with our own medicines."

She gently picked up Amy's arm, brushing the salve over a scrape. Amy hissed for a second as the balm burned, but then sighed as it switched to a cooling sensation. As Amy ate, Maven gently applied balm to the scrapes and cuts she could see.

"So, where did you come from, Love? Few on Earth knew about Reven and the gates, and I don't remember hearing your name in the reports."

Amy sighed, staring into the depths of her cup. She shrugged. Her innocent life on Earth seemed so long ago that it was only a dream. "You know of the Hub?"

Maven nodded.

"I was a hacker. Recruited to search for stuff. People I guess. Only I didn't know what I was searching for. They were just words. Then I found Reven, or at least his name. I don't know why it changed. Before I knew I was spying. But suddenly I had a problem with it."

"Words stopped being just words."

Amy nodded. "You could say that. If I'm being honest, I just got tired. Tired of being cooped up. Tired of being lied to. Once I found out the word was a person, I wanted to know more."

"Seems odd to throw everything away on a curious mind."

"Yeah, tell me about it." The words were bitter and she

spit them out. "It was Whisper that did it. They brought me in. They're mean and cruel. Anyone they get sent after can't have a peaceful time. I guess I just wanted to know..."

When she didn't continue, Maven prodded her. "Wanted to know what?"

"That they were bad people. The people I was spying on, the people they tasked me with finding. Like I said, they sent Whisper after me, and I wasn't a criminal, just a hacker going after corporations and other bad people. It was hard to condemn people they went after as bad."

"So you defied orders and went to see Reven. That's when they caught you."

Amy nodded again. "I wanted to help him. I didn't realize..."

"Realize that your world view was about to be broken. I know how that goes." She got up and filled Amy's cup again.

Amy cradled the cup, but didn't drink. Tears filled her eyes, but she wanted to fight them back. She didn't cry. She wasn't weak. But she had already shed so many tears. It was like Maven had cracked the dam, and Amy couldn't patch it up again. The more water that pushed through, the wider the cracks became, until Amy could feel the whole thing teetering on dissolving in her mind.

A hand softly landed on her shoulder. "I know."

That simple touch disintegrated the dam completely, and

Amy started sobbing. Maven took the cup and knelt down, pulling Amy into her. Amy collapsed against her, the sobs ripping out of her chest. She felt ashamed of crying, ashamed for being so stupid, for being so weak. Maven's arms wrapped around her, holding her with a safety and warmth she hadn't known for a very long time. It had been twenty years since she'd felt a touch like this. A mother's touch. Her own mother had died when she was five, leaving her with an alcoholic father who hadn't really cared whether she was around. But this feeling felt familiar. Safe. Amy felt herself melting into it, forgetting that Maven was a compete stranger and falling back through the years until she was a little girl.

Slowly, the sobs subsided as both the tea and the warmth from Maven soothed her overwrought mind and body. Amy sniffed, and Maven released her, reaching for a napkin. "Here you go, love."

Amy nodded and took it, wiping her nose. "Thanks. I'm so sorry. I don't usually…"

"Don't think of it, dear. We've all had more than our share of crying here."

"This is not at all what I expected when I woke up yesterday morning." *Had it really only been yesterday morning that this strange trip started?* A hiccup laugh burst out. Just as the crying before, it seemed to unleash other nervous laughter. Pretty soon, she was crying again, this time from not being able to stop laughing. Several minutes passed before the hysteria faded and she gained control. She wiped her eyes. "Sorry, I don't know what came over me. When you live in the Hub, you get used to the fact that they are hiding secrets from you. I mean, it's the government. What would be unbelievable would be them not keeping secrets, especially considering how they 'recruited' me. But this? All of this? No way."

"How did they recruit you?"

"I told you Whisper brought me in? They showed up at my door, stuck a gun in my face and gave me a choice. Rot in a dark cell all by myself, or live in a semi-private cell under the ground and work for them. I figured with option two, I could have movies and video games to keep my mind off the kidnapping."

"So you weren't with them?"

"Hell no! Had I realized what they were up to, I might have taken the dank hole. Definitely would have been safer."

Maven was quiet for a minute, digesting what she had said, when Amy looked at her. "You knew a lot of this already, didn't you? You're interrogating me."

Maven sighed but didn't deny it. "Letting you vent. But I also need to make sure you aren't a threat. Like I said, I protect many people in this city. They're my family. I know Reven trusts you, but I don't really know him. Nothing but stories, really. How would he know if you were some government plant setting us up?"

Amy's battered pride growled. *After everything I've been through...*

But her rational mind piped up. *What would you do in her shoes?*

Amy smiled. *Do exactly what she's doing.* "Well?"

Maven smiled. "I think you pass, for now."

She settled back into her chair. "Besides, you looked like you really weren't up to the crowds. As a friend of Reven, they'd be clamoring all over you."

"What is the story with that? I didn't even know who he was and they treat him like some kind of god."

Maven smiled. "That's because, for a lot of us, he is. His people were one of the first to stand up against the Tark. The Tark extinguished their race, their home world destroyed and left in cinders. The Tark tried to use them as an example of what happened to those that opposed them. But then along came Reven, standing up and fighting, even when it was just him. Of course, it was just small stuff. But to those who were captives or slaves of the Tark, who had their own homelands destroyed, it was something. It was a chink in the Tark's armor. It was hope."

"Sounds like a lot for a mortal to accomplish. I mean, he is mortal, right?" Amy half-laughed, hoping it was true. But hearing Maven talk, she wasn't so sure.

"Oh, aye. His race age slower than humans, but weapons can kill him. Just like any of us. But the idea of him, David standing up against Goliath, that's what makes him a god and will survive long after we all are gone. Like any legend that's steeped in just a little truth."

Amy just shook her head, staring into her cup. "This morning I was just a hacker. Now…"

"I know. I used to be a secretary."

"You are human, then?" Amy took a deep breath. "From Earth?"

Maven nodded. "Most of us are right now, although there are a few other races mixed in here and there. Most look very different from humans, like the Tark. But we're their main source right now. See, they're smart about military tactics. They only capture a few planets at a time as feedlots. That way, they don't get stretched too thin. Makes them harder to attack."

"It's still hard to believe. We all laughed about it being a secret base, conspiracies and all that. But to see it in person…"

"You did not know?"

Amy shook her head. "There are two rules at the Hub: don't ask questions and do what you're told. Looking back, I know I was living blindly. But I didn't care."

"And now?"

Amy let the question hang, staring at her tea again. How did she feel? Her only answer was more swirling emotions underneath a layer of numbness blanketing it all. "I don't know."

"Now there's an honest answer. Most people either collapse or put on a brave front. When the most logical thing to be is numb and confused."

"Which one were you?"

Maven laughed and stood up, crossing over to a cabinet. "I was one of the brave ones, right until I had a nervous breakdown."

She opened the cabinet, pulling out some cotton pants and a tunic. "Is the tea helping?"

"Yes, thank you. Although I think I'm going to need a lot more tea to feel alright again." Amy tried for a weak laugh.

"Well, maybe after we get you washed up and in some new clothes, you'll feel better." She walked back over to Amy. "Time to get you settled in your new home."

—

The crowds dissipated as Reven, Tam and Tyler reached an enormous tower of black stone in the middle of the city. At the top, a huge bonfire burned, casting its light over the entire city. Corresponding towers on the outskirts of the city communicated with it by signal fires and mirrors. If an attacking army approached anywhere near the Refuge, they would spot it. But it was not the lookout tower that interested the trio right now.

Soldiers guarded a doorway set into the bottom, nodding at Tam and Tyler as they escorted Reven through with only the briefest of questioning glances at Reven. He sighed in happiness. It was a welcome change after the mob in the city. His face ached from smiling so much. Being a leader and God was more than he had bargained for.

They descended underground to the Inner Chamber, which contained the throne room and private residences of the One, the leader of the city and the Resistance. Here, Reven found another pair of soldiers guarding a metal door. Only these soldiers were different. They wore red tunics emblazoned with a strange creature surrounded by vines. The symbol looked familiar, but he couldn't place it. They also wore every weapon imaginable. They stood ready, and one challenged Tam as he approached.

"I am here to see the One. I have brought the rebel called Reven, who has traveled to see her."

The guard glared at them all for a moment, then nodded. The one on the left pulled a hidden lever, and the giant door split down the middle, opening with a groan. Silently, Tam and the others walked in.

The One sat on a throne atop a dais, working behind a desk. She wore simple white robes, her silver hair pulled behind her in a ponytail. Her face seemed youthful, with smooth milk white skin and crystalline blue eyes. But lines by her eyes told of a different story. She was talking to one of her advisers when the door opened and she paused, watching as the group came forward. Her face split into a grin just as the adviser started complaining about the interruption. She waved him off and came out from behind the desk, descending the dais.

The trio stopped short, and she walked up to them, nodding at Tam and Tyler. "Your mission was a success. Well done, you two."

Then she turned to Reven, and a huge smile broke out on her face. "Finally. After all this time, you are here, Brother."

He smiled and walked forward, sweeping her into a hug. "Sister. It is so good to see you again."

She released him and stepped back. "Come. We have much to discuss."

The One turned to Tam and Tyler. "Your thanks indeed for bringing him home safe."

Tam and Tyler bowed. "Your Majesty."

She nodded. "Now, back to your posts. I fear things will move quickly now."

They nodded and left. She smiled at Reven. "Let us go to

my private chamber. So much better than this cold room."

Her adviser cleared his throat as they passed the dais, and she glared at him. "I must speak to my kin. Those things can wait. Have the kitchen staff bring food to my quarters."

He opened his mouth to interrupt, then closed it with a sigh, staring glumly at the stack of papers he held in his hand. He knew better than to argue with that tone of voice. "As you say, your Majesty."

She led Reven to a small door set into the stone wall. Inside was a small living area. A brazier was lit with some odd fuel source, heating it without smoke but filling the air with a thick spiced scent. Thick rugs littered the floor, along with some battered but well-stuffed chairs. Beyond a curtain lay a gigantic bed. She waved a hand at a chair. "Sit. You must be exhausted."

He just stared at her. "You are looking well, Alia."

She paused, smiling. "No one has called me that for a very long time. It is usually 'The One' or 'Your Majesty'. It is good to hear it from your lips."

Reven sat in a chair across from hers, slumping down into it with a sigh. "It's been a long time since you first sent a message to me while I was on the planet Aven. You cannot believe how amazed I was to get your message."

"Not as amazed as I to hear that one of the Ra'shek had escaped, and from a family so closely aligned with my own.

For so long, I thought I was the only one."

"As did I."

"So." She reached for a nearby table, pouring him a glass of water from the pitcher on the tray and handing it to him. "What happened on Earth? I hear you arrived with another human in tow. One of the group you spoke of in your last message?"

"Amy. She isn't part of my group. Just an innocent bystander thinking she was doing the right thing."

Alia frowned. "A plant?"

Reven shook his head. "No. No way. She really is who she says. Although the Colonel approached me."

Alia raised an eyebrow. "Really? What did he want?"

"He wanted to know how to destroy the Tark."

Alia mulled this over for a moment. "Do you think he could be an ally?"

Reven snorted. "NO. That is one man who looks out for himself. He only does what is helpful to him. He would sell us out in a moment."

"Pity. It would have been nice to have tried to smuggle more ammunition and explosives over to our side. Were you able to conclude anything else?"

Reven shook his head. "No, I didn't have time. I underestimated how organized and ready to act they would be. Whisper captured myself and the group I was with before

I got them out of danger, and then shipped Amy and I over here almost instantly. The Colonel took me to the Tark scouts. There are only two, but the security surrounding them is impenetrable."

Alia sighed. "Well, at least you are here and we got you safe. Perhaps this is even better. We can go ahead with our plan to attack them at their source."

It was Reven's turn to be skeptical. "You put a lot of faith in me. I couldn't even deal with the scouts."

"I understand your hesitation, but this time, you are not alone. Time is running out." A worried look crossed her face. "The Tark are getting braver. They know of us. Our group and city are too large, our attacks and raids too much for them to ignore. It is only a matter of time until they recruit enough humans to have an exploratory force."

"You've had spies?"

She nodded. "A few. Fortunately, we have friends among the slaves, some of the same few who travel through the gates with their masters and carry our messages. They've alerted us to the incursions. We've been able to catch them and deal with them before any damage was done. Except for my personal guard and a few select others, no one in the city knows how many have tried to get through. Fortunately, humans hate being slaves as much as most and when faced with working for the Tark or being free down here, they chose us every time. Or almost. It's hard for the Tarks to extend their control down here. But they will find the right key to motivate the greediest humans. Like any species, give them a prize big enough and they will sell out their own kind."

"The tunnels?"

"Too small for most of the Tark. We have a heavy guard over the largest tunnel, but there are so many it would not be hard for a human to slip in."

"Your people would notice them as a stranger."

"True, but they could cripple us before that happened." Alia sighed. "Which is why I feel we must strike soon. These rocks have given us protection and freedom. But many miss the sun, the wind. I know I do."

"Kaphisia flowers." Reven smiled.

Alia turned a quizzical look at him. "What?"

"That's what I miss. The smell of the Kaphisia flowers as they bloomed by the waterfall near my village."

A sad, reflective look passed over Alia's eyes even as her lips smiled. "I had almost forgotten about them. Our garden had a natural spring they grew by."

She reached over and placed a hand on Reven's knee. "I am so glad you are home, brother."

He put a hand over hers. "As am I."

14

***

Maven led the way through the city. Amy's head swiveled this way and that, trying to pick up all the information she could. People, mostly humans, wove back and forth through the streets performing their daily activities. Once in a while she would catch sight of another, some with feathers, scales, or spines wandering amongst the crowd. Some towered and some were small and yet all mingled freely in this town.

A dull roar in the distance grew sharper and louder. Amy inhaled as they broke free from the rows of stone buildings and an unfamiliar sight towered above her. From a hole high in the wall, a great waterfall fell, emerging from the depths like a hungry dragon cascading down to a series of pools in the floor. The upper pool connected to a series of troughs that bore it into the city. After the pools, it flowed out as a stream, disappearing into the rock in the darkest parts of the cavern. Here, rows of bio-luminescent lights lit the edge, giving the water an eerie green glow. Other women gathered at the edge of the lowest pool. And stripping?

Amy coughed and averted her eyes. They were bathing out in the open where anyone could see!

Maven turned her eye and laughed. "Don't be shy. We aren't. We don't have running water but fortunately we have the Khao. When all the water fled from the surface of the planet, it found a refuge underground. It's said the power of the water carved this cavern and some of the original tunnels that the One found. Now it gives us our lifeblood. We drink and bath in the waters which are warmed by the planet's depths. It allows us to exist down here."

Still doesn't explain the nude bathing. Amy had never thought of herself as a prude, but as they drew nearer to the pool, she could feel her cheeks redden. She glanced down at her slight form. *Not that there's much to show, but still...*

Some young women and men were off to one side washing clothes in tubs of water. The soapy mess kept well away from the drinking pool. Other young women lounged on the side of the pool, taming wet hair or chatting and laughing with the others who were swimming. They all looked up at Amy's approach, and she felt her cheeks redden a little more.

A tan beauty with sleek black hair swum up. "Good day Maven! Come for a swim? The water is very warm today."

"Aye, I would if I had time, Mai. I just came to introduce a newcomer. Hoping you girls could get her settled."

A round of murmurs and assurances flowed through the group and Maven looked down at Amy. "Girls, this is Amy. Just came through the gate and she's still a little shaky on her legs."

Rounds of hi's and welcomes echoed around her and Amy bravely smiled back. Her introvert alarm was rioting. *There are way too many new people here. And they're naked.*

Not that it's distracting or disconcerting.

"They rescued her with Reven?" Mai asked, an odd gleam in her eye.

Amy didn't answer but stood there rooted to the spot, silent as a stone, even though every fiber of her body wanted her to run and hide. Find some shadowy corner and just hide until this nightmare ended. Or she died, one of the two. An awkward silence descended that clawed at Amy's brain and started waking up the anxious little voices that liked to pick on her in moments like this. Thankfully, a small sprite of a girl who looked to be in her teens stood up. She had short, spiky blonde hair and sported a pair of well-worn breeches and a white shirt. Her blue eyes sparkled as she held out a hand. "Hi. Welcome to the Refuge. My name is Jess."

Amy took a deep breath and held out her hand. "Hi. I guess you know my name already."

Ice broken, Maven laughed and clapped her on the back. "Good. I'll just leave you here to get acquainted. Jess, make sure she makes it to lunch, ok?"

Jess nodded. "Of course."

For the second time, Amy felt her stomach sinking as Maven walked off. Was she ever going to meet someone who actually stuck around to help her? Everyone leaving her to fend for herself in a giant swirling vortex of uncertainty. Just like when she was young. What she wouldn't give to be back in her little van, just her and her computer and the ingenuity of her mind.

Jess gently touched her arm. "Hey, let's get you cleaned up. You'll feel better after a swim. I know I did, my first day here."

Amy slowly let Jess lead her over to the edge of the pool. Mercifully, the others had ignored her for the moment and had become absorbed in their own conversations and duties again, although Amy saw Mai studying her at a distance. Her eyes darted over to the other nude swimmers. "Do I . . . I mean, do you always . . ."

Jess barked a laugh. "Don't worry. It can take some getting used to. My upbringing was super-prudish. My mom would have a fit if she saw me now. But it's really not that bad. It's actually kind of nice. Freeing. We all look the same naked, you know?"

Amy hesitated and Jess smiled encouragingly. "Well, why don't you just sit and dangle your feet? Start small if you're not ready to dive in."

Amy sat down on the edge of the pool, taking off her socks and sneakers and rolling up her pant legs. She slipped her bare feet into the pool and, without thinking, sighed with pleasure. The water was warm, and it tingled as tiny bubbles swirled around her skin. The warmth seeped into her, dispelling the cold and fear that lived in her bones. She must have had a blissful smile on her face, because Jess laughed again as she sat down beside Amy. "Pretty wonderful, huh?"

Amy just nodded. After a moment, she hesitantly asked, "You came through the gates? Oh. I mean, obviously you did, but I mean, if you don't mind me asking. Is it ok to ask?"

Jess smiled warmly. "It's ok. Some people don't enjoy talking about it, or their lives before, but I don't mind. I came here a couple years ago. Just a little kid, really."

"How did they get you?"

Jess's eyes darkened, but she talked strongly. "I was stupid. Remember how I told you my upbringing was super-prudish? My dad was a strict religious guy. Laws and rules and all that. Yelling at me to do everything right. Nothing was ever good enough. 'Question nothing'. Everything I had to do had to be perfect, so he looked good. Finally, I had it. I had it with his rules and told him that. He said I could either obey the rules or leave. So I did. I ran away. Didn't get very far though before these two jerks in a black van grabbed me. Was sure they'd rape or murder me. Little did I know it was my government wanting to send me as food to another planet."

She shook her head. "It seems insane unless you've lived through it. But I got lucky. A raiding party hit my convoy as they were taking us to the holding pens. Now I have a new home and family here with the Resistance. You'll find one too, I suspect."

"Holding pens?" Amy shook her head. "How do you all say things like that so matter-of-fact?"

Jess patted her shoulder. "It's hard finding out that you are food for something after being at the top of the food chain. But we're all food for something at some point. After a while, you have to just accept it. It's a part of our life. But down here, at least we are safe."

"So you're okay with all of this?" Amy couldn't help the slight rise in her voice of anger, concern, frustration.

Jess let the anger flow over her, understanding she wasn't the target. "No, I didn't say that. It's just one thing you figure out. However, just because they see us as prey doesn't mean we have to lie down and take it. I mean, deer grow antlers and rhinoceros have horns. So, we've grown to protect ourselves."

Amy sighed and cradled her aching, burning head. All she wanted to do was lay down in a nice, cool place. "This is all too much."

Jess smiled sympathetically. "It'll get better. Traveling through the gates can be nasty. But the transport sickness passes pretty quickly. You're lucky. Most don't survive with their brains intact."

What a sad thing to be happy about, that the gate didn't scramble my brains. "About the gates. There's something that's been troubling me. You can go back through the gates, right?"

Jess frowned, but nodded. "That's the theory. The Tarks move back and forth all the time, obviously."

"What do you mean 'that's the theory'? Has no one tried?"

"Of course people have tried. But as far as we know, no one has made it. The One finally outlawed attempts to try it."

"Who is this One? I keep hearing people talk about them."

"The leader of this place. She's been fighting the Tark longer than any of us. She keeps us safe."

"Why would she outlaw your way home?"

"I'll tell you why." Mai swam up with a couple of other girls. "Because it's suicide. They're guarded around the clock. You also have to know how to manipulate the energies to get you to where you want to go. Try to go through without doing that and you find yourself in the nothingness of space. At the worst, you get fried to something between charcoal and beef jerky."

Jess sighed. "Amy, the over-dramatic one there is Mai. The other two are Sephora and Drail."

A buxom woman with short blond hair and a tall, leggy, dark-skinned woman with curly hair nodded their greetings. Mai scowled. "It's not over-dramatic. Remember Peter's scrounging team? The only one who made it back was Sam, and he's a blithering idiot now."

Jess looked like she was about to start an argument when Amy held up a hand. "I'm sorry. Scrounging team?"

Mai nodded. "You know we send raiding parties to hit shipments? Well, we find things that the Tarks have abandoned or we steal things from the marketplace. It's dangerous work, but without us, this town couldn't survive."

If she had been a bird, she would have been puffing out her chest and strutting down the street. But Amy supposed she had a point if the reason for the team's existence was true. An idea was forming in her head. *They go to the surface. Where the gates are.*

"Are you all scroungers?" She asked Jess.

Jess nodded. "Yeah. Everyone has to have a job. Some people stay here and make clothing, tend the few crops that we can get to grow down here, things like that. Some are soldiers who protect the city and guard the One. Others are the Elite patrols, like Tam and Tyler, who get sent on critical raiding and military missions. The rest of us are scroungers."

"So, what job will I do? If everyone has a job?"

Sephora smiled. "Oh, you just got here. You're allowed some time to rest and recoup."

"But more than likely, you'll be a scrounger." Drail interjected. "Most of us who are young are. We can evade the

Tark patrols and navigate the tunnels easier than the elders."

Sephora shot Drail a look. "But you won't go to the surface for a while. You need to rest."

Before they could descend into a fight, Mai rose out of the water. Amy tried to act nonchalant, like the others at being confronted with the woman's nakedness, but could feel herself blushing. *When did I turn into a prude?*

Mai grabbed a towel from a nearby rock and started toweling herself off. From the glint in her eye, Amy knew the other woman was aware of the effect she was having. The message was obvious. *You aren't in Kansas anymore, little girl.*

Amy would have to watch this one.

Mai grinned like a Cheshire cat. "I don't know. Our new comrade looks pretty rested. Perhaps she should get a taste of her new life. I'm leading my patrol out this afternoon. Care to join?"

The others had uneasy looks on their faces, but none would speak against Mai. Another interesting clue, Amy thought. Her instincts told her this was a trap. But above was where the gates were, and she had no intention of staying on this planet one second longer than she needed. If that meant playing Mai's little game, she would deal with it. Amy nodded. "When and where?"

"Meet us in an hour at the red building by the Arch." She

pointed over the city to where a vast arch of rock jutted out of the floor. "We'll give you your first taste of life here. Welcome home."

She laughed as she wrapped the towel around herself and walked off. Jess shook her head, but said nothing until Mai was well out of hearing distance. Even then, it was only a whispered "Bitch."

Amy caught the imperceptible nods from Sephora and Drail. Sephora finally sighed. "You shouldn't have agreed."

"But what could she have done? Remember the last girl who made an enemy of Mai?" Drail slipped deeper into the water. She darted a glance at Amy. "Sorry, Amy. Mai doesn't like competition and any new person is competition in her eyes."

"Competition?" Amy snorted, looking down at her thin body and pasty white skin. "What competition am I?"

"You're an unknown. Until she knows who you are, you are competition. Mai looks out for Mai, and woe be to anyone who gets more attention than her. Unfortunately for you, arriving with Reven is about the most star power we have around here." Jess sighed. "How did you hook up with him, anyway?"

"We're not 'hooked up'." Amy scoffed. "I . . . he . . . it's complicated. But I really don't know him. We just got captured and sent here together."

"Well, don't let Mai hear that." Sephora clung to the edge of the pool. "Reven is your shield, in this case. If she thinks he protects you, she won't mess with you that bad."

"So what? Is he some kind of god or something? I mean, he looks normal."

Jess laughed. "For those of us that have been living this nightmare, he's become something of a legend. He and the One were the first to fight the Tark. The One began this place, began rescuing people from the holding pens. We found out Reven was doing similar things in other worlds. It became something of a magical thought. That they were our saviors. That if one day he came to this world, together he and the One would take down the Tark forever. We could all go back home."

Home. Jess emphasized the word with such heartache and longing. Amy could see the wound inscribed into her eyes, her very soul. The others hung their heads as well. They might put on a brave front, but they all wanted the same thing. *Home.*

Amy had never had much of a home. After her mother had died, her father had turned his abuse towards her. Amy had run as soon as she had enough money for a car and some necessities. She'd been on the run ever since, living in her van and making money through hacking. Then of course she'd had the Hub. She'd never really thought of it as *home.* But she yearned for it now. Yearning for a thing she'd never known she had. Until someone had ripped away it.

It was all too much. Alien worlds. Conspiracies. Her stomach wanted to revolt, thinking about all those people piled up at the gates. Her people were being harvested by their own government.

She shoved it away. She had to focus. There was only one thing that mattered now: getting home. Getting back through the gates. "So the only way home is through the gates, right? How will you get home if no one knows how to use them?"

Jess shook her head. "I didn't say that. Rumors say the One knows, and maybe a few of their trusted advisers. But if they know, they're guarding the secret carefully."

Damn. She'd have to figure out that information quickly. That or take her chances. *Maybe getting fried wouldn't be bad. Just end it quickly.* Amy shook her head to dispel the thought. She was smart. She could figure this out!

"I bet that with Reven here, she'll let us assault the gates. At least some of us could get through." Sephora's voice had a wishful tone.

Reven! That's the answer. I bet he knows how the gates work. Amy was about to voice her thought when she heard a sharp voice call. "Amy!"

She looked over her shoulder. Reven was walking up fast,

a serious look on his face. The other women whistled quietly. Jess whispered. "He's even more gorgeous than I pictured. Lucky girl."

Amy grimaced at her and got up. *Reven's okay, but he's not that hot.*

Although he looks a little hot under the collar now. She paused, watching Reven stalk over to her. His body tensed. He stopped short, his fierce gaze turning slightly softer. "Are you okay?"

"Of course." His demeanor puzzled her. "What is wrong with you?"

He took a breath like he wanted to yell, but just sighed. "I just came from the One. Some girl named Mai asking for permission to take you on a patrol today? I thought you were safe with Maven. How did you get signed up for a scrounging patrol?"

Amy weakly pointed behind her, where Jess and the others unabashedly waved back. Amy noted happily that Reven blushed as he saw them. *So, my 'Gorgeous God' isn't as used to dealing with the ladies as he'd like you to believe.* "Maven brought me here to wash up and meet the others. Mai was with them and invited me. I thought it sounded like fun."

Reven recovered and looked at her. "You should take it easy. The One was telling me about the patrols. It's dangerous."

She knew she should be happy that he was concerned, but something pricked at her. "Any more dangerous than coming to get you?"

"Amy . . ."

"Don't Amy me. I hardly know you. But in the last few hours, everything that I've ever known has self-destructed. All because of you, and these creatures, and my stupid government. I mean, I fucked up. I could have, should have, just stayed out of it. But I'm here now, on a freaking alien planet where the locals want to eat me. Nothing in my entire life has ever looked at me like a meal before. You're telling me that all of that wasn't dangerous?"

"No. I just . . . you should rest. It's an enormous shock. Especially being thrown through the gates."

The gates. Home. She took a deep breath. "I have to get home. The more I know about this place, the better chance I have of doing that."

His eyes grew sad. "Amy, you can't. The gates..."

"Are dangerous. I got that. But I have to do something. I can't stay here. I need to go home."

"So do these people. Even if you could get through a gate, what are you going to do? It's going to dump you right back in the Hub."

His rationale stung her vision. He was right. But her heart

hurt too much right now. Saying the words had opened up a canyon in her soul. Tears pushed at her eyes and she could feel the darkness wrapping around her. She missed Jeff. Her laptop. She missed not having to deal with things. "I have to do something. I can't just sit here."

He reached out like he wanted to comfort her, then pulled away, scared to push too far. He simply wiped a tear off her cheek with a finger. "You need rest. Let all this settle. I promise I will get you home."

"But when?" Her frustration leaked out in her voice. "You have a mission here. To defeat the Tarks. Everyone is talking about it. Looking at you like you're some sort of God. I'm just the accidental tag-along. They will not let you risk yourself for me. Put your mission first, right?"

She wanted him to deny it. But he didn't even address it. He let it die, which told her the truth more than any words. "I'm responsible for you. I will get you home."

A heavy weight settled in her stomach. "Thanks. But I'm not really one for relying on other people."

"But the gates..."

"I won't go to the gates. I promise. I just want to look around."

"It's too dangerous. Or wait and I'll take you."

"Like your keepers would let that happen."

"You're angry again."

"Of course I'm angry!" She balled up her fists. "Everything normal in my life is gone. I've gotten arrested, beaten up, tossed around, marched through darkness and thrown into the most terrifying thing anyone can imagine. Now I'm being told to just sit on my butt and let other people take care of it. I don't know what to do and I feel absolutely helpless."

"Sorry for caring about you."

She took a breath. She saw the hurt on his face, but her anger was flooding out now and she couldn't control it. It lashed out of her mouth like a whip. "Care about me? The second we got here, you forgot about me. Admit it. I'm just the third wheel in your little hero party."

His eyes hardened. "You came after me, remember? I didn't ask for your help."

"Well, that's good, because I'm not asking for yours now. I'm going to go with Mai, and I'm going to find a way home!"

His eyes raged. He whirled, hurrying away. "Fine. I have other things to do than babysit you."

She watched him stalk off. Immediately she wanted to run after him, apologize, grovel and break down at his feet. She had just pissed off the closest thing she had to a friend, and why? Because she was a whiny brat who wanted to go home? She opened her mouth to call out to him.

Then she closed it. Maybe it was better this way. He

wouldn't be watching her every move. She wouldn't distract him from his mission. Amy looked out over the city. The Arch stood towering over the town. She had her own mission now.

15

***

Amy approached a long, one-story building that sat by the Arch, the courtyard outside filled with lounging young people. They eyed her as she walked by, but returned to their conversations. Scroungers, she figured. Self-consciously, she pulled at the brown tunic Maven had given her, along with a white cotton shirt, brown breeches and well-worn but sturdy leather boots that molded to her legs like they had been hers for a lifetime. Swallowing her fear, she stepped into the darkened building.

The building was one big room set with windows and glow lights. At one end, people gathered talking to each other. Mai looked up at the intrusion and the glower on her face turned to a predatory smile. "Ah, the recruit. Amy, right? C'mon in. We're just getting ready to go."

The group stared at Amy for a moment, then went back to their conversation about the upcoming raid. Amy stepped to the outside of the group, relieved when a familiar face showed up. Jess came towards her, carrying a bundle of cloth and a hard metal collar. Her face was anxious, and she turned her back to Mai, whispering to Amy. "Are you sure you want to do this? Mai wants to take you as her partner. She doesn't do that with newbies."

"Do you really think she'll do something to me?"

Jess hesitated. "I don't . . ."

She glanced over her shoulder at Mai, then shook her

head slightly. "Just be careful."

Amy's nerves itched, her intuition telling her to listen to Jess and Reven. Yet the allure of home pulled harder still. She had to get home, whatever it took. "Don't worry. I can take care of myself."

"I hope so." Jess handed over the bundle. "Good luck."

She left Amy holding the bundle. It contained a hooded brown cloak, and a silver collar. She looked around the group, noticing that some already wore a similar collar around their necks.

"Slave collars." Mai smiled as she walked up. "Or at least a reasonable facsimile. It allows us to pass as slaves on the upper world and helps avoid detection."

"Slaves?" Amy's throat clenched at the word.

Mai nodded. "Most of the stock brought to the Tark home world become food. But they keep some people as slaves to assist the Tark in their daily routines, running errands, running messages, cleaning, things like that. They all wear the brown cloaks and the collars to signify that they are a slave. Usually the owners engrave the collars with the holder's seal and name, but it's hard to see unless you're looking, so we don't bother."

"What happens if you don't have one?"

"Oh." Mai chuckled. "They peg you as Resistance or an escapee. If you're lucky, they kill you on the spot. If not..."

Another person came up and asked Mai a question, and she turned her back to Amy. Amy stared down at the collar. *Do I want to get home or not?*

Summoning up her courage, she slid the collar around her neck, her skin crawling as the cool metal touched it. Her stomach flipped as the locking mechanism clicked shut. Her fingers ran over it, contemplating what it meant. Mai turned around, smiling. "Good. You got it. Some people have trouble first time. Ready to go?"

Amy slipped on the cloak. "What do I need to know?"

"Just keep your head down and your mouth shut. You'll be with me, so just follow what I say. We'll take to the tunnels as a group, but the others will split off along the way. The Tark don't allow slaves to congregate in large numbers, so going together to the marketplace as a group would arouse too much suspicion."

She turned to the others. "Everyone ready?"

The group nodded. Jess came up beside her, quietly squeezed her hand and gave her an encouraging smile, then walked off towards another member of the group. Mai turned, handing her an empty basket. Amy saw the others grabbing baskets as well. Then as one they left, silently and quietly. Amy followed as well as she could as they slithered and crawled through the cavern streets, heading for a dark hole in the side of the stone wall.

Her exhaustion forgotten, Amy stepped into the tunnel with the group. She kept her eyes focused on the backs of the others, focusing on Mai. Focusing on her mission.

She had told Reven she wouldn't try for the gates. As much as her heart yearned to disobey that pseudo promise, she knew it was suicide. The two sides squabbled for a moment before the rational one won out. Yet adrenalin pumped through her system. Even if she wasn't trying for the gates, she could keep her eyes open and learn. She could get out of the tunnels and figure out what in the hell was going on. If she saw an opportunity? She would take it.

Most of all, it felt good to be doing something other than running and hiding. Maybe she should have been wary of this adrenalin, the same that had rushed through her once she had decided to rescue Reven. *After all, look how well that turned out.*

But she brushed off the nagging thoughts. This felt right. The cold metal of the collar reminded her of the handcuffs. First when Whisper had come to her van, then again back at the Hub. Her skin shivered. No one was going to make her a prisoner again.

The group moved silently through the tunnels, the only sounds their footfalls and the dripping of water. Soon enough, little side tunnels started branching out. Every time they passed one, a couple of people would peel off, disappearing into the darkness without a word. Amy kept throwing questioning glances at Mai, which she didn't acknowledge. She just kept plunging forward down the tunnel, and Amy followed. Soon enough, they were the only two left. Mai turned down a small tunnel, pausing before what looked like a large, loose rock. She turned to Amy. "Remember. Stay silent and stick with me. Watch what I do, and learn."

Amy nodded. "What about the basket?"

"It's part of the cover, but we also use it to hide items we are taking back. Don't worry about what to take, I'll tell you. Now, c'mon."

She pushed the rock aside with some effort, peeking her head out. Apparently satisfied with what she saw, she slipped out. Amy quickly followed. Together they pushed the 'rock', which was part of a wall of a courtyard in a private alley, back into place. Brushing herself off, Amy peered around at her surroundings.

"Going to stand there all day?" Mai prodded. "Let's go."

Amy took a deep breath, pulled her hood over her head and followed Mai down the shadowed alley towards the sunlit street. As she peeked around the corner, she saw a wide street lined with stalls and stores. Her breath caught in her throat as she spied the crowd of Tarks. Even though the citizens were smaller than the soldiers, they towered over

Amy, their teeth and claws shining in the sunlight. Here and there, she spied a human, but they were fleeting glimpses. They disappeared quickly amongst the mob of alien flesh.

Mai snorted, seeing Amy shrink into the shadows. "C'mon. What are you scared of? Citizens don't pay any attention to slaves. Just watch out for soldiers."

Amy reluctantly left the alley and followed Mai through the crowd. The push of heavy warm bodies nauseated her as the stench of sweat and rancid meat rolled off of them. She fought down the nausea, trying not to gag. Thankfully, Mai stopped in a shadowed corner by a shop selling meat. Amy gulped in a breath of warm but clean-smelling air.

And almost lost it the moment she inspected the shop.

Arms. Human arms dangled from the roof, slowly rotating in the desert air. Legs lay piled on the table, alongside mounds of ground red meat. The worst were the small babies laying in a place of honor on a platter in the middle. Amy's gorge rose, and she turned, fighting desperately not to throw up while her mind screamed in horror.

Mai gave her a disgusted look. "Hold it together."

"But those . . . that is . . ."

"Human. What did you think? You knew they ate us." Mai's eyes gleamed.

Realization dawned. "You brought me here on purpose."

Mai snorted. "Just wanted to judge your reaction to the

truth. Don't seem that tough to me. Not for someone traveling with Reven."

"That's why you invited me? To size me up?"

"Of course. What did you think? That I wanted to be friends? This isn't high school. Grow up."

Jess's words rang in Amy's ears, but she shoved them away. "I just wasn't expecting to see that."

"The Tark eat us. End of story. Just like they eat the Kalapaks and Dauquins and Treshauk and any other planet they can open a gateway to." She grabbed Amy's arm. "And we eat what they eat because it's all we have."

"You mean..." The nausea rose again, bile filling her mouth. "I won't. I won't be a cannibal."

Mai smiled that evil smirk again. "Fine. Then starve. But don't get in my way."

With that, she turned and melted back into the crowd. Realizing that Mai had been teasing her about eating human flesh, Amy swore and followed. Mai was an evil bitch, that she was sure. But Mai still knew her way around this world and Amy didn't. No way she was letting the woman drop her.

Mai didn't think Amy was worthy of Reven. Amy wasn't sure why it was so important to this woman, other than what Jess had said about attaching to his star power. But with the stories and tales elevating him to god status in the Resistance, it made sense for a narcissist and power-climber to want to be near him. This was a test to see how hard it would be for Mai to replace Amy, and Amy had failed. She knew that in Mai's eyes, Amy was fair game.

Still, Amy was in between a rock and a hard place. Putting herself at that woman's mercy was insane, but she didn't know how to get back down into the tunnels. Mai had curled and swerved so much Amy wasn't sure she could make it back to the alley. Cursing herself, she plunged forward.

What was that you were saying earlier? That you knew what you were doing?

Shut up.

She caught up to Mai, who only acknowledged her with a slight glance. The two kept weaving their way past stalls. Every so often imperceptible to all but those watching for it, Mai's hand would dart out as they passed a stall, grabbing what looked like a melon or an odd spiky fruit. Slowly, her basket filled. Amy's was empty as she didn't dare attempt the maneuvers Mai did, especially under the glare of the Tark store owners who yelled and screamed at the passing crowd, looking at each one who wandered close as either a potential sale or a potential threat.

She was so intent on keeping up with Mai that she almost bumped into her back when the woman stopped short. Mai turned and shushed her, tilting her head to the side. Amy's eyes followed it. A small clearing had appeared in the crowd, which had not stopped but was flowing around two large Tarks with red crests. *Soldiers!*

Amy shrank into her hood, preparing to turn the other way, when suddenly Mai grabbed her arm. Without a word, she flicked a hand at Amy's collar and it fell to the ground. All Amy saw was her wicked smile. Then Mai shoved her roughly towards the soldiers.

Amy stumbled on the rough stone street and fell, sprawling at the feet of the soldiers. Quickly, she scrambled to her feet, but not before a clawed hand clamped on her shoulder. She inhaled as the claws pushed at her skin, not daring to breathe in case they skewered her. Trembling, she raised her head. The two soldiers were glaring down at her, all teeth in the shining sun.

"Pah!" One spat, disgusted. "Human scum. Watch where you are going."

"I'm sorry." She stammered. "Please, I..."

"Enough." The one growled. "Don't inflict your tongue on me. Cunt creatures can't even learn our language."

"Look." The one holding her pointed at her neck with a clawed finger. "No collar."

The other raised an eye ridge. "Runaway?"

"Mmmm or escaped transport."

"Pah! Stupid fool. Let's drop her off at the Breeding Pits,

then go get some food. I'm starving."

Amy tried to twist away, even as the claws threatened to pierce her skin, but the Tark was too strong. He picked her up and threw her over his shoulder. She tried to push away and fight, but he snarled. "Be good or I just eat you right here."

His hot, rancid breath washed over her, and she subsided to her panic, trembling and cursing. Her eyes drifted to the crowd where Mai had been. The woman was gone and Amy cursed her name a thousand times. *I swear if I find a way back, I'm going to kill her.*

The soldiers moved through the crowd easily, and Amy saw the furtive glances at their unusual burden. More than once she thought she saw a cloaked and hooded figure that might have been one of the Resistance, but she didn't dare cry out, not with the soldier's claws pressed against her back. She finally dropped her head and closed her eyes, resigned to wherever they were going to take her. A single tear fell off her cheek. *Oh Reven. I should have listened to you. I'm so sorry.*

—

"You shouldn't have let them go."

Alia raised an eyebrow, watching Reven pace in her chamber. "Are you going to second guess all my decisions now that you're here?"

He turned. "No, it's just too soon. I mean, the uproar of

our escape today must have the entire city on alert."

Alia sighed, setting her cup down. "I know you are worried about your friend, but it will be okay. My people are good at what they do. We need supplies, especially if we are going to make our move soon."

"I'm not worried about her." Reven countered, although his blushing cheeks said otherwise. Alia wisely chose not to comment. He cleared his throat. "I just think we're vulnerable right now and I'd hate to have something happen. I feel responsible for her."

"I don't see why. From your story sounds like she stuck her nose where it didn't belong. She'd be out of this otherwise."

Reven sighed. He walked over and dropped into the chair. "She didn't know. Hardly any of them know. Haven't you picked that up from your people? Most humans don't believe in aliens and they labeled the ones that do crazy. She knew what she was doing was dangerous, but I truly believe she did not know how deeply this thing went. So, I'm responsible."

"As you wish. I understand what you're saying. But she's also an adult and needs to be part of the community. Everyone here has a job."

Reven sighed, resigning himself.

Alia smiled. "Relax. She's with Mai."

"You say that like I should know who Mai is. I don't remember."

Alia laughed. "Of course. Mai is an interesting creature. She likes to be in charge and she can act like a tough guy to cover just the normal fears that this situation brings. But she would never endanger this place or any of her fellow Resistance. Also, she worships you like you are some kind of god. She won't let any harm come to Amy."

"I hope you are right." He took a big drink. "So, what's your grand scheme for attack? I mean, I hope you have one after all this time."

Alia smiled. "We haven't been sitting around, if that's what you mean. I guess you are ready to meet the council."

She rose and walked to the door, having a word with the soldier standing guard. She returned to her seat, smirking at Reven's raised eyebrow. In a few moments, there was a tentative knock at the door. "Come in."

A group of five filed in, three humans and two of the humanoid Dauquins that were the Tarks' other choice of food at the moment. The two, a male and a female, wore simple tunics and breeches. Their pale blue skin rippled like water and they walked with a languid grace as they moved to arrange themselves in a semi-circle around Reven and Alia. The Dauquin were a semi-aquatic race with orb-like eyes and smooth skin. Their race were masters of poetry and art and people said their architecture was a thing of beauty. The two bowed before sitting.

The other three humans, two males and a female, bowed as well before taking their seats. The female spoke first. "Your Highness..."

Alia held up a hand. "Audra, how many times have I told you to call me Alia in my chambers? Your Highness sounds so stuffy."

"Alia." Audra's mouth twisted as if she had to work to get the word out. *If she's a born soldier, it probably was hard,* Reven mused. "Our spies report quite a furor over the events of the morning."

Alia nodded. "As to be expected. Go on."

The taller of the two males spoke this time. He was lean but muscular, reminding Reven of a taunt bowstring waiting to be loosed. His eyes were small and dark, his posture reminiscent of a hawk. "Shipments have stopped. They also doubled patrols in the city and they are snatching everyone up, collared or not."

Reven squirmed in his seat. *Snatching everyone collared or not? What did that mean?*

He had been in contact with Alia enough to know the workings of the Resistance, but he was suddenly realizing that he was woefully unaware of how the Tark city worked. He shot a glance at Alia, who just calmly nodded like she was expecting all of this. A smile quirked at her lips. "Tavros, what say you?"

The Dauquin male looked up at her. "Our warriors are ready. Talna and I have examined the structural weaknesses of the fortress and have found several likely avenues of entrance. Once the distraction is in place, of course."

Tavros looked pointedly at Reven, who fought hard not to squirm under the glare. He suddenly realized that the entire group was staring at him. He struggled to get himself under control.

"Alia? Something you want to tell me?"

She chuckled. "You wanted to know the plan. Here it is. General?"

She pointed to the dark-skinned male. He was shorter than the hawk man, but much more muscular. A scar ran down one cheek, but his eyes spoke of confidence and leadership. He stepped forward, bowing slightly to Reven. "General Kwon at your service, sir. But most around here call me Rail."

Reven nodded. "Nice to meet you."

"Rail was one of the first that I found. Audra and Hawk came soon after. They were all warriors in their respective realms, so they became a good fit for the council. Tavros and Talna weren't soldiers, but each brought certain skill sets which have proved useful." Alia interrupted.

Reven's head spun with all this new information. "So, Rail, what is the plan?"

"Simple. The Tark are too much to take head on with a small force. But they have a weakness. While they have individual thought, they are all connected in a hive mind to the Queen. This link helps her direct the troops in large armies. However, this link could be used to our advantage. If we can kill the Queen, we believe her death would send a shockwave through the link, possibly incapacitating or even destroying all those that look to her."

Reven couldn't believe his ears. He had told this scenario to The Colonel as a joke. They were seriously thinking about taking on the queen? "You call that simple?"

Rail shrugged. "We understand that there are some logistical issues with the plan. Which is why we needed you to come to this world, sir."

Reven's stomach dropped. "Why me?"

"A distraction." Tavros picked up the speech. "We need to have someone taken before the Queen. If the Tark arrested any of us, they would either kill us immediately, or imprison us until we died. However, there is one person in this universe that the Queen would take pleasure in dispatching herself."

Reven's stomach dropped to the floor. "Me."

"Correct. Not only would the soldiers celebrate your capture, but the Queen would crow with delight. It might provide just enough of a distraction to allow the attacking party an opportunity to access the fortress."

"As my counterpart has intimated," Talna spoke for the first time in her light, bell-like tones. "We have already figured out several structural weaknesses that should allow our soldiers safe passage, granted that you can keep the guards distracted. Once inside, we will make our way to the Queen's quarters, dispatching her and rescuing you."

"We have spies and allies within the fortress." Audra spoke. "They will help make sure you stay safe until the teams can make their way to you."

Reven couldn't believe what he was hearing. He knew taking down the Tark would be a gamble, but this? "What if she wants to kill me right off? I mean, I pose a threat and everything."

Talna spoke. "Tavros and I have conceived of several weapons you can hide upon your body. While they may not be enough to kill a Tark, they should be enough to allow you to incapacitate any nearby. That should give you sufficient time to get away."

Was she joking? He wanted her to be, but the serious look she gave him answered the question. At least they hadn't thought about him being defenseless. He looked at Rail. "When?"

"Tomorrow. The Queen and her guard will not be

expecting so swift an attack. If we wait longer, it may give them time to counter anything we can do."

Reven was about to speak when there was a frantic knocking at the door. Without waiting, one guard burst in. "Your Highness. The patrol is back."

Alia's stormy look spoke bad things to the soldier. But within a second, she picked up his frantic tone. "What has happened?"

The guard looked silently at Reven for the split second he needed to tell him what was wrong. Without a word, he rushed out of his chair, surprising the others. He grabbed the guard by the lapels. "Where is she? Where is Amy?"

The guard moved to the outer chamber, Reven on his heels. He heard the others coming, but didn't acknowledge them. The guard led them out of the main quarters up into the courtyard. There a large crowd had gathered, circling around two women who were yelling at each other. They were both dressed in brown cloaks and silver collars around their necks. One woman looked to be of Asian descent, while the other was a blond woman who looked barely out of her teens.

"You bitch. You just left her there!" The blond one yelled.

The other woman sneered. "I told you. They captured her. What could I do?"

The group parted as they realized the One approached. The blond woman looked like she was going to respond to the other woman when she caught the movement in her eye and melted back into the crowd. A twitch betrayed that the other woman wanted to run, but then her pride caught her and she stood her ground, taller, defiant. Alia took charge of the group and spoke up.

"What is going on here, Mai?"

Mai's smile was contrite and sweet as she swept a deep bow. "Your Highness, a most awful thing has happened…"

"She let Amy get captured!" The blond growled. She made a move to step forward toward the other woman, but subsided under Rail's glare. Two other females stood behind her, the dark-skinned woman flipping a knife angrily back and forth in her hands. Belatedly, the blond looked at Alia. "Sorry, Your Highness."

"Enough Jess. We'll deal with the outburst later." She glared at Mai. "Is that true, Mai?"

Reven's heart dropped. He knew Amy was in trouble! He should never have let her go.

Mai looked up with innocent eyes. "I was showing her around, as I do with all newbies. There were soldiers. One of them saw her. What was I to do?"

Reven growled and murmurs fluttered through the crowd, but Alia held up a hand. "Did they know who she was?"

Mai shook her head. "No. Seemed to think she was just a normal runaway. But that's all I heard. What could I have done?"

"Not been a jealous bitch." Jess muttered under her breath. Reven wouldn't normally have heard it, but the crowd had fallen silent so that the words of the two speakers could carry.

Alia glared at Jess again, who subsided. Then she sighed and turned to Mai. "You did what was right. It would have been too risky in the marketplace to attempt a rescue."

A growl rose in Reven's throat. "We have to go rescue her."

The crowd murmured their approval, but fell silent as Alia glared at him.

"No! No one is to go to the surface."

She turned to Rail. "Double the guards. No one may leave or enter. I confine everyone to quarters until we can figure out what is going on."

She turned to the crowd. "That means everyone. We are on lockdown."

The murmurs rose again as Reven steamed. He walked to Alia's side. "Alia we . . ."

She turned stormy eyes to him, hissing. "I am Your Highness or the One in public, Reven. I have to keep appearances. No, you are not to go out after her. No one out means that, no one. We are going ahead with the operation tomorrow."

"I can't leave Amy!" He argued.

"You will have to. I understand you feel protective of her, but I have an entire city to think of. Entire planets! I will not risk it for one girl." She turned to Rail. "Carry out my order."

She turned to Reven. "My decision is final. Go find your quarters until I send for you tomorrow."

She stalked off while the crowd dispersed. The one called Mai walked up to him. "Lord Reven, it is so good to meet you, even if it is under these harsh circumstances. But perhaps I could be of help."

He whirled on her. She stepped back under the assault of his angry eyes. "What? What could you do for me? You already lost her!"

"Mai!" The two looked over to where Alia stood at the entrance to her chambers. "Come. I want a full report."

Mai threw Reven another wanting glance, then meekly walked over to Alia. Reven watched her go, seething. *I have to find you Amy; I don't care what Alia says. I should never have let you go!*

A hand tugged at his shoulder. He whirled to see the small blond woman Alia had called Jess. For a moment, she stepped back, afraid. Then she straightened up, summoning up some courage. "I saw it."

"What do you mean?"

She swallowed and licked her lips. Reven tried to breathe and calm himself. He was scaring her. She seemed to be the one person who gave a damn in this place about Amy. Jess finally got her fear under control and spoke again. "We aren't supposed to leave our partners on patrols. I could get in a lot of trouble if they find out."

Reven nodded and motioned her to continue.

"I knew Mai was up to something. I mean, she's normally not that bad to newbies, but I could see she zeroed in on Amy. The One and the other Elite don't see it, but Mai will do anything to make Mai look better. You follow?"

He nodded.

She continued. "I knew she was going to do something to Amy. I just didn't know what. So, I broke away and worked my way to where I thought they would be. I found her just as . . . just as . . ."

"Jess, what?"

A tear slipped down Jess's cheek, but whether from sadness or anger, Reven wasn't sure. She spit out the words like they were rotten juice on her lips. "Mai. She took off Amy's collar. Then she shoved her into the soldiers and ran away. They weren't even looking at Mai and Amy before. They would have been fine!"

Reven shook his head. "I don't understand. She took off her collar? What does that have to do with…"

Jess fingered her own collar for a moment, before flicking a latch and shoving it at him. "We wear them above ground. They mark us as slaves, those that work for the Tark in exchange for not being eaten. With these on, the soldiers don't give us a second look. Without them . . ."

"They assume you're a runaway." Comprehension blossomed in his mind, his throat constricting with fear for Amy, filling with anger. He glared over his shoulder at the tower. He couldn't see Mai, but knew she was in the depths. "Where will they take her?"

Jess shrugged. "Hard to say. But probably to the Breeding Pits."

He looked over his shoulder one more time. *I'll deal with her later.* "I'm going after Amy."

"I'm coming too." When Reven looked like he was going to object, she crossed her arms over her chest and gritted her teeth. "You won't get past the guards without me, and I know the layout of the city better than anyone. Besides. I didn't know Amy well, but I know she didn't deserve what Mai did to her. She's your friend and I feel like she could be mine, too. I knew Mai was pulling something, and I didn't push hard enough to stop it. So, I'm coming."

Reven opened his mouth to object again, then shut it. He

nodded. "How do we do this?"

Alia was going to be furious. But right now, he cared nothing about her plans. Maybe she had a city to save. But Amy was in danger and right now that's all that mattered.

Hang on Amy. I'm coming.

16

* * *

Amy lost track of how long they walked, but soon saw a long stone building surrounded by chain link fencing. Groups of women milled around inside. Tark soldiers stood around the perimeter, most looking bored and laughing with each other. As the duo passed the fence, the women turned dead eyes up to greet her. Then glanced back down again.

As the two soldiers approached a door set into the side of the building, a matronly woman with gray hair pulled into a severe bun walked out. She wore a red robe with a silver collar. The Tark holding Amy dropped her to the ground, causing Amy to cry out in surprise. Quickly, she rose, dusting herself off. The woman turned sharp black eyes onto Amy, making her flinch. "What have you brought me this time?"

"Runaway. Caught her in the street." The other Tark barked.

The woman huffed and, with a quick movement, reached forward and flipped the edges of Amy's cloak back. Amy flinched again and took a little step back but couldn't move much with the Tark soldiers standing behind her. The woman critically eyed Amy's body, then sighed. "A little scrawny, but that'll improve with food. She'll do."

With that, the woman grabbed her arm and yanked her towards the door. She quickly led her through a small room filled with cabinets. She locked the door, preventing escape, and motioned to Amy. "Get yourself stripped."

When Amy hesitated, she reached out to help her and Amy shrugged her off, quickly pulling off her cloak and clothes and letting them puddle on the floor. The woman tossed a thin white cotton dress to her. Amy slipped it on. The woman grabbed her arm roughly and dragged her into a short hallway that intersected with a longer one that looked like it ran the length of the building. Amy heard a sharp cry echoing down the hallway, a piercing scream that made her dig in her heels and stop for a second. But the woman merely grunted and twisted Amy's arm, making her wince in pain and follow meekly.

The woman led her down a set of stairs into darkness. They descended into a larger cavern carved out of the rock. A room filled with more chain link breaking the room into small cages. In each cage was a cot and a pail. A stench that was born of fear hit her, and she wanted to retch, but the woman persisted in hauling her down the walkway. Most of the pens were empty, but here and there Amy's blurry eyes could pick out a single woman staring up at her as she passed.

Finally, the woman stopped at an empty cell and threw her inside. Amy fell to the stone floor. She quickly pushed herself back up, but not before the woman closed the door with a clank, locking it shut. Amy threw herself against the fence with a cry, the metal vibrating under the impact but standing firm. "Please. Stop. What is going on? Where am I?"

The woman merely glared at her. Then a hand whipped out, slamming into the fence and mashing it into Amy's face, knocking her back to the ground. Amy looked up helplessly as the woman towered over her. The woman sneered. "Be quiet and learn your place. Everything will go much easier if you do."

With that, she walked off. Leaving Amy alone, cold and shivering on the stone floor.

What in the hell have I done now?

"Welcome to the Breeding Pits."

Amy looked to where this unfamiliar voice came from. It was soft, but strong. In the cage next to her, a woman lounged on her cot reading a tattered paperback book. She had dark hair pulled back in a braid and wore the same simple white cotton dress. Amy dragged herself up off the floor and sat on the edge of her own cot, facing the woman. "I'm sorry? What did you say?"

The woman turned bright blue eyes onto her. "The Breeding Pits. Or should I say, Hell."

Amy looked around and shivered. "I can imagine."

"Can you? I doubt you can." The woman gave a barking laugh. "At least not yet."

"The Breeding Pits. What do they breed?" Amy asked softly. She already knew the answer. But she wanted the woman to deny it.

Another barking laugh. "They breed us. Small children are a delicacy here."

Amy felt her gorge rise. "I think I'm going to be sick."

The woman pointed to the pail. "Be sick in there. We only get so much water and if you're sick anywhere else, they'll make you use it to clean up."

Amy just sat on her bed, forcing her stomach back down. The woman eyed her, then nodded. "Strong. That's good. Or bad, depending. Anyway, my name's Kallie."

Amy nodded. "Amy."

Kallie put down her book, propping herself on her side to face Amy better. "Well, I'd say nice to meet you but…"

She waved a hand to show the room, lit from overhead by faint glow lights. "It's not much, but then again, it's not much."

She chuckled sadly. Her eyes grew somber. "Seriously, it's not the worst. The nights here, that's when you'll see. But other than that, we get food, water, books, and for the most part, they leave us alone."

"They? You mean the Tarks?"

Kallie shook her head. "The slaves who take care of us."

"The woman?"

"No one knows her name, but we call her Grim. But there are others who take care of us. The only time the Tark get involved are the soldiers outside. They're okay. They treat us pretty nice. The human guys, though? Twisted."

"Twisted? How?"

Kallie shook her head. "You'll see. I'm sure they were normal once. I mean, the Tark gave them the same choice they gave us. Do what we say, or die right here. So, you do what you have to do. Only they've grown to like their job a little too much. They're monsters now. All of them. They think of us as nothing but cattle."

Amy swallowed and hugged her knees, rocking slightly back and forth. *I promise if I ever get out of here I am so going vegetarian!*

Kallie's voice softened. "I know it's horrible. But like I said, other than the nights, it's not too bad. Considering the alternative."

A tear slid down Amy's cheek, but she fought to sound normal. "I saw women outside when they brought me in."

Kallie nodded. "The yard. They let us out to get sunshine every day. My group went out this morning. You'll probably be in my group now. It's nice. As nice as this place gets."

Amy shook her head. "I can't believe other humans do this to them. To you!"

Kallie sighed and sank back on her pillow. "Like I said, I get it. My choice was this or to be killed. Even with as horrible as this place is, I enjoy breathing too much."

"But you said the men . . ."

Kallie's eyes grew dark. "You get used to it."

"No. I won't let them." She gritted her teeth. *Reven will find me soon. Won't he?*

"You better." Kallie sat up again, sternly glaring at Amy. "You don't and they'll kill you. Do you want to be dead?"

Amy was silent. She knew she didn't dare voice the thought that had popped into her head, the thought she had held since she'd come to this place. The thought she'd held since Whisper had come to her years ago. She'd locked that thought away, too scared to let it out of its cage.

Just then there was a loud clanking sound, and the low rumble of footsteps descending the stairs. The dead eyed women were back, filing meekly into their cages. Amy silently watched the procession. No one fought. No one tried to run. They all just filed in, finding their places, organizing themselves without a word. *Broken.*

Amy gasped as she saw the pregnant ones. They were all sequestered into cages at the end of the rows. Kallie followed her eye line.

She answered a question Amy didn't ask. "So they can keep track of us. Who's mated and who's not."

She said it so matter-of-factly it made Amy want to retch again. Would that be her fate? To be so calm about being impregnated, bearing a child only to have it ripped away from you to be eaten. Her memory stirred of the dead child in the marketplace and felt her stomach revolt again. This time, she couldn't stop it and lunged for the bucket.

Kallie wrinkled her nose but said nothing. When Amy finished, all she offered was a faint, "You're strong. Most of us never made it that long without throwing up."

She didn't feel strong. She felt stupid. Stupid for going after Reven, stupid for arguing with him, stupid for ignoring Jess and letting Mai manipulate her. The tears welled again as she thought of Reven. *He was right, and I told him to fuck off. All he did was care for me. He knew it was going to go wrong. I don't think you can get much more wrong than this place.*

Amy sank to the floor, leaning against the chain link. She looked over to where another silent woman sat, watching her. She was a slim black woman with short curly hair. Yet even wearing the simple cotton dress, she looked like a supermodel or a queen. Haughty brown eyes stared at her. Questioning.

Kallie spoke up. "Christa, meet our new one. Amy. Christa."

Christa nodded, a smile flitting on her lips. "Sorry to have to meet you, Amy. But welcome to the group."

Amy nodded at the greeting. "Nice place you got here."

She was being snarky, and she knew it, but the words slipped out of her lips. It was all too surreal. "How long have you all been here?"

Christa shrugged. "Who knows? You lose track. Long enough I know."

Her face twisted as it does for one struggling with inner scars. Amy avoided her gaze, looking down at her hands. "When will they come for me?"

Kallie and Christa looked at each other, then Kallie sighed and spoke gently. "A day. Maybe two. Depends. Sometimes they really like the fresh meat."

Amy's skin shivered only a second before she lunged for the pail again.

—

Jess led him to a small building tucked back amongst the barracks that was reserved for the Elite soldiers. She looked around to make sure no one was watching, then ducked inside, motioning him in quickly. She closed the wooden door behind him. Reven looked around, realizing they were in a supply room. Extra clothes, food, packs, and weapons lined the walls and shelves. Jess quickly started hunting.

"What are you doing?" They needed to get going, to get out of the city before Rail had the extra patrols up.

Jess had grabbed a bag and was stuffing it with weapons and food. "We don't know where she is at, or how long we'll be up there. Besides, you can't believe Alia will welcome us back once she knows, do you? I mean, you maybe, but me?"

Reven stared at her. "What are you talking about?"

Jess stopped and stared at him, her blue eyes somber. "Exile. If I'm lucky. If not . . ."

Reven shivered at the iciness of her voice. "She would throw you out?"

Jess nodded. "It's the fate of any who defy her. We get escorted to the Outlands, the desert lands that the Tarks destroyed and abandoned. Nothing lives or grows out there."

"That's . . . that's . . ." He couldn't think of the words to finish the sentence.

Jess shrugged. "We don't have to worry about people betraying us to the Tarks. Exiles don't come back, and the ones here won't face that fate, so they toe the line. Works pretty well for the One."

"You would face that for Amy? Why? You don't know her."

Jess's eyes drifted off, staring at something far out in space for a moment. Then she shook her head, coming back to the present. "I didn't need to know her long to see she was innocent. Like all of us. She understood nothing about this world and Mai threw her to it. You've not seen the Breeding Pits. I have."

Reven's anger rose again as he thought of the woman. "If you all know Mai is like this, why is she allowed to do things?

Alia talked like she was a gift from God."

Jess sighed again, filling another pack. "People let Mai be because they are afraid of getting on her bad side, or her beauty fools them and they want to follow in her wake. The One needs her because she's a talented spy. Most don't know that. They think she's just a scrounger. But I know she works for Alia by helping her rout out undesirables in the camp."

"She spies on you?" Reven stared at where he thought Alia's tower was. *There is a lot about her I don't know, it seems.*

Jess shrugged again. "All it would take would be one spy for the Tarks to take this place down, so it becomes a necessary evil. The problem is Mai is a narcissist and uses the role to her own personal advantage. Only a few of us have figured out who Mai really is, and we're keeping our mouths shut less we find ourselves on her list."

"You said she did this to Amy on purpose. Why did she have it in for Amy?"

"My guess?" Jess tossed him a loaded pack. "You. Mai is star struck with you. If it's one thing Mai likes, it's attaching herself to the most powerful person in the camp. Hence her spying for Alia. If she could capture your attention, that would be the ultimate. Unfortunately . . ."

Reven's stomach fell. "Amy was in the way."

"In Mai's eyes, yes." Jess started stripping.

Reven turned around, embarrassed. "What are you doing?"

"I need better clothes for sneaking and fighting. Not that I want to be doing much of that." Clothing muffled her voice for a moment. "There. It's safe."

Reven hesitantly turned to see Jess smirking at him. She was now dressed in tight fitting black pants and shirt with a weapons belt around her waist, archer's guards on the inside of her arms and fingerless black gloves. She also had on a pair of soft black leather boots that moved without a sound. Her eyes twinkled. "Didn't know you were shy."

He felt himself blushing and covered it up. "Just manners."

Jess laughed, which was a cheerful sound in the tense air. She shouldered her pack. "Come on."

Instead of going back outside, she led him deeper into the room. Crouching down on the floor, she lifted a trapdoor. A set of stairs were set into the wall of a stone tunnel that led down through the floor.

"A back way?"

"Escape routes. They are in all the supply huts. Hopefully, Rail won't think to cover them."

"Hopefully?" He looked questioningly at her as she started making her way down the tunnel.

Reven sighed and followed her, swinging the door shut

behind him. They descended into darkness, searching blindly for the rungs of the ladder. Soon, he heard Jess hit solid ground. A faint light illuminated his last few steps. He jumped down, landing softly beside Jess, who held a torch.

They were in a small tunnel. Jess looked at some strange scratchings on the wall, then started moving confidently to the right. Reven followed, glancing at the scribbles. "You read that?"

She nodded. "I dated an Elite for a while. He taught me. Thought I could become an Elite someday."

"What happened?" Reven asked, noting the past tense.

"They were trying to ambush a transport. Only they got ambushed instead." Her voice grew bitter. "He died a warrior."

Reven fell silent as they walked. Finally, he whispered. "I'm sorry."

Jess's voice grew tight, the tone of one speaking words she knows by heart but deep down doesn't feel. "We all know the score. Better to have a few moments of happiness and die fighting for others than to go meekly into the teeth."

Silence descended again as they walked on. After what seemed like hours, Reven dared to speak again. "You think Rail won't think of the tunnels?"

"Oh, he might think of them." She stopped at a break in the tunnel where another tunnel intersected, studying the scribbles. Then she kept on the main tunnel. "But he won't think anyone would use them. He'll lock the gates, have patrols on the wall. But this tunnel is special. It comes up in the main tunnel, not in the no-man's-land beyond the wall. If we're lucky, we'll escape notice."

"Lucky?"

"If he sends patrols outside the walls, one could spot us or hear us. It's hard to be quiet in a city of stone. It's one reason the Resistance has grown. You can't sneak anything past our guards."

"Except for this tunnel."

She nodded. "Only the Elite use it, and no Elite would dare challenge Rail or Alia, so he'd have no reason to keep them guarded."

"He doesn't know about scrounger girls who used to date Elite fighters?" Reven said.

Jess turned slightly to smile at him. "Let's hope not."

17

***

The Grim came and passed out bowls of gruel and water, and that was the only hint that night had fallen. Amy eyed the lumpy, gluey mixture and her stomach turned. She curled back up on her bed, wishing this was all a nightmare. Kallie said nothing except a faint. "I know. But you should eat. It's all we get."

They came soon after, drunk and stumbling down the stairs. A blur of tall, muscular men reeking of booze and testosterone. Amy curled up tighter, shivering. She held her breath as they passed her cage. One slowed, eying her, but another punched him on the arm. "C'mon. You know they're no good the first night."

She closed her eyes. But nothing drowned out the noises.

Christa was sitting with her back to the fence where Amy's cot was. She started singing under her breath, a sweet song with words of hope and light. Amy concentrated on the words, willing them to fill her ears, to drown out the screams and cries and laughter of the men.

Hours passed, and finally silence fell.

Christa stopped singing.

Amy whispered. "Thank you."

They had left her alone for that night. But she knew they would be back tomorrow.

—

* * *

Breakfast was the same bowl of gruel and small bowl of water. Amy forced herself to choke down two bites, and she gulped the water, being careful not to spill a drop. The Grim came through, unlocking the doors. The women, including Amy, calmly filed out. Amy eyed the Grim and contemplated knocking her down and making a run. But the woman carried a long stick that sparked every so often at the end. Amy eyed it warily for a moment, before Kallie nudged her and shook her head. Amy subsided, and meekly followed the flow of women as they walked up to the outside yard.

Amy blinked as the blazing sun blinded her. Sorry, *suns.* She shielded her eyes with her hand, wishing she had her hood back.

"The planet has two suns." Kallie had come up beside her. "It's part of why it's a desert. Legend has it back when there was only one. This place was a fertile land. Then the Tarks learned how to mine the earth for metals to make their weapons. One metal worked to help stabilize the planet's orbit. As the Tark removed it, the planet destabilized, its orbit started rocking and become irregular. The planet got sucked into the grasp of a cluster of stars which scorched it to the desert it is today."

"Is that true?"

Kallie laughed and shrugged. "Who knows? Who cares?

All I know now is that it's fucking hot out. But it's still better than down below."

Amy felt a smile cracking her lips. She knew what Kallie meant. It somehow didn't seem as bad out here, even with the fence and guards. The heat warmed her skin and drove out some of the cold that had seeped into her bones. She looked around her. Tall fencing surrounded the area on three sides, the building making the fourth wall. There were no trees or shrubs in the yard, just a tarp stretched over some poles, allowing some shade. Along the fence, armed Tarks with whips and swords watched carefully.

Other Taken and Tarks flowed along the street, going about their business, not even giving the women a second glance. Amy licked her lips. *Maybe I could shout at one of them. Have them get word to Reven.*

But even as her mind came up with that insane plan, Kallie spoke again. "Don't even think about it. You go near the fence and the guards will kill you. You call out to a passerby, and they will kill you."

"But . . ."

Kallie shook her head. "You don't think we've tried? It seems so simple. They're all right there. But the Tarks don't care, even the citizens. We're their food. Their only way to survive. And the slaves? They're too beholden to their masters and just glad to still be alive. They won't risk that for us. Besides, where would you go?"

Amy thought about telling her about the Resistance, but stopped. She had to remind herself that she didn't know Kallie, as nice as the woman seemed. The way Kallie talked, the only way ahead was to throw your fellow humans under the bus. Amy had already taken a chance with Mai, which had landed her here. Trusting Kallie and talking about the Resistance might make things worse.

"The gates. You could go to the gates and go home."

Kallie snorted. "Child's dreams. Nice ones, but no. The gates will destroy you. We were lucky enough to get through with our brains intact the first time."

Amy sighed. Her eyes drifted around to the other women. She pointed at the pregnant women with a nod of her chin. "Is that all they want from you? The children?"

Kallie followed her gaze and grimaced. "It's not too difficult to understand. You get pregnant. They take the kids. As long as you keep giving them children, you can stay. If not . . ."

Amy shivered. "How . . .?"

She stopped. How do you even ask that question?

Kallie smiled to ease her pain. "We all ask in the beginning. I've only been here for a little while. I haven't had one yet. Some here, though, they've had over ten. Although most die from complications before then. But it's not something we like to talk about."

Amy fell silent, the bites of gruel souring in her stomach. Kallie touched her shoulder affectionately, then left her alone and drifted over to talk to Christa, who was standing under one of the shade tarps. Amy let her eyes drift over the courtyard. She shivered as one of the Tark soldiers glared at her, smiling to show razor-sharp teeth. She turned away, catching the sight of a small girl outside of the fence. The little girl had brown hair drawn into a braid, and wide green eyes. A slim silver collar was around her neck and she wore a thin brown cloak. The girl locked eyes with her. Amy opened her mouth, wanting to call out, then stopped. The girl looked over at the soldier, then back at Amy. Then she turned and sprinted down the street.

Amy felt her energy drop. She looked at the fence again, remember Kallie's warning. *Maybe it would be better to end it. Leave this world with some dignity rather than face what the night would bring.*

Her mind crackled with the memories of the screams of last night. Doors opened and choked whimpers filled the air as women realized it was their night. The laughs of the men as they held the women down. Or just the realization that many were so used to the visits that they just let them do what they came to do, no fighting, no crying, no sounds at all.

As she looked at the fence again, she knew she couldn't

end it. She was too weak. Or too strong. She couldn't decide which was closer to the truth.

—

"What do you mean, you can't find him?" Alia's icy voice chilled the air.

The guard gulped. "No one can find him, Your Highness. He's not in the quarters you assigned, nor is he at any of the commonplaces. We haven't instigated a known search yet, not wanting to alert the populace, but . . ."

She waved a hand to cut him off and glared at Rail. "I thought you shut the city down."

He shrugged, not withering under her stormy glare. "We locked the gates. There are doubled patrols on the walls and I grounded all scrounging teams until further notice. But you know as well as I do we can't cover all the routes out of here. Not with the personnel I have."

Alia sighed. "Damn him. Risking everything for that stupid girl. What a fool."

She looked over at Mai, who was leaning against the fireplace, but directed her words at Rail. "Does the rest of the council know?"

"No. Just that there is a delay in the plan, but we were conferring with you first."

"Damn him." She hissed. "We had the perfect time to strike. Without him . . . do you have any idea where the girl is?"

She glared at Mai.

The girl simply smiled. "Oh no, my Lord. Last I saw was her getting captured by the two soldiers. After that . . ."

She shrugged and held up her hands, still giving Alia her 'cat that ate the canary' smile. Alia's stomach twisted. She looked at the others. "Leave us. Rail, tell the Council that we are holding off. We'll meet in an hour to discuss the developments."

Rail and the guard both bowed. Rail spoke. "As you command, Your Highness."

They left, the door closing securely behind them.

Alia turned to Mai, hissing. "What in the hell did you do to that girl?"

Mai's eyes blinked in surprise a few times before she quickly recovered. "Why, whatever do you mean?"

"Oh, cut the sweet and innocent crap. I know you threw her to those soldiers. I asked for one day from you, one day of putting away your jealous insecurities and ladder climbing. One day! You couldn't even do that. Now you're jeopardizing everything!"

Mai's eyes grew stormy. "Me? Not my fault he ran after that tramp. You're the one who told me to sideline her. That you needed him to focus on your mission. So, I got rid of her."

"There you go again, making stories up in your head. What did you honestly think? That Reven would welcome you into his arms. You're delusional. I just wanted you to keep her occupied. Keep her busy so that he wouldn't have to worry about her."

"Be careful how you talk to me. Without me, the Tark would have destroyed us long ago."

Alia sighed and sank back into her chair. "I knew I was making a deal with the devil when I hired you, but I didn't know that the demon was also an idiot."

"What do you think the people would think if I let slip that you encouraged me to spy on them?"

"Blackmail? Is that what you're stooping to now?" She shook her head.

Alia stood and stormed over to Mai, getting in her face. "What do you think the people will do when they find out you ruined their salvation, all because you got jealous? What did you do, huh? Claim she was a runaway? Tell the soldiers she was stealing? Forget to tell her about the collar? I should never have agreed to let you take her out!"

"I did nothing. I told you. The soldiers grabbed her. I took off."

"Yeah, I don't doubt that's the truth you've told yourself

in your head. What is that human saying? Tell yourself lies long enough, you believe them?"

"So, what are you going to do? Ground me? Then what? Lose your only chance of finding the spies in your camp? I don't think so."

"I can always get another spymaster. What I can't get back is this time we've lost."

"Don't be mad at me. You told him not to go. Not my fault that he disobeyed."

Alia realized she was grinding her teeth and forced her jaw to relax. "Yes, he did. But the reason he did was you! You are a conniving snake, and I'm tired of being bit."

"Well, if I'm a snake, then what does that make you?" Mai walked away from the fireplace, walking over to the drinks, pouring herself a glass and taking a long swig. "You think you're so high and mighty because you came from one of the oldest races. But didn't stop the Tark from taking your asses out, now did it?"

She smirked over the cup rim, and Alia's heart raged.

Seething inside, she fought for calm. "I think you've done enough damage for today. Get out."

Mai smiled and slowly set the cup down. As she sashayed out of the room, she threw a parting glance at Alia. "Once Reven gets back, I'll be more than happy to keep him in line for you."

She left, closing the door and leaving Alia alone. Until a black hooded figure stepped out of the shadows at the back of the room. Alia did not turn, did not acknowledge him.

She asked, "Did you get that?"

"All of it." The somber voice answered. "What would you have me do?"

"Find Reven and bring him back to me unharmed. Kidnap him if you have to. I can't let him undermine what I've built here."

The figure nodded and bowed, preparing to leave.

Alia turned to face the figure. "The girl. Mai."

The figure's face was unreadable, hidden in the shadows of the hood. "What about her?"

"See that she disappears. She's become too much of a liability."

The figure nodded and bowed, disappearing back into the shadows without a word. Alia turned back to stare into the fireplace. The fire was nothing but coals now, orange-red flickers of light within the darkened embers. Her plans were going up in flames. But she hadn't survived this long by being a fool. She would rise from this like the Phoenix. She would destroy the Tark and have revenge for her home world. Then she would rid herself of these disgusting humans. Every single one of them.

* * *

—

"Where do we start?"

Jess and Reven had emerged into the main tunnel a while ago. She'd stopped before they got to the surface, rummaging in her pack. Reven watched in confusion as she stood with two brown robes and twin silver collars. He was even more perplexed as she handed a robe and collar to him, but mimicked her as she put hers on.

She looked up. "The Breeding Pits. It's the most likely place they would have taken her. Besides, if she's anywhere else…"

"What?" Reven asked when she hesitated.

Jess gave him a sad look. "If she's anywhere else, she's probably already dead."

Reven's stomach sank, but he shook away the dark cloud. *Focus on the positive. She is still alive. I know it.* "So, tell me about these Breeding Pits."

Jess grimaced. "I've only seen them up close twice, because they're guarded. There are several buildings, one for each race the Tark currently harvesting. Which should make it easy to find her if she's there. Getting in though, that could be tricky. The buildings are out in the open, surrounded by high walls and metal doors. Tark soldiers patrol it and inside its guarded by a contingent of slaves whom are very loyal to the Tark."

"Loyal to the Tark?"

She shrugged and started working on removing the metal covering of the entrance. "You know how it is. When your choice is to do this or die, you loosen up your morals. The men get food, shelter, power. And they get to breed the women. There are plenty of lowlifes who will line up for that job."

Reven felt his soul twist in revulsion as he caught her meaning. "You mean the men, they rape the women?"

Jess turned dead eyes on him. "Women can provide children, which are a delicacy on this planet. But there's only one way that happens."

She turned and opened the door, cutting off the conversation. Reven watched her go for a moment before shaking himself out of his paralysis. *Hold on Amy. I'm coming.*

He stepped out into the alleyway, pulling his hood over his face to conceal himself. Jess replaced the door, the seams fading into the face of the stonework of the building. The system was ingenious, and even though he knew it was there, he had trouble seeing the door. "Dauquins?"

Jess nodded. "Yes. Their knowledge of architecture has helped us hide the tunnels right under the Tark's noses. Oh, they know they exist and that they are there. But few know where they are. There are too many alleys for them to watch them all. So they don't even try."

"Confident."

"It's their one weakness we exploit. They think they are so powerful that it doesn't really matter what we do. Not that it would stop them from destroying us if they could."

"So, do we go out to the street now?"

Jess grinned and walked over to what looked like a ladder stuck in the side of a building. "Nope. We go up."

Reven looked in surprise as she quickly scaled the building and followed her. The stone was cool in the night air, but he knew it would bake during the day. She led them to a small chimney that stuck out of the stone that would shelter them from both the sun and wind.

"Won't they think this suspicious?" He hissed as they settled in.

She shook her head. "They won't see us here. I scouted it. Besides, the Tark pay little attention to the slaves. As long as we don't attract attention, we are safe."

"What are we doing up here? I thought we were looking for Amy."

"We are. I brought us up as close to the Breeding Pits as I dared. Now wait here."

She walked over to the edge, throwing a note tied to a rock down to the ground. Reven stared at her odd behavior.

When she returned to the shade, he asked. "What was that?"

"You'll see. Just wait."

"Shouldn't we be rescuing Amy?" He asked impatiently.

Jess shook her head. "First, we need to figure out if she's there. They lock the Pits up at night, the women kept underground. By this time, there will be alarms. If we set those off, the Tark will descend on us. Plus, we're both exhausted. It'll be light soon. We should sleep and get our strength. Once daylight comes, they'll let the women out for some air. Then, it'll be easy to see if Amy is among them. Then we can make a plan."

"But what if she's not here? What if she's in the kill lots? We could miss our chance to get her." Reven wanted to argue, but the strategist in his mind told him Jess was right. As much as he hated it, he had to wait.

Jess laid a hand on his arm. "You don't know the kill lots like I do. They don't keep humans in there long, mere hours. If she was there, she's gone already. I'm sorry. But if she's in the Pits, she's as safe as she can be for now."

Reven and Jess made makeshift beds, using their packs for pillows. He slept fitfully, his mind full of nightmares and shapeless demons. As the sun rose, he awoke. He and Jess breakfasted on some dried meat. After a few hours, a small girl slipped over the edge of the building and rushed over to Jess. She leaned down, whispering in her ear, then fled back the way she came.

Jess nodded and turned to Reven, a slight smile on her face. "Amy's there in the Pits."

Reven sighed. At least she was alive. He made to get up. "C'mon. Let's . . ."

Jess grabbed his arm and yanked him back down. "Sit."

He did as she commanded, surprised by the firm tone. But even as he sat, he wiggled impatiently. "If she's there, we should . . ."

"Get ourselves killed facing the Tark soldiers? No, thank you." She stared up into the sky. "I told you, we can't do anything during the day. Nighttime is our safest bet. At least we have confirmation and don't have to waste the day tracking across the city."

"We wait? But that'll take all day. Hours! They could hurt her."

"Relax." She laid a soft hand on his arm. "We haven't been sitting around on our butts, you know. We've done a lot of surveillance and we know the Tark pretty well. They like routine. The men only get to go to the girls at night."

Reven shook his head. How was she so calm about this?

His face must have reflected his question, because Jess just threw him a sad smile. "I may be young, but I get it. We all hate it. Every single one of us women. Every month, One has to deal with a new one whipping us up about it. Wanting to storm the gates. Rescue everyone. It's almost happened twice. But each time she stops us. As she should. There's no way the Tark would let us survive it. We'd be throwing our lives away. But every single one of us wants to. Every single one of us knows we escaped the horrors of that place. I think it's why so many of the women fight. Because every day they remind us that we should be there. But there is a part of us that accepts it. After all, it's not like things like that didn't happen back home. Here it's just out in the open. Sanctioned."

She shivered. "Anyway, it's suicide to hit the place during the day. But at night the women are below ground and the Tark soldiers go home. It'll be harder to get inside, but my scouts think they have a way."

"Your scouts?"

She grinned. "Mai isn't the only one with spies. Children are children no matter if they are slaves. And children will do anything for a bribe."

"Sneaky."

She shook her head. "Prudent. Children see everything, and adults ignore them."

"So, why couldn't we just get everyone?" Reven asked.

Jess sighed. "Because getting one person out will be hard enough. Forty or fifty? No way we could move through the city fast enough to disappear."

Reven thought about the logistics, warring with his emotions. He sighed and leaned back, feeling defeated.

"I know it's hard. Maybe someday it will all end." She paused and looked out at the city. "We should rest. Worrying about things we can't do will only rob us of energy."

"Do you really think we can do it? Save her, I mean?"

Jess was silent for a moment. "If we don't, her fate is sealed. As is ours. "

18

* * *

The porridge sat like lead in Amy's stomach. She had managed to choke down a few bites of dinner, but now stared at the gray sludge. Her eyes focused on the metal spoon. With enough force, maybe she could use the handle...

"Don't even think about it."

Amy jumped and looked at Kallie, who's kind eyes met hers. Her voice was soft, but firm. "We've all thought about it. But you get punished for fighting."

Amy looked down at her bowl again. "Can it be worse than the alternative?"

Kallie sighed. "Better you don't find out. At best, they'll send you to the slaughterhouses. At worst...well...we've heard the screams."

A shiver ran down Amy's spine and a tear threatened to roll down her face but she closed her eyes tight to deny it.

Could she just do that? Not fight? Let them *breed* her?

A low rumble in the doorway heralded their presence. Amy's muscles tightened and her head swiveled, as did every other woman's in the room. They approached, drunk and laughing. Beating on gates as they passed, cackling as the women shrank back. Finally, she saw him. The one who had stopped at her gate yesterday. He was standing at her gate, leering. Kallie and Christa retreated to the farthest corners of their cages, not hiding, but not looking at her either. Shrinking was the only word that came to her mind. Trying to blend in and not draw attention. Trying to ignore what was about to happen.

Her heart beat faster, leaping up into her throat. Her brain exploded, wanting to cry and scream and attack the man all at the same time. Her muscles jerked slightly at the onslaught of the mixed messages, the flood paralyzing her as the man started unlocking her cage. Her bowl slipped out of her numb fingers, the spoon bouncing out and disappearing into the dark depths underneath her cot. Her ears bled with the sounds of the other men laughing and cheering the man on, all of them waiting to pile into her room. But her eyes were only for the one man. Lank blond hair fell in his eyes as he swaggered into the room.

"Well then darlin" he drawled as he undid his belt. "Time for you to join the party."

—

Reven and Jess crouched in the shadows of the roof, watching as the sun dripped lower and lower into the sky. Jess managed to nod off, but Reven's nerves were too keyed up. It grated on him that they were so close to Amy but could do nothing.

At one point during the day he had dared to peek over the edge into the yard. His heart had leapt as he saw her milling around with the other women. His body ached for action. To run and snatch her back into safety. Yet even as his heart contemplated this suicide mission, his eyes drifted over to the Tark guards. Perhaps he and Jess together could take one, but not the six that patrolled the perimeter right now. Even if some miracle happened and they could get past the six, it would be mere seconds before a flood of them rushed to the scene.

He forced himself to wait. He tried to imitate Jess's relaxed but wary stance as she wiled away the day. But he just ended up switching between pacing on the blazing roof and crouching in the shadows worrying about Amy, about everything that could go wrong. About everything he had done wrong.

Silence had ruled the day as neither had known what to talk about. Finally, the twin suns hovered over the horizon. Reven broke the silence. "What now?"

She eyed him. "Now, we wait for the guards to leave. The woman who runs the Pits will retire soon after she feeds the women dinner. The men will arrive after that from their own work quarters. If we can slip in after she leaves but before they get here, we might have a chance of getting her out before they signal the alarm."

Reven ground his teeth. *More waiting!*

"So, is it true?" Jess suddenly asked.

Reven startled, taken aback. "What?"

"I've been wanting to ask you all day but didn't know how to phrase it. But are the tales true? That your entire planet was destroyed by the Tark? That your people refused to give in?"

Reven sighed, pushing away the heart pain that always came with thinking of his home world. He started to tell Jess that he didn't tell anybody about the wars on his planet, but realized that he already had with Amy. *Perhaps its time to start bleeding off the poison.* "We were the first the Tarks found with the gates. Our planet was what you would call a conveyance point, much like this world is. The energies were stronger allowing the gate energies to find it easier than other planets, like Earth."

The words started flowing, the rote of someone who had spoken the same speech a thousand times if only to himself. "They sent their scouts, to give us an ultimatum. Surrender or die."

"Your people chose to fight?"

He shook his head. "My people were not warriors, but we also were not weak. The people had never seen wars. But we were hunters. We had powers the Tark did not have. We knew our world. The elders thought we would be a match for the Tark. They were wrong."

"What about you?"

"I was a young boy so I wasn't privy to much of the discussions, only what I overheard people gossiping about. On the day of the invasion my parents had sent me out to gather food. I saw the Tark army coming for the village. I tried to hurry back, but I was too late. Only now I realize my father knew what was coming and did what he could to save me."

Jess was silent for a moment. "So, they came for everyone?"

He nodded. "After the destruction of my village, I tried to get to the other villages, to warn them. But they were the same."

"How did you get away?"

"I hid, surviving as best I could. One day, I went through one of the gates that they used. I thought it would take me to their home world. I had this crazy idea that I would find my parents and free them, that they were somehow still alive. But it didn't take me here. It took me to another world. I lived there for a while. It was nice. The people took me in. In time, I felt like I was healing. Then the Tark came for that world. That's when it started."

"The start of your fight against the Tark."

He nodded. "Why do you ask? I mean, I'm told I'm something of a legend here. Don't you know this already?"

"You are. Although I never knew about a lot of that. Just

that the Tark came for your people." She shifted slightly. "I may be young but I'm not stupid. You're not a god. But you are a warrior. I just wanted to know how much of the mythology was myth and how much was true."

He shrugged. "That's about it for the truth. I'm not a God. I'm not even sure I'm a warrior."

"Well, its nice to know you're human, so to speak. Humble." Reven saw her stare wistfully off into the distance, into the sunset. Jess sighed. "So many tell your tales as one of hope. You're their savior. They're convinced that you will come and defeat the Tark and we will all go home."

"And you? What do you believe?"

She gave him a sad, wistful smile. "The mere fact I didn't end up in the Pits or the slaughterhouse has been enough saving for me. I know I will die fighting on this world. But your story still comforts me."

"How's that?"

She smiled again, that shy smile that never seemed to blossom but died on her lips. "You are the last of your people, or at least you thought so for a very long time. Yet you fought, giving everything to save others. That's what I wish. For my fight to save someone else. Someone who might just be the one to end this war once and for all."

"And you didn't want my story to be fake. Because it would cheapen your wish."

She nodded. "You know how tales and stories get. Especially when it comes to the hero, the savior. I don't feel like dying for some asshole."

She looked over in the direction of the Pits. "I have to admit. I'm kind of surprised you wanted to do this."

"Do what? Rescue Amy? Why wouldn't I?"

Jess pulled out her dagger, wiping it off absently with a cloth. "Defy the One. Risk yourself for one person when you've been trying to save the whole universe. It's just not something I was expecting."

"What were you expecting?"

Jess laughed. "I guess I was expecting the normal let down. You know, the God figure who had drunk too much of his own Kool-Aid, where mere peons were too lowly for you to worry about. You're less God and more Prince Charming, rushing out to save the damsel in distress."

Peons. That's what Amy called herself back in the Hub. Reven shook his head. "Is being the Prince better or worse than God?"

"Better in my opinion." Jess stood up, sheathing her dagger. "Being a God is impersonal. The One is a God. Apart from her people. You? You would risk your life to save Amy. That's being human. That's someone I can follow. So, is it worth it? Defying the One?"

Is it worth it? I've been working forever with Alia for the chance to get here, to take down the Tark. But I rushed into that base without a real plan. Without backup. Knowing I was going to my death. I didn't care about the people who got caught up in it. Amy. Jess. Kevin. Tosh, All of them. Then I jumped without hesitation at the chance to rescue Amy. He nodded. "Yes. Amy came to rescue me, risking everything, when she had no idea what was going on. She was an innocent swept up into all of this, like every human who comes through that gate. When we got to the Refuge, I just threw her to the wolves. I didn't mean to, but it happened. I know I could never live with myself for leaving her there. The One will just have to deal with that. If she's not willing to save the One, she doesn't have the heart to save the hundred."

Jess grinned. "Good to hear. Because I couldn't live with myself either."

Carefully she walked to the edge of the roof and peered over. Reven followed. The streets were empty. He watched as a Tark guard yawned and stretched, gathering with his fellow soldiers, talking to an elderly woman in a black robe before they took off down the street. The woman turned and walked the opposite way down the street. Jess whistled low. "Just as planned. C'mon. We won't have much time to get inside before the men show up. If we're lucky we can get at Amy before the chaos starts."

* * *

Time stopped for a moment. Two men stepped in the cage behind the first man. Amy bolted blindly as they rushed her, but she only took a few steps before running into the cage wall. The men grabbed her arms roughly, laughing as they threw her down on the cot. One covered her mouth with his hand as she tried to scream.

The first man towered over her, laughing and leering. One of the other men pulled up her dress, exposing her hips. The first man's eyes glinted in the glow lights. He opened his mouth to speak to her.

Suddenly, an arrow sprouted from his throat. His eyes went wide with surprise.

The men released her as they stood up, startled. The first man tried to speak, but nothing but a wet garbled noise came out. Bubbles of blood filled his mouth and popped, before he fell to the floor. Revealing Jess standing in the doorway. With her crossbows aimed at them.

The two other men didn't have a chance to yell before she aimed and hit the triggers. Two silver arrows flew like lightning across the small space, burying themselves in the men's chests. They staggered backward, slumping to the floor.

Amy's ears registered more yells, the quick yells as men's lives were ended, the thump of bodies. Jess ran over to her. "You okay?"

Amy sat up and hugged her friend, tears running down her face. "You're here. You're really here."

Confused questions started rising from the other cages as the women started realizing what was happening. From somewhere overhead, an alarm rang. Jess's head whipped upward. "Damn. We got to go."

Reven stepped through the doorway, a sword in his hand and blood splattered on his clothes. He stopped, smiling as he caught sight of Amy. "Amy."

He ran to her and hugged her, picking her up in his arms. She wanted to protest that she was okay, but the second he held her she wrapped her arms around him and started crying.

Jess went to the door. "What happened?"

"One of them got upstairs. I guess he hit the alarm."

"Damn. We have to move. The guard will be here in seconds."

He nodded, and they left the cage, heading for the stairs. Amy lifted her head slightly as the women started screaming. She saw Kallie, and yelled. "Stop!"

Reven paused. "What?"

"The others. We can't leave them!"

Reven looked at Jess, and she shook her head. "No way."

He looked sadly at Amy. "I'm sorry."

"No. No, we can't!"

But her words were lost as they headed to the stairs. She wanted to struggle, to fight, but her body refused. All she could do was watch as Kallie and the others disappeared from view as Reven ran up the stairs. Tears flowed down her face, and she buried it in his shoulder. Blocking out their faces. Blocking out their cries.

Jess and Reven ran quickly through the building and burst out onto the empty street. The alarm rang through the night, and noises rose from the vicinity. They sprinted down the street.

"The alley's just ahead!" Jess panted. "If we can make that, we'll be okay!"

A Tark red crested soldier stepped around the corner of the building, sword brandished, snarling. Jess and Reven both slammed to a stop. Jess started swinging her crossbow to position, only to remember it was empty. She looked over at Reven, but he couldn't fight carrying Amy, and she looked in no shape to run. She swore and reached for a dagger, hopeless against a Tark soldier. But if they were going to go down, they were going to go down fighting.

The Tark soldier snarled, advancing on them. "Rebel scum. I will be rewarded for this."

Suddenly, his body arched and a scream issued from his

throat. An arrow blossomed through his chest, thick green blood oozing from the site. The Tark staggered toward them, infuriated. Then, his eyes flew wide open and his body stiffened. His muscles jerked and twitched before he fell to the ground.

Jess, Reven and Amy stared in silence, stunned. Jess shook herself quickly. "Whatever. We got a friend. Let's go!"

Reven's eyes drifted to the rooftops. A single shadowed figure looked over for a moment, then turned and disappeared.

"C'mon! You want to wait for the others?" Jess yelled from the alleyway.

Reven shook himself out of his revelry and ran for the alleyway. Jess was already at the door, pulling it open. Jess climbed down, followed shakily by Amy. Reven climbed in, replacing the door mere moments before numerous feet pounded the ground outside.

He moved back into the tunnel, finding Jess huddled over Amy. Jess stood and walked over to him, pulling him further away and whispering. "Everything ok?"

"No pursuit." He looked over at Amy and whispered. "She ok?"

Jess sighed. "I don't think anythings okay. But she isn't seriously wounded beyond some scrapes and bruises."

"Thanks for that."

"We need to get her to the city."

"I thought you said if we go back you'll be exiled."

Jess inhaled sharply, her eyes troubled. "Probably. But there's nowhere else to go. I had originally thought to try for one of our safe houses with an ally, or try for the mountains. But the Tark will be looking hard for her above and the mountains are too far to make with the city on high alert."

Reven thought for a moment. "The One needs me. Perhaps that will be enough to protect us."

Jess wanted to believe him, but the hope was a sputtering flame. "One can wish. Can you carry her some more? I don't think she can walk."

"You said she wasn't seriously wounded."

"I think she's in shock. She just collapsed on the floor and won't move. "

Reven's eyes grew concerned, but he just walked over and crouched next to Amy. "Amy."

She lifted tear stained eyes. A weak smile wavered on her lips. "You came for me."

Instinctively, he reached toward her face, gently tucking her wayward hair behind her ear. "Of course. You came for me, right?"

She barked a soft laugh. "What was it you said? You don't know what you're getting yourself into?"

He smiled. "The adventures just starting."

Tears started pooling in her eyes, and he picked her up, cradling her against him. Her body vibrated in a muffled sob, but he just pulled her closer and turned to Jess. "Ready?"

She nodded, leading the way down the tunnel. Reven hugged Amy tighter, her sobs quieted but her body shaking.

"Don't worry." He whispered. "We're going home."

19

***

"Are you sure about this?" Reven asked. They were crouched at the end of the tunnel, looking out toward the city. "Why can't we just go the way we came in?"

Jess took a deep breath. "And say what? Mai was mistaken and Amy was here all along? We found her sleeping it off somewhere? No, they'll know we left. Better to face it up front then sneak around waiting to get caught."

"Okay. Lead the way."

They had just started into the open ground when a voice shouted. "Halt!"

Jess and Reven stopped. Jess held up her hands. "Taiki. It's me, Jess."

The man startled for a second, then lowered his crossbow. "What the hell Jess? You know you're not supposed to be out."

Reven shifted uneasily. *They didn't know we were gone. Why would Alia keep that quiet?*

Jess straightened, taking advantage of the situation. "We were running a secret mission for Alia."

Her eyes flicked to Amy.

Taiki's eyes widened for a moment, before he nodded. "Right. We'll escort you to the city."

Taiki whispered something to a runner, who ran ahead. Then he motioned for them to walk, the patrol loosely encircling them. Anxious static filled the air, the tension growing as they approached the looming wall.

The silent walk across the open ground rankled with Reven. *Why would Alia keep their disappearance quiet? Because she didn't want to appear weak? She didn't want to appear like she couldn't control me? Did she send that person on the roof? Were they supposed to be helping us, or was there another reason?*

The group reached the main gates, which opened. A crowd had quickly gathered, news of the patrol relayed quickly through the town. Rail was waiting with some of the Elite guard. His expression was calm, but his eyes were stormy. As the group cheered at their return, he walked up to them.

"Welcome home." His tone was even, but Reven detected the restrained growl underneath. "The One sends her thanks for returning Amy and asks you to wait in her special quarters for the doctor."

Reven forced a genial smile to his lips, even as his hackles raised at the tension in the air. *Ah. House arrest. But we want to make the impression we're welcoming the returning heroes.* "Lead the way."

Jess looked at him quizzically. He shook his head slightly, and she calmly moved her hand to her dagger. Nothing in her posture changed, but he felt the electricity as her body tensed. *She's young, but she's good.*

They followed Rail, surrounded by the guards as the crowd fell away. There were some murmurs and inquisitive looks, but Alia had her people trained well and they melted back into the streets, returning to their routines.

The guards led them to a small one-story building near Alia's headquarters. The interior was brightly lit and filled with comfortable furnishings and a fireplace. It looked to be an apartment. Except there were bars on the windows.

"The doctor will be here soon. The One will send for you when she is ready." Rail said.

To tear my head off. Reven finished the thought. But Amy came first, and he needed to take care of her. "Thank you."

Rail left, not even acknowledging him. Reven shook his head and headed to what looked like a bedroom. Jess moved to the window, searching the shadows outside. She nodded at him. Rail hadn't taken their weapons, but that didn't mean they were safe. He nodded his thanks, knowing she had their backs.

He moved into the dimly lit bedroom, carefully laying Amy on the plush bed. She stirred slightly, looking up at him. "Where are we? What's going on?"

"Home. You can rest now." He filled a glass with water from a nearby stand. *At least they gave us some comforts.*

Carefully, she sipped the water, then fell back on the

pillows. She turned her head, facing the wall. He sat there for a moment before asking. "Amy?"

She didn't answer. "Amy. Are you okay? Did they hurt you?"

There was no answer. After a few seconds, she whispered. "We just left them."

He didn't have to ask who. "I know. But we didn't have time. The patrols were coming."

Silence. She did not speak, and the more the time stretched, he wondered if she was angry with him. Finally, her hand reached behind her, the fingers searching for his hand. He grabbed it. She turned to face him. Her eyes brimmed with tears. "I hate them."

Again, he didn't have to ask who. "All of us do."

"What do we do now?"

"Now you rest. Leave everything else to me."

She nodded and closed her eyes. He tucked a blanket over her, watching for a moment. Then he walked to the door.

"Reven."

He stopped and looked back. Her eyes glimmered in the dim light from the doorway. "What?"

"They need to be stopped. All of them. It has to stop."

He gave her a sad smile. "Get some rest. We'll talk about it when you feel better."

He returned to the main living room. Jess looked over at him. "Some prison, huh?"

"You picked up on that too?"

"Kind of hard not to. How is she?"

Reven's eyes drifted to the door. "Like you said, she's hurt."

Jess just nodded sadly. "Did . . . did we get to her in time?"

"I don't know. I think so."

"Good." Jess turned back to staring out of the window. "What do we do now?"

Reven settled on a chair in front of the fire. "We wait. We take care of Amy. Then I'll deal with Alia."

"The One?"

Reven nodded. "She'll send for me. I know she will. Then we'll see what game she's playing."

"What are you talking about?"

"Didn't you think it was odd that the patrol didn't know we were missing?"

"Yeah. It surprised Taiki to see me."

"Right. They weren't out looking for us, just looking for anyone. Alia didn't tell anyone we were missing. Why? If nothing else, it would look good for her. Going off to save one of their own. That's a moral booster. But she kept it silent."

"We disobeyed her."

Reven quirked a smile. *She's a smart one.* "Right. And that means?"

"She can't let the city see her not having absolute control. Which means she'll make an example out of me."

"You?"

Jess turned to face him. "Well, you're her friend and hero to the community. She may slap you, but she can't do anything to you, can she? Not and keep the support of her people. But me? I'm just a nobody. She can make an example out of me. No one may challenge her will."

A shiver ran down Reven's spine, but he dismissed it. Alia was strong, she had to be, but she wouldn't be that harsh. "I won't let that happen."

Jess barked a harsh laugh and returned to the window. "You may not have the choice. You've not lived here. People go . . . missing . . . when the One gets angry."

Reven stared at her. "Missing?"

"Just what I said. One day they're here, the next . . ." She made a helpless gesture with her hands. "They get sent on suicide missions. Or they're just gone. Rumors have been circulating for a while that the One has a secret guard to take care of things for her, things she doesn't want people to know about."

Reven's mind drifted back to the shadowy figure on the

roof. Whomever they were, they had been good. A single arrow at night to the one chink in a Tark's armored skin. Wielding a bow that could deliver an arrow with that much force took skill. Hitting that small of a target at night was the work of a master. His soul shivered. If Alia had even one warrior of that caliber under her complete bidding, ruthless enough to kill for no reason other than her word, she was more than just powerful. She was dangerous.

A knock at the door startled him, and the guard outside opened it to admit the doctor. He was a tall, lean man with graying hair and a scar down his cheek. His eyes were hard, and he had the demeanor of someone not interested in being summoned, but he sniffed and extended his hand. "Doctor Clemson. Are you the patient?"

Jess merely kept looking out the window, although Reven saw her back tense. Reminding himself to ask her later, he shook the doctor's hand. His skin itched with the man's negative aura, but he shrugged it off and tried to smile. "No. It's Amy. The Tark captured her."

The man waved him off, and Reven stiffened at the interruption. "Enough. Where is she then? Let's get this over with."

Reven turned and led him to Amy's door. He knocked lightly as he opened it. "Amy? The doctor's here to look at you."

She was curled on the bed, facing away from him. At his voice, she slowly turned over. A faint smile crossed her face. Until the doctor stepped into the doorway. He watched as her eyes grew wider as the doctor approached. He crossed the room quickly, pushing past Reven. As he approached the bed, Amy sat up, shifting across the top to put her back to the wall, retreating from the older man. Her muscles tensed as the man eyed her.

"Well then, you look well enough to move." He eyed her disdainfully. "Let's get this over with."

Reven saw it, the moment Clemson reached for her arm. He watched something in Amy shift. It wasn't her eyes anymore, but that of a wounded animal. He watched as time slowed down, as the doctor's hand contacted Amy's skin.

Amy exploded, screaming and kicking out with her leg, catching Clemson in his abdomen. The doctor folded for a moment, cursing and sputtering. Then he snapped straight up, his facial muscles twisted by rage. He raised his arm as if to slap her, but Reven strode forward and grabbed it. "Enough!"

"She kicked me!" Clemson sputtered, fighting against Reven's grip. "Stupid, ungrateful bitch. Doesn't even know I'm trying to help her."

Amy snarled, a dark, beastly sound that made Reven shiver. But he only tightened his grip, pulling the doctor away. Jess stood in the doorway and nodded to Reven as he pushed the older man out the door into the common room. Reven felt more than saw her go to Amy's side.

"Why I've never . . . lying bitch . . . she's not hurt . . ." Clemson's mutterings increased in anger and velocity as Reven roughly pounded on the door for the guard to open it.

"Unhand me!" Clemson finally wrenched his arm free as the door opened, trying to pull himself into professionalism. *Playing up for the guard,* Reven mused. He wanted to deck the man. What the heck had all of that been about? But his mind drifted to Amy and he let the impulse pass. He had enough to deal with without being charged with pummeling this idiot.

The guard had a confused look on his face. "Is everything alright?"

Clemson pushed past Reven and the guard. "The girl is fine. She attacked me! I'm going to see the One about this!"

The guard side-eyed Reven and he shook his head. "I think there was a misunderstanding. I'll take care of it."

The guard rolled his eyes at Clemson, then smirked at Reven. "Not the first time."

Reven sighed as the door closed. At least Clemson's non-bedside manner was not a secret here. He'd deal with Alia later, anyway. Surely she wouldn't punish Amy for reacting to him that way.

Jess was just leaving Amy's room, silently closing the door. He strode across the room, intending to go in, but Jess stood in his path, holding a hand to his chest. "Stop."

Her voice was soft, but commanding. He glared at her. "Is she okay?"

"She's hurt. Clemson's an idiot and he hates women. How he became a doctor in any sense of the word escapes me. But the way he came at her, well . . . the men in the Pits may have done nothing to her body but her mind is another matter."

"She thought he was attacking her?"

"She's hurt, angry, lost, and confused, not to mention feeling guilty. That's just the little that I got out of her. She's not processed any of it yet. She needs time, something I don't think she has."

"It just . . . her eyes. That snarl. She sounded like a beast."

Jess shook her head. "How do you react when someone hurts you? We are all animals, deep down inside. It's just we grow beyond those base instincts to have other emotions and thoughts. But those instincts are still there, buried deep inside."

"She didn't react that way to me."

"Because you are her hero, even if she doesn't realize it. You saved her. You came for her."

"I'm the one that got her in this mess."

"True. She should hate you. She might at some point, trying to work through this. But right now? You are the one thing she can trust and cling to, her touchstone to sanity. You came for her. That's everything right now in a world where nothing makes sense."

"How'd you get to be so smart?"

Jess quirked a smile and shrugged. "My mom is a psychologist and wanted me to follow in her footsteps. I didn't have time to decide if I wanted that before I got taken, but doesn't mean I wasn't listening."

Reven shook his head. "You are wise beyond your years, young one."

She sighed. "Not wise enough to have stayed out of this mess."

"We'll get out of it. Together. We're a team now, the three of us."

She nodded. "I think there's more out there that would join that team. But you're going to have a tough time defying the One and getting people to agree to it."

"Who said anything about defying her?"

Jess raised an eyebrow. "I know you feel it. How wrong this feels. Not anything you can put your finger on, but something. It's been like that for a long time. We've all been too busy just surviving to pay it much attention, but every so often something happens that makes the hairs on your neck stand up. Something that betrays the lie of the idyllic Refuge for the hunted. But you forget it because it's always off to another raid, worrying about an invasion, something. It's never something solid enough to say 'yup, something's weird'. All overshadowed by the thought of you coming to save us, all of us banding together to make it home. But now with you here? I don't know. Maybe the whispers are growing into something more."

"You think my coming here makes the problem worse?"

"I think your coming here was a blessing for the One, but also came with a curse she wasn't expecting. I think our defying her order and going for Amy put a crack in her control, a crack she can't afford to have. Now she has to do something about it."

"What do you mean?"

"I mean, she is our leader. She has protected us. But you? You are a god. You are the fighter that made the Resistance a thing. You are the brave hero traveling between lands, battling to save them. The One? She is a government official. Keeping us safe, yes. But she's not the hero of the story. Only she has been until recently. Because you were just a story. Now, you're real."

Dawning reached into Reven's mind. "I'm a threat, even if I don't want to be."

"Just like Amy was to Mai. Ir might have been just a little

thought in her head she tried to ignore. *With this little stunt, you proved it in her mind.* The populace will love us for rescuing Amy, because in their minds it could have been any of them that were captured. You came for Amy. The One didn't. What about the next time, when it is one of us? Will she just leave us to rot?"

Reven sank down in a chair. "I defied her and she can't make me disappear."

"No. You vanish, and here goes all the hope and morale of every single warrior in the city. Me? I'm just a scrounger. Accidents happen all the time. Amy disappears? Poor child, just didn't understand how this world works."

"I won't let that happen." He felt the anger in his voice. Then suddenly, his soul felt cold, and he looked toward Amy's room. "She tried to get rid of Amy."

"I didn't put the two together until after Mai pulled her trick, but yes. I think the One told Mai to keep Amy away from you. She probably only wanted Mai to distract her, not get her captured. I think that was Mai improvising because she wanted a rival out of the way. But the One used Amy, and will continue to do so. To manipulate you."

Reven took in a deep breath and stirred, walking over to Amy's door. He stopped, turning his head slightly to look at Jess. "I won't let anything happen to either of you."

Jess just looked at him sadly, her tone the one of the

realist who can't believe in dreams anymore . "I really hope that you can."

He opened the door slowly into Amy's room. She was curled up with her back to the door again. Slowly, he crossed the dark room, sitting on the edge of her bed. He felt her tense, so she wasn't asleep. But she did not move or acknowledge his presence.

He waited.

Finally, she turned over; her face drained. Her eyes were downcast and red with shed tears, but they had dried. She stared at him with wide eyes. Ashamed. "I'm sorry."

It was a whisper, but it knifed into his heart. "For what?"

"The doctor. You told me he was a doctor, but I didn't hear. I just felt . . . it was like . . ." Her body started trembling again with dark memories, and Reven broke. He pulled her into his chest, feeling her tremble against him. Slowly, he felt the trembling subside. He expected her to pull away, but she just lay against his chest.

"It's okay. He was an ass." He hoped she could feel his smile.

She hiccupped and laughed. It was small, but something.

They stayed like that for a while. Reven knew in some part of his mind that it should feel weird or uncomfortable. They didn't even know each other. They weren't even of the same species. But in that moment, nothing felt more natural.

She needed him and his strength. Not his words, because words wouldn't heal. But strength, that was what she was lacking right now. A touchstone, as Jess said. So he just sat there, holding her.

He felt the moment she fell asleep, the moment her tense muscles eased and blessed peace settled over her. The moment where her exhaustion overwhelmed her need to be alert. Carefully, he laid her down, covering her with the blanket. *Rest easy, little one. You've got a long road ahead of you.*

Reven realized that, until this moment, revenge had been the driving force of every minute of his life. Revenge for his family. For his planet. Revenge for his pain and loss. But that pain and loss had been a part of him for so long, he had forgotten what it was like to have other emotions. Happiness. Laughter. Love.

And fear. Not fear for himself, but for another that he couldn't protect. Images flashed through his mind of his mother, sister. Of their broken, burned bodies. His stomach and soul twisted at the thought, the senses flooding in fresh as the day. The smell of the charred flesh, the blood splashed upon the walls, the frozen screams of terror on the faces of those he had loved.

He tore himself away from the flashback, gasping, hoping the noise hadn't woken up Amy. How long had it been since he had buried those memories? How long since he had felt the pain?

How long had his life been about pain, revenge, hatred?

He looked at Amy's fragile form. Her tear-stained face. Her thin body. He remembered her laughing eyes when they first met, her surprise, the fire of adventure flowing out of her. He remembered her eyes from that moment before, the dark haunted beast that plagued her soul peering out at him.

The Ra'shek were an emotional species with a highly tuned psychic ability. It was one reason theirs had been such a peaceful society. It was hard to inflict pain when you intimately felt what the other person was experiencing. But he had closed himself off to that psychic side long ago. In fact, he had sworn off so many of the things that made his people what they had been. Because he had tired of hurting. So tired of being in pain constantly. Of being reminded of what he had lost. So, he had blocked it out. Shoving it deep inside, locked within a safe. His only thought, his only emotion left, had been revenge. Driving him. Focusing his thoughts. All these years.

But he felt Amy's pain now. The sudden, stabbing, choking pain of one who has never really known pain before. Not really. Not that deep, searing pain of fear. Where you face your own death. Your own mortality. The darkness and ugliness of the universe. The depths of darkness within your own soul, or another's. He remembered losing himself.

Falling into the bottom of a well. And never coming out.

He had to be more now.

He had allowed his world to get out of control, and it had swallowed Amy whole. Now she needed a lifeline to get out of the well. To deal with the pain and anger and fear. Now, her only lifeline was him.

Not knowing why, he bent over her still form, kissing her lightly on the forehead before tiptoeing to the door. He stopped, turning one last time to look at her sleeping form. *I am done watching those I care about get slaughtered. I promise you I will protect you. I will get you home. I promise you will laugh again.*

20

* * *

The door opened without warning, and Rail strode through, a grim look on his face. Reven could see the patrol of men standing outside. Rail stopped a few feet away, far enough to be polite but close enough to force an issue if need be. Reven tensed his muscles instinctively, but

Rail spoke first. "The One requests your presence."

"Amy's not well."

"It is only your presence she requests."

Reven had no intention of leaving Jess and Amy alone, not with what he had learned from Jess. He eyed Rail, trying to read the man's mind. But his mental touch hit a wall, feeling like it was slipping against glass. Rail smirked. *So, he knows about my kind's psychic powers and how to block them. Interesting.*

Reven's eyes scanned the room until he caught sight of Jess. He made what he hoped was a subtle *be wary motion.* Jess merely nodded and placed a hand on the dagger at her hip as she slipped across the room to Amy's door. It wasn't perfect, but Jess would guard her. He could only hope she could handle whatever might come. Reven turned his attention back to Rail. "Lead the way."

The patrol surrounded him the moment he stepped outside of the door, and they walked swiftly through the streets. Reven noticed the crowds of people dawdling on the edges. Trying to appear busy in their day-to-day lives but eying the procession. Waiting. Watching. The entire city hummed with nervous tension. Something had changed. But what? And why? Was it merely as simply as them defying Alia's orders? Or was there something else that he didn't understand? Whatever that was, he hoped he figured it out soon. Something told him their lives depended on it.

They led him up to what he now thought of as Alia's palace, into the throne room. *Ah. No more cozy, informal setting. Now I get to see the queen.*

He didn't want to believe anything bad about Alia. After all, she was the last of the Ra'shek. She had created this home and helped save these people. But the subtle wrong that Jess had brought up itched at the back of his mind, bringing up all the odd things that had happened since coming here, piecing them together. Now, as he approached her throne set high above, surrounded by the grandness of the room, he saw that gleam in her eye. She glared down at him, dressed in rich robes of white and gold. She did not have a crown, but her posture left no doubt that there should be one. Gone was the tired leader of a rebellion. Here was a displeased tyrant.

"Leave us." She waved her hand, and the patrol dissipated, the doors closing behind them with a heavy thunk. Her eyes weighed down on Reven, the fury blazing. "You disobeyed me."

There was no question. No asking for explanations. Just

damnation. Reven stood tall. "Only because you let her go to the surface. Amy needed me."

"So, you're not repentant?"

"I wish you would not have made it wrong for me to go. I regret having to disobey you. But going? No. That I do not regret."

"So, you would do it again?" Her voice became soft, but stronger than steel. It vibrated in the air, a snake coiling to strike. She glared at him, her eyes like daggers.

Reven knew he was on thin glass. "I don't plan on letting Amy out of my sight again. So no, as long as she is safe, I don't see a reason to disobey you again."

A small smile quirked on her lips, and the anger drained. But he still saw it, simmering beneath the surface. She shook her head, sighing. "Do you know what they are saying, out on the streets?"

"No. You've had me under house arrest."

If that provoked her, she showed no sign. She stood, descending regally from the throne, her eyes locked on his. "They're hailing you as a hero. 'He went to save her' they cry. 'He will rescue us'. They are looking to you instead of to me to save them. In one day, you've undone everything I worked to achieve all these years! One day!"

"I really doubt—"

"Don't speak!" She snarled. Her eyes blazed with fury.

He refused to shrink. "Do you know what it's been like these years? Hiding. Scavenging. Cringing at the slightest sound, worried that they've found some way in. Do you know what it's been like, hiding like moles under the very feet of the people that destroyed my world?"

"It was my world too, don't forget."

"Ha." She turned her back, returning to the dais steps. "Do you even remember who you are?"

Reven felt icy fingers running over his skull, the sign of a not-too-subtle mental attack. Quickly, he threw up a block, a wall of steel surrounding his mind. Alia's lips quirked in an odd smile. "Well, at least you remember that much."

She withdrew the attack and sat back down on the throne, glowering at him. "You denied everything, driven by revenge. But you got to flit around being the hero while I was here, doing the hard work, keeping these people safe, and for what? To be forgotten the moment you stick your nose in the door?"

"So, is that your problem?" Reven attacked. He was tired of the cat-and-mouse game. "Not enough recognition?"

She glared at him for a moment, then threw her head back and laughed, a short, harsh barking laugh that made his insides cringe. "You think I'm jealous? Hardly. You were supposed to come here for one purpose and one purpose only. To attack the Tarks once and for all and get revenge for our planet. We had the perfect opportunity! Then you throw it all away on a stupid human girl."

"She's not stupid."

"Why do you care so much for her, anyway? You admitted to me you didn't know her. Or have you grown soft in your elder age?"

"I care for her as you care for anyone in the city."

"Ha." The same short barking laugh. "You presume a lot about how I feel about anything. But you haven't answered my question. What were you thinking? Here I was expecting a blazing avenging angel, a warrior of pure steel, yet I find one made of sand."

"It was the right thing to do."

"It was careless. Not only have we lost our window, but the city is on an even higher alert. We raid shipments all the time, but an invasion into the Pits? That's something new. We can't sneeze without the guard bearing down on us now. Our perfect moment of revenge lost because you went soft on a human curr. Do you even remember our homeland?"

The memory flared up, the scent of burning flesh sharp in his nostrils. He clenched his hands and willed it back down again. "How dare you even ask that?"

"I ask because it boggles my mind how you threw away your, our one chance at revenge for a simple human girl. Not to mention how you made me look like a fool. I don't think I have to tell you I don't enjoy looking like a fool."

"That wasn't my intention."

"Wasn't it?" He felt the icy fingers and threw up a block. She smiled.

She's trying to wear me down. She knows I can block her. What game is she playing? It's against the code of our people to invade another's mind, so what is she doing with me?

Alia rose and descended again, smiling broader now, *like a cat that found a mouse.* "I invited you here. Told you about our little commune. About our plan. Then you just go off and do whatever you want."

"I'm not one of your subjects."

"Oh. But you are. Or have you forgotten your station?"

Realization dawned. "You can't be serious. Just because your family was part of the noble class. Those obligations died when the planet did."

"Did they?" She glared. "I am a member of the Tashavik family. I am royalty. You are a servant. Yet here you are, disobeying me."

He stared at her in disbelief. "Are we really doing this? Our entire planet was destroyed. We are the only two left. You're pulling rank on me?"

"Perhaps my heritage means more to me than it does to you. I honor my family. I will honor them more with my revenge upon the Tark. What about you?"

The words slapped him in the face. She continued. "You threw away your revenge. Revenge handed to you on a silver platter to go haring off after a girl. A human girl. A human girl you didn't even know. How could you turn your back on your people?"

The stinging bite punctured him to his core. But he stood there, staring her in the eye. Her words boiled around inside of him, twisting around with all the other emotions and events until they became this unintelligible mess. Reven took a deep breath. He had done what he had to do, and it had been right. But his mother . . . the memories of her face flooded back. He shoved it back with a bitter laugh. "We are not a people anymore. We are two bent on revenge. But those out there—"

He turned his head, looking through the stone to where the city lay. "They are the innocents. They still have a world and life they can go back to. If I don't do everything I can do to save them, to return their life to them, that's when I have turned my back on my family."

"Even if saving the one meant sacrificing a chance to end it all?"

It was his turn to laugh. "I think you overestimate our chances with your little plan. Even if we knock the Queen out of commission, there will be another to take her place at some point."

Alia snarled. "At least I am trying something."

She returned to the throne. A calm peace settled over her, the calm of a queen with an empire to rule. She glared down at him. "What's done is done. But you will pay the consequences."

She snapped her fingers. Out of a secret door, a hooded figure stepped. Dragging Jess beside him. Bound and gagged.

Reven took a step toward her, but stopped when the figure raised a knife to Jess's throat. Jess's eyes boiled with fear, but she shook her head slightly. Alia laughed. "I figured you cared for this one as much as Amy. Always like a Vaushin to take the lost little ones under their wing. A shame that you weren't of a higher class. When I had heard fragments of rumors that a Ra'shek had survived out in the Universe, I had clung to a faint hope we could resurrect our race. Yet it wouldn't be good to mix. Still, we might have been good allies and friends. But I cannot abide one that does not know his place."

"Let her go. I don't know what changed, but your anger is with me."

"Yes, it is. And nothing changed. Except my feelings of compassion towards you. I thought we could work together in our mutual revenge. But you are a loose cannon. Following your heart and all that. Meanwhile, I have taken the burden of protecting these people. Sacrificed myself. Taken their pain. Then you just waltz in like nothing and undo all of it. All the respect, loyalty and reputation I worked so hard to get. Poof. Now, you're the hero. You're the one who cares for them."

"That wasn't—"

"Stop with the excuses. I don't care what you intended or not. What I care about now is what happens next. Like I said, there must be consequences. So, here is the plan. You and Miss Amy, since I know how desperately you want to watch over her, will allow the Tark to capture you and take you to the Queen. Once there, we will enact the plan as before. The Dauquin assures me we still should be able to get in. When they take you to the Queen, our Elite guards will swoop in and kill her."

"And if I say no?"

"Then Jess dies. Simple as that. You were so willing to put the populace at risk to save the one. Are you willing to risk the one in order to save yourself?"

Reven locked eyes with Jess for a moment, and her body sagged. He couldn't put Amy in danger again, especially not waltzing into the Queen's castle. But neither could he risk Jess. At least if he was with Amy, he might do something. "Fine. You win."

"Good." She smiled. "See, wasn't that easy?"

Alia waved her hand, and the figure dragged Jess back

into the darkness. "Don't worry, I'll keep her safe. For now. Let's hope your mission goes well."

"What happened to you? No Ra'shek would ever inflict pain on another."

Her face turned to stone. "No Ra'shek ever dealt with watching their entire world burn before them. What other Ra'shek dealt with escaping the clutches of a sadistic race bent on destroying an entire Universe. No Ra'shek ever dealt with ruling over another race and trying to keep them protected under the noses of said sadistic race. I rose to that challenge and have done what I needed to do it."

"I watched our people burn too!"

"Ha." She snarled. "You ran away. You are a disgrace!"

Alia took a breath, struggling to regain her composure. "So, here are the rules. You will return to Amy and you will not speak another word of dissent. There will be no discussion of this conversation. You will await further instructions. If I hear anything, any inkling of disobeying me or dissent from the populace and I find out the source is you, I will kill Jess. If I find out anyone learns of her being held here, I will kill Jess. If I hear of any part of the plan not going right, I will kill Jess. Do you understand?"

His stomach twisted. "Please, she had nothing to do with this. Punish me, but let her go."

"Punish the hero of the story? No, we can't have that.

Your death would only devastate the people. But her? Well, accidents happen."

Reven's breath chilled at her tone, the very echo of Jess' words before. He shuddered but fought to not let it show on his face. Icy fingers playing over his mind again, softly, almost caressing him. He grimaced and said, "It doesn't have to be like this."

Alia smiled. "Oh, but it does. You saw to that. Now you understand how far I'm willing to go to have my revenge. Either you play by my rules willingly or by force. You chose force. So, we have a deal?"

Amy's and my life for Jess's. Yeah, I hear you. "And when it's done and we're safe?"

She shrugged. "You can all three go on your merry little way."

Somehow he doubted that, but he nodded. "Deal."

"Good. The patrol will see you back to your new quarters. You will stay there until the council and I figure out how best to enact the plan."

She dismissed him. Reven turned around and headed to the door, which opened as if by some mysterious signal. Once again, the patrol circled around him and led him back to Amy. This time, he did not notice the stares and questioning looks of the populace. Reven's mind was whirring madly, trying to think up a plan.

I promised to keep Jess and Amy safe. How the hell do I do that now?

Reven cursed Alia for putting him in this position. Something had warped her mind. He was helpless. She had been playing him all along, using him and his status within the community. While he had abandoned his heritage, she had embraced hers and the inflated ego that went with it. She was an avenging angel, the savior of this world and the destroyer of the oppressor. She wasn't about to let him step in the way of her glory and adulation.

Helpless, the only thing he could do to save Jess was to walk Amy and himself into the teeth of the lion.

He had hardly stepped into the door and watched it swing shut behind him when Amy flung herself into his arms. She was weeping, gasping, and sobbing as she tried to speak. He hugged her close, trying to comfort her.

"They—they came—and Jess, Jess, they took Jess. I tried—I tried, but they just—"

"It's okay. I know. I know. She's okay." *For now.*

"You saw her?"

"She's okay." He led her over to the couch. She collapsed against him, exhausted. "She's with Alia."

"She is using Jess as her hostage."

Even in her emotionally wrought condition, Reven marveled at how quickly Amy's mind worked. "Yes. But she's safe. Alia will have to keep her safe to keep my cooperation with her little plan."

"What does she want?"

He let it hang. She wasn't ready to hear the agreement. "Later. Right now, are you okay? They didn't hurt you, did they?"

She shook her head and sighed. "I'm ok. They came in with some hooded figure. I couldn't see their face. Jess thought about fighting them until she saw the hooded figure, then she went with them. She looked so scared. I've never seen Jess scared, even when you were rescuing me and the alarm got triggered. I tried to fight, but the guard just pushed me on the bed and they left."

She looked up at him with wide eyes. "What the fuck is going on?"

Good question. "Things that are bigger than us."

Amy let out a heavy sigh and laid down on the couch, cradling her head in her arms. All he wanted was to get Jess and go through the gates and get all of them out of there. But that wasn't the script Alia had written.

Reven whispered. "Are you mad at me? I got you in all of this?"

Amy reached for his hand, grasping it. "You came for me. You saved me. You and Jess. I owe you my life."

Amy released his hand. "So, what now?"

Reven sighed, relaxing, only now realizing that he had been holding his breath. *I was worried. Worried what she thought about me. What does that mean?*

He shook his head, banishing the thoughts. *It doesn't matter. I need to focus on the now.*

"We wait. Alia has plans and if we don't agree with them, there are consequences."

"Like puppets waiting for her to pull the strings." She grimaced.

"What?"

"I am so fucking tired of being a puppet. First as a kid, then for the government. Then being in that . . . place." She spat the word out like it was poison on her tongue. "Now this woman with a god-complex is threatening my only two friends in this world. If I'm not her good little puppet, I put my friend, both my friends, in danger."

"I won't let anything happen to you. Or Jess. It's me Alia wants to use. You just got caught up in it. I'm sorry. I didn't understand."

She smiled a wan smile. "Something tells me none of us did. Would you do me a favor?"

"What?"

"Teach me to fight."

It startled him. "Fight?"

"I know we don't have long. I can't imagine Alia giving

us time to come up with a counterplan and ruin her ideas. But please just teach me something. Something so I don't feel so weak."

She shivered and wrapped her arms around her knees. He covered her back with a nearby blanket, concerned. "Are you okay?"

She nodded. "Just thinking. It's hard not to think of the past day or so. That place . . . I can't even describe. Not even sure of all I felt or went through yet. It's like my brain refuses to process it. But I know one thing. I never want to go back there again. Only I don't know how to make it stop. People taking me."

She's not just talking last night. She's talking about before as well. "Okay. I'll teach you."

"Really?"

He nodded. "I don't know how much I can teach you before they come. But everyone should know how to protect themselves."

She smiled, resting her head on her knees. "Thank you."

Amy stared off into space for a moment. "So, what does Alia want us to do?"

Reven sighed. "She wants us to turn ourselves over to the Tark. Both of us. Then a team will sneak in while they are all distracted and take out the Queen."

Amy was silent for a moment, drinking it in. "And if we

die, all the better for her. We can become martyrs while she comes out the hero.”

“I won't let that happen. I will protect you.”

She gave him that wan smile again. “It's nice that you think that. I wish it was true.”

All he could do was grab her hand, pulling her to him. At first, he thought she'd resist, but she snuggled into his chest. He could feel her heartbeat, feel it thudding fast. Feel her trembling although she fought to remain calm on the outside. Jess's words came back into his head. *You are her touchstone. You are the only thing that makes sense in this messed up world she finds herself in.*

“I will fix this. I will rescue Jess. I will deal with Alia.”

“Sounds like a lot for one man to shoulder.”

“Good thing I'm not a normal man. I was so focused on revenge I brought you here. Then I got Jess involved. So, now I'll get you two out. No matter what it takes.”

She was silent. Finally she spoke, softly. “I'd forgotten you weren't human. You and Alia.”

She didn't pull away in fear. He smiled. “Right. We're Ra'shek.”

“Tell me about your people.”

“Well, mostly, our tribes were peaceful. We all lived in different tribes, all under a ruling family who would govern all the tribes in an area. The rulers would work together to deal with any issues. We were pretty advanced for a civilization, but we tried to live in harmony with the earth. Rumor was that some Ra'sheks could even communicate with the animals, the soil, the sun."

"That must have been nice."

"It was." The memories of the sun upon his face, the wind blowing through the trees, the smell of rain on the wind flooded his senses. "My family was a part of a tribe called the Vaushin. My family served under Alia's family."

"So, you knew her?"

A sour taste filled Reven's mouth as he remembered Alia's speech back at the castle. He shook his head. "No. I knew of her, I guess. But they lived apart from our tribe. Only people who went to work for the ruling family ever saw them."

"That must be hard. Although I suppose its not much different from what we do. I mean, we 'see' the people we elect, but we don't really know them."

"It wasn't bad. There were never any wars or things to worry about other than storms or things of nature like that. So, as long as everything was peaceful, no one cared."

"Until the Tark came."

"Yeah."

She paused. "They destroyed your planet. But not mine."

He sighed. "Your leaders must have made a pact. They feed the Tark in exchange for not being destroyed."

She growled, that same guttural bestial sound from before. A thing of hatred and anger. But it subsided into a whisper. "All those people. All these years. I helped them."

"No. You didn't know." He hugged her tighter, afraid she might slip back down into the darkness. "You can't think like that. At least you know now."

"Yeah. I know a little too well." She rubbed her wrists. He could see they were red and bruised from where the men must have been holding her down. He felt a growl rising in his own chest, but suppressed it.

"So, that's it then." She sat up suddenly, staring him in the eyes. "We do as Alia asks and we get Jess out and we take down the Tark."

"You make it sound so easy."

"We have to make it out. All of us." She turned her somber eyes to him. "I'd rather die than go back to that place."

Reven saw it then, deep within her eyes. A spark within the darkness. It was coalescing within her. All the pain. All the fear. The government kidnapping her. Being sent here. The Pits. All of it. Something had coalesced within Amy. She was angry and was already learning to focus on that anger.

He nodded slowly. "Okay. We fight and we get out."

"It has to end. All of it. Your people. My people. This place. All of it. Especially the Pits." He could feel the poison and terror draining off of her. The steel of decision replacing the vague cloud of despair.

He nodded again, standing up. He reached out a hand to her. "Well then. No time to waste."

"What?" Her eyes were confused.

He smiled down at her, eyes sparkling with hope. "Time to train. If we're going to fight, you better know some basics."

21

***

It was three days later that Rail knocked on their door.

Amy looked up from her dinner plate. She met Reven's eyes, and he shrugged. He rose and went to the door. His hand had just touched the knob when it flung open, smashing into the wall. Rail strode in carrying two cloaks, tossing at them without ceremony.

"C'mon." He growled. "We have little time. Be quiet. We don't want to alert the populace. I don't have to remind you what happens if there is any disobedience."

Interesting that Alia wants to keep this quiet. Amy thought. *Why doesn't she want to trumpet it from the highest, the culmination of her plans, the finale of the Tark? Could it be she believes there are spies? Or want to deny everything in case it all goes bad?*

The stoniness in Reven's face told her he was having similar thoughts. She pulled on the cloak, pulling up the hood, careful to not draw attention to the weapons she had concealed on her body. It still felt weird, having the dagger in her boot and the one hidden at the small of her back. They were all Reven could find in Jess's things that would fit under her clothes. She had drilled with them almost instantly, but still felt like she was more a danger to herself than others. Yet their weight felt good as the butterflies started flitting around in her stomach. *No matter what happens, I will not be weak again!*

"We're going at night?" Reven asked.

Rail said, "We want it to look good, right? What would be more natural than you two sneaking around at night? Moving behind people's back?"

Amy's body tensed. Anger boiled within her, and that emotion wanted to shout a few choice words at the man. But she pulled herself back, burying the impulse. There would be more than enough time to tell Rail what she really thought of him. Once Jess was safe.

Speaking of her. "Where's Jess?"

Rail said, "She's safe. For now. But only if you do as you are told."

He turned around and stalked out of the room, ending the question session. She locked eyes with Reven. He said nothing, but nodded. Amy took a deep breath, the butterflies dancing in her stomach, her muscles trembling. *What in the world are we walking into?*

Reven put a hand on her arm. "Relax. You can do this. We can do this."

Amy took another deep breath, letting it out slowly. She nodded, biting her lip. *I have to do this for Jess. I can do this.* "Let's go."

They walked out the door into the waiting darkness. Awaiting them were a group of cloaked figures, with no torches to light their faces. There was enough ambient light in the cavern that Amy could tell shapes, but not much else. Silently, they turned, herding Amy and Reven towards the gate. She stifled a laugh. *If I didn't know they were marching us to certain death, this would be hysterical. Somebody around here has been watching too many of those old Hollywood horror movies.*

At any moment, she expected Dracula or Frankenstein to come lunging out of the shadows after them. Instead, the group proceeded out of a side gate in the wall, heading to a tunnel. The group proceeded to street level, stopping just where the alley went into the main street.

The street was quiet, unlike her other trip to the surface. She shivered with the memory, but fought it down. A stray thought popped into her head that she had never wondered what had happened to Mai after her return, then realized with an internal laugh that no one had asked her story. They were in this mess because Reven and Jess had come for her. The One had been perfectly content to leave her to die. Grimacing, she returned her attention to the street. *The One.* Worthless as any other leader she had ever known back on Earth. Just as corrupt, just as in it for their own glory and how they appeared. Woe be to the underling who got in the way; they just got ground underfoot.

She felt Reven beside her, a tense energy radiating off of him. She took a deep breath, steeling herself. Whatever happened now, the only way out of here was together. He would need her to be something she had never been, to find depths within herself that she had never known.

There was no failure here.

"There" Rail whispered, pointing down the quiet street. She could just make out a group of Tark soldiers coming out of another alley. "Let them 'catch' you. We will follow."

Reven nodded, standing up and leading the way out onto the street, Amy a beat behind him. Her heart thumped so hard she could feel it in her throat, the vibration growing until she swore her ribs would crack under the pressure. Her throat threatened to close and her mouth ran dry, her hands sweating. She could see them, laughing and growling, joking with each other as they walked. She could smell their fowl stench, feel the claws on her arms.

Reven touched her, and she jerked, but looked up. He smiled at her. *Steady. It will be ok.*

She heard the voice in her head, shaky and quiet, but there. For a moment, she startled, wondering if she had just imagined it or if it had really been there. But Reven smiled again and Amy suddenly remembered him talking about his kind having psychic powers. She took a deep breath. *No weirder than anything else I've encountered. I can do this. I have to.*

One of the front of the group noticed them moving and

came to attention, his clawed hand flexing. The others snapped to attention, their eyes burning like embers in the dark. The leader barked at them. "Who goes there? What are you doing out after curfew?"

"Run!" Reven cried, whirling on his heels.

Amy stood there frozen in confusion for a moment. *Aren't they supposed to catch us? Isn't that what we want?* But she quickly took flight behind him, her own fear now unleashed, propelling her forward. She could hear the patrol behind her. Her breath burned in her lungs, but she knew it would only be a matter of time before they caught up.

A few steps later and she felt a clawed hand grasp her arm, yanking her upward. Amy screamed, but tried to remember not to struggle, although her muscles twitched and jerked in instinctive responses. She wanted to grab her knife, to plunge it deep into whatever vulnerable soft spots she could find in their bodies. She wanted to claw their eyes out, to kick their teeth in. But she held herself still.

Amy watched as they grabbed Reven. He gave up a token fight, but she was pretty sure it was only so his hood could 'accidentally' fall from his face.

The guard who had him growled and hauled him closer. "What are you doing, you stupid human? Who owns you?"

The leader walked up and eyed Reven. His lips curled in a leer. "Look closer, you simpleton. No collar."

"A rebel then?" The soldier vibrated in happiness. "Shall they reward us, sir?"

The others in the group growled happily at the young soldier's words, but fell silent as the leader chuckled. He was bending down now, looking eye to eye with Reven, a sneer crossing his lips as comprehension dawned in his eyes. "Oh, if I am right, the Queen will reward us handsomely. What is your name, boy?"

Reven stared at him defiantly. "You're so smart, you tell me."

The leader rapped him lightly on the stomach with a curled fist. Reven doubled over, coughing as Amy winced. Reven slowly stood up, and the leader growled. "Your name, human scum."

"Reven."

The others crowed with laughter and celebration at their find, too stupid to realize the trap.

Although I guess that's the point, Amy mused. *Not that it makes any of this any better.*

Suddenly, the guard holding her pushed her forward. "What about this one? Shall we take her to the Pits?"

A small cry escaped her lips. *No. Not that.*

Then the leader walked forward, eyeing her. "Walsh, what was the description of that girl who broke out of there earlier?"

A thin, tall Tark stepped forward, a scar over one eye. He hissed when he caught sight of her. "That is she. I'd know her everywhere. And that one. They were there with another girl. They were the ones who slew Tarquin."

The mood now turned hostile, filled with low growls and hisses from the group. The leader reached out a hand, silencing them. He leaned down, snorting at her, the thick musky decaying odor making her want to gag, but she threatened her stomach to stay in place. "Settle. I know we all want a chance to bite the heads off of these murderers. But we have our orders, especially with that one."

He inclined his head toward Reven. He stood up; the others mumbling murderously, but quieting under the leader's steely eye. "Cheer up, lads. Who knows? Perhaps the Queen will give us the honor of biting their heads off, anyway."

The group descended into laughter as they grabbed Reven and Amy, surrounding them in a wall of teeth, claws and muscle. They herded them through the streets, and Amy saw their destination. The castle that she had spotted the first day. Huge spires of twisted red rock reached into the sky, looking like the artist had somehow melted and twisted them into being instead of carving and assembling them, while bridges of the same rock connected the spires. It towered over the city, flames licking out of the tops of the spires. Amy shivered, but forced herself to keep walking.

Reven reached for her hand, squeezing it. She could feel his warmth flowing into her. Again, the super shaky voice reached into her mind. *It will be alright. I'll protect you.*

Nothing about this was alright. This was a nightmare, a dream caused by too many Twinkies and playing too much Dark Spire with Greg. That was it. She would wake up back in the bunker, clueless and ignorant, just like before.

She was definitely not marching to her death on an alien world with the only other person she could trust and depend on marching right beside her. But she walked on. Because she had made a promise to herself. She was going to survive, and take down these bastards anyway she could.

22

***

Amy twitched as the heavy iron door slammed behind them. They had reached the castle at dawn, but instead of being led to the Queen, the Tark had led the pair down into the bowels of the earth into what appeared to be the dungeon. Someone had carved the cells out of the solid rock, and set them with heavy metal bars. The rock was so cold that water condensed on the surface, giving it a slick sheen that shone in the Tark's torchlight. Somewhere in the distance, she could hear the water dripping like a rhythmic gong sounding their doom march. Other than the torches, there were no windows or light, only a faint glow off of some bioluminescent moss that covered the stone floor.

"What's going on?" she asked after she was sure the Tark had disappeared down the hallway.

Reven was pacing the cell, looking for any weaknesses or ways out. Finally he sat, slumping against the iron bars at the front of the cell. "We're waiting, that's what."

Amy stood against the bars, looking out into the small hallway beyond. Directly across from them was another empty cell. She knew there were other cells down the hallway that they had passed, ending at an enormous iron door guarded by an equally enormous Tark. Reven was right. Even if they could find a way out, there was no way they were fighting past him.

She sighed and slapped the bars. "Why do you think they

put us in here? Why not take us right to the queen?"

"I don't know. Probably to let us soak a while."

"Soak? What are you, a 70s cop show?"

That finally got a smile to crack his stern face. "I've watched a few. But it wouldn't surprise me if they had ears within the walls."

Amy looked around a little, then chided herself. *Like it would be obvious.* She went to sit down beside Reven. "It's hard not knowing what's going on."

"I know."

"So out there. You were talking to me in my head, right?"

He grew hesitant. "Does that freak you out?"

She shrugged. "Not really. It's like I said before. I forget you're not from Earth. Then you do something that reminds me. But I think it's cool. You're different. I've always been different, too."

She leaned her head against his shoulder. It should have been awkward. She had always been awkward about boys. But somehow, in this place, in this moment, all those childish notions of worrying about what people thought seemed to evaporate into the air. She wanted to laugh at the absurdity of all of this, but was afraid that it would open the floodgates of the pent-up emotions. All held behind the wall of her mind, shoved there to deal with another time. Only when would that time be? She was supposed to be back in the Bunker, safe behind her computer screen. Not a million light years away on a distant planet, a thread's tension away from having her life snuffed out.

Reven should have scared her. He was an alien. A lifetime of monster movies and alien blockbusters had trained her she should fear him. But she didn't. He was different, that was all. He was the closest thing she had to normal in this place.

But it was more than just the situation. It was the reality of the whole scenario. Aliens. Gateways. Rebel forces fighting against an immeasurable threat. She'd landed herself in the middle of one of those sci-fi movies that she loved so much. Only this was not a game, or a script. *If I ever make it home, it's comedies from here on out.*

She stared at her palms, looking at the scars from the Pits when she had curled her hands so tightly the nails had bit into the skin. It was real. All of it. The Tarks were real, not some animatronic or CGI-imagined props. Jess. Cara. They were real people, not actors waiting for the director to shout cut so they could go hit the catering table or go back to their million dollar mansions and yachts. She had been a part of a government entity, not only hiding the existence of aliens, but cooperating with them. Feeding them humans! She had helped them all along. She had helped give them Reven.

"I'm sorry." She whispered.

"For what?"

"For helping them find you. I didn't know."

He said, "There's nothing to forgive. You were doing a job. Considering how they took you, I'm assuming quitting wasn't an option."

"No, definitely not. I was one of the few who they kidnapped, others volunteered, if you can believe that. Some really got gung ho about it, with salutes and yes sirs all over the place. Playing soldier, we called them. But most of us were just hackers who weren't smart enough to not get caught. I'm pretty sure if most knew what was really going on, they wouldn't be so compliant. I know I wouldn't have been."

"Would you have believed it? If they had told you what was going on?"

Amy thought for a moment, then shook her head. "No. I mean, I still have a hard time believing it and I have the bruises and scars. I've seen them and it doesn't seem real."

"That's what they were going for. Deniability. They worked with Hollywood and misinformation campaigns to make aliens seem imaginary, the people that believed in them crackpots. That way, even if the truth got out, people would still believe it wasn't real."

"Jesus. I knew our government was shady but that . . ." She shivered, and he scooted closer to her. His warmth steadied her.

Amy said, "How can they do it? I mean, they're sending innocent people to be food. To be raped so the children can be food."

Her stomach wanted to revolt, but thankfully was empty. Reven wrapped his arm around her, holding her.

"People will do strange things to protect themselves. That is what the Tarks offer. Protection for the mighty few in expense of the innocent." Reven said.

"Now we're sitting in their cells. You're sitting in their cells. Because of me."

He sighed. "No, we're sitting in these cells because I was stupid."

"What?"

"Alia outsmarted me. I never realized that she and I weren't the same. I thought we both were working for the same end, to stop the Tark and protect the Universe. But she was working her own game, for her own means, and I was so blinded and stupid I didn't see it until it was too late."

"What game is that?"

Reven shook his head. "I don't know the end game. Her family was royalty back on our planet, and apparently her ego still thinks she should be one. Instead of working together, she's thrown me to the wolves so that she can gain the power and glory."

"Very astute."

The crisp voice cut through the air, startling them. It was sharp and clear, not the low growling tones of a Tark. Reven and Amy both jumped to their feet, whirling around to face the unfamiliar presence.

Beyond the bars, a young woman stood. She was tall and willowy, with a lean, muscular look. Her skin shone like white stone, her piercing blue eyes contrasted against the whiteness of her skin, her silver hair pulled down her back in a braid. She wore all black, tight fitting clothing and armor with leather archers' guards and knee high leather boots, along with a hooded cloak that, when pulled up, would make her nothing but a shadow. Suddenly, Reven knew who she was.

"You! You were the one on the roof."

The woman eyed him with that same serene, stonelike quality that her voice held. "It was I."

Anger built in Reven. "And the one who took Jess."

The woman shook her head. "Not I. That was another of my group. We are the Sh'vren."

"The elite guard? Here?" Reven noticed Amy's confused look. "The Sh'vren were the elite guard of the royals on my planet. They lived in shadows. No one knew their identity. We considered them the deadliest warriors, and to see one meant your death. But you don't look like a Ra'shek."

"I am not. My name is Mira, and I am Tallir. My people

were warriors before the Tark came. Like you, a small group of us hid and survived, pledging vengeance for the lives of our brothers and sisters. We came through the gate, hidden from them, and found the rebels. Your queen was quick to buy our services for herself."

"So, what are you doing here?" Reven growled. "Here to finish the job for your One?"

The tiniest of smiles ticked the corner of the woman's mouth. "I am not. You already have sniffed her deceit. I am here to make sure it is not coming true."

"What are you all talking about?"

The woman turned her icy glare on Amy, but kept the tiny smile to throw some warmth into the words. "I am a friend. It is why I rescued you that night, and why I come to you now. I serve my queen, but her recent actions have not been that of a loyal leader."

"You're not here to kill us?" Amy questioned, confusion filling her voice. "I mean, thanks. But I don't understand. Reven?"

Reven just looked at Mira, his eyes serious. "I told you earlier, Alia is playing her own game and I knew that she wasn't telling us the whole truth. That's why she refused to let Jess and I come for you. She wasn't worried about us setting off the Tark, or messing up a time frame to attack. Alia was worried it would mess up whatever secret plan she has. She wants to be the savior, the ruler of everything."

The woman nodded slowly. "You do not know the depths of that truth, but I am here to try to reset the path."

"Why? Why would you betray her?" Amy asked suspiciously. "Why wouldn't we believe this is a trap?"

"The Tallir are ferocious warriors and once we give an oath, as we gave to this One, we do not turn away. But there are also three truths we hold in our hearts, truths set into us from the moment of our birth. Three truths your One did not bother to learn and has disrespected."

"What are those?" Reven asked.

She locked eyes with him. "Secrets are a poison that will kill the entire tribe, and so all must live in the light. A leader puts themselves below their people, to protect and guide them for the safety and survival of all. Above all else, a ruler must NEVER shed an innocents blood."

"This plan of hers . . ."

"She has already shed much innocent blood. With this plan, more will fall."

"The others Sh'vren. They are with you as well?"

Mira shook her head. "No. She has infected them with her words, her mind. They are hers, they are no longer Tallir. But I have something that protects me. I see what she does, and know my heart will not rest in death unless I try to stop it."

She pulled a thin chain from inside her shirt, a large black gemstone dangling from it. Even in the dim light, the dark stone flashed with a blue and red living flame caught inside of it.

Reven's breath caught in his throat. "You have an emberstone?"

"What's an emberstone?" Amy asked.

Reven looked in awe at the stone. "They were rare on my planet, and we had little use for them because most people learned to block their minds. There is something about the properties of the emberstone that blocks psychic powers."

"Yes." Mira spoke up again. "My mother gave this to me when I was small. It is a protective stone in my world. It has protected me from the powers of your One."

"She is not my One." Reven growled. "If she has an elite guard in her control, if she coerced them with her mind, she has broken more than your truths. We need to get out of here and stop her before the guards realize what is going on. I'm surprised they haven't already heard us."

"Oh, them." Mira's smile broke a little more, a sharp sparkle in her eye. "They will not be a problem."

Her hands flashed forward with a large key she produced from under her cloak. It clicked in the lock and the door swung outward. "Hurry. We must go to the throne room."

"I'm not interested in taking down the queen. I want to

get to Alia."

Mira's eyes glittered dangerously. "That is where the One is."

Reven stopped cold. His voice grew ice. "Explain."

"She cares not for the people of the underground. She has spoken with the Tark queen and made a trade."

"What?" Reven's voice thundered, and Amy flinched, straining to hear any approaching footsteps.

Mira scowled. "Who is being loud now? Do you want to bring them all down on us before we even begin?"

Reven breathed deeply, his muscles and hands still tensed. "Mira, tell me what the hell did that stuck up royal bitch do to my people?"

Mira's solemn eyes locked with his once more. Her words sliced through the air like an arrow. "I believe in the words of the humans you would say she sold them out."

23

***

Dead. They were all dead.

Amy stared in horror at the throne room floor, the bodies splayed out around her, dark sticky liquid spreading out from them covering the orange-red stone of the floor. Blood. Their blood.

She tried not to look at their faces, eyes frozen wide in horror and betrayal. She didn't know all of their names, but she knew enough to know who these people were. Rail. The twins. These were the squadron sent to kill the Tark queen. Only they were now lying dead on the floor.

They had left the cells, Mira giving them dark cloaks like her own to help them hide in the shadows, and had given them a couple short swords she just had found. Quickly and quietly they had stolen through the palace. They had found the throne room after a few missed turns, expecting to find the Queen, or maybe Alia. Not this.

Reven grabbed her arm. "C'mon."

Amy startled. "What? Huh? Reven, they're . . ."

"We can't help them." His eyes scanned the room, Mira taking a defensive stance, her hand on her weapon. "Now I understand why we were able to get up here so easily. It's a trap, we need to leave."

"So right you are."

Alia stood beside a throne chair. A chair occupied by an enormous thing.

Words failed Amy's mind. It contemplated that *something* sat there, but after that her brain just shut down.

This thing had the same leathery, reptilian skin of the Tark and was smaller than the soldiers. The skull stretched upwards, glowing orange through translucent skin, veins black against the surface. Out of this skull grew tentacles that stretched behind the creature, attaching to an enormous membrane sack that stretched from the floor to ceiling.

Egg sac. A voice in her brain helpfully replied.

The egg sac pulsed the same orange as the queen, with dark indistinct shapes swimming in it.

The Tark queen.

A voice nudged at her mind. Reven.

The Tark function much like insects from your world. All Tark are born from the queens. It is what allows the queens to control all of them at once, like a hive mind, if she needs to.

Amy grimaced. *And we just walked in here like it was nothing? Maybe we should have thought about her being guarded?*

Reven didn't respond to her internal thoughts. It didn't matter, anyway. They were all about to die.

Alia stood beside the queen in a white gown, the grin of triumph that lit her face blaring her superiority to the room. "Welcome fools. But I'm afraid you're a little too late."

At an unseen signal, Tark soldiers stepped out from

hidden doors in the walls, surrounding them. They growled and snarled, their weapons and claws bristling, but made no move towards them other than surrounding them. Amy, Reven and Mira instinctively moved back to back, swords leaping into their hands. Amy's knees trembled and threatened to buckle, her mind frozen in fear.

"Mira, Mira, Mira, I'm so disappointed in you. Siding with the losing team."

Three more black-robed figures stepped out around Alia, surrounding her in a ring. Her face was glowing with power and pride. Amy's eyes flicked to the queen, wondering why she was just sitting there.

Mira growled, "I do not serve one who is not worthy."

"Pity. Because I now control all the Tark and soon, all the universe will bow down to me."

"What?" Reven growled. "How could you—"

"How could I do what? I told you, Reven, you had your chance to serve me as your lineage dictated. These monsters destroyed my chance to rule, but it does not change the fact that I am a Queen! Rulers are to be praised, not hiding in the muck watching over a city of idiots. So, imagine my surprise when I learned the Tark operated with a hive mind. They are all born from one queen, and even when she is close to death, a clone is born to take her place, so that clone has all the same ties to the Tark horde as the previous queen. Even though individual Tark's have minds and thoughts of their own, the power of the queen can override all of that, turning them into her obedient slaves at a moment's notice."

"So, this was your plan all along. You wanted to take over the queen's mind?" Reven said.

"Very perceptive. I learned long ago how to bend others to my will but I had to get within her presence to enact the mind control. What better way than warning her of an impending attack?"

"And now that you're in control?" He growled.

Her face beamed. "No one can stop me. Even if an individual Tark wanted to take me out, I control the queen, who controls all of them. I'll know the thought and stop it at a moment's notice."

"All of this. All of this so you could sit on a bloody throne?" Reven yelled. "Betraying all of us. Everything we've fought for."

"Wrong. Everything I've fought for. While you gallivanted around the planets, I sat here in the muck and dark, listening to these people crying and mewling. Figuring out how to feed them and keep them alive. And for what? Nothing! All you had to do was come sweeping in with a smile and a wave and suddenly you're the hero. But I'm a queen! I deserve to live in the sun, surrounded by riches and adoration. Not living in the mud forgotten by all."

She walked down the dais, her guard following her. Her eyes locked on Reven. "Now I will. All the realms will bow before me and serve my name. With the Tark as my army, I will take my rightful place as ruler of the universe."

"You're mad! All the people you will kill."

"There will be some deaths, sadly. Those who cannot understand my greatness and choose to deny it. But for those that choose to follow, I will be merciful."

"As long as they are obedient."

"I must make sacrifices. Besides, that is the rightful place of anyone who is not me. Bowing at my feet."

She laughed, the sound grating and piercing. Amy's hand tightened on the hilt of her sword. *Jesus. And I thought our politicians were bad. This chick has more ego than a dozen CEOs.*

Reven stood tall, facing Alia. His eyes blazed with a fierce light. "You are a disgrace to our people. Our rulers were benevolent, taking care of the people. Not punishing them into obedience!"

"Look where that got them." She snorted. "Dead. Because they never learned that you cannot reason or talk to people. You can only dominate them."

She turned and walked back to the dais. Two Tarks emerged, carrying a new throne, larger than the queen's, and setting it beside her. Alia sat, leering down at them.

"So, kill us already. You know you're going to." Reven said, "Stop playing with us."

"Oh, my dear Reven. Of course, I'm going to kill you. But not before I show you exactly why you are the servant and I am the queen. There is a natural order, as much as you would like to deny it. I am here to restore that."

"Look." She gestured with her hand, bringing their view to the arching openings that overlooked the city.

The city hung silent in the dawning light, as if the entire world was taking a breath. Suddenly, a tremendous boom exploded and reverberated through the air, the stone trembling underneath their feet. As they watched, breathless, a spire of black smoke rose from the middle of the city, rising into the air. A tortured scream filled the city as a tower of fire erupted from the middle of the city, mixed with the screams of thousands of innocent people.

Amy stared in horror. *Why would she destroy the Tark city?*

"What did you do?" Reven's voice was a whisper.

"I told you. Exerting my power so no one questions me. What you see there is the Phoenix, rising from the ashes of the Refuge."

Amy didn't realize a scream tore out of her throat, until she felt Reven holding her, pulling her back. *All those people in the city. Drail. Sephora. Tam. Jess!* "You're a monster! All those people trusted you to protect them. You betrayed them! You killed them!"

"Sacrifices were necessary to make this work. You humans are too independent for rule. The Tark are much better suited for abject obedience."

"So, all of this secret plan was to get those out of the way who would oppose you?" Mira spoke, her voice as sharp as a dagger.

"You do not know how far my plans go. I have been dreaming of this day since I first set foot in this place. The only thing that went wrong was Mira not bowing to my control. Who would have thought you would have a protection stone? Oh well. To the best laid plans."

She flicked a hand and the three guards stepped forward, swords drawn. "Now, you three have a choice. You can either die easy, or hard. Personally I pick hard, it's more entertaining for me."

"Your plan is almost perfect, Alia." Reven called out, cying the advancing guard.

Alia quirked an eyebrow. "Almost perfect? Tell me. What thing is it you think I forgot?"

"That you're not the only mind speaker in the room! Halt!"

With that one word, the guards stopped in their tracks. They blinked furiously, like they were unaware how they got where they were, looking down at the swords in their hands like they didn't know they had drawn them.

"No." Alia snarled. "My control is perfect."

"Brothers!" Mira cried. "This One has deceived you!"

Her hands flashed, throwing three stone shards at them. With cat reflexes the trio caught them out of the air. Suddenly, their eyes completely cleared, and they turned to stare at Alia.

"No! I demand you obey me!" Her eyes hardened as she concentrated on their minds.

"It's no use, Alia." Reven called. "We all have protection from you now. A funny little thing I found out on my travels. Protection stones work no matter how small or big a piece is. You also forgot why our people outlawed complete slavery through mind control. You may make them behave, but they know what you asked them to do. They know how you forced them."

"Brothers!" Mira called, her face breaking into a grin as she strode up between the others. They looked at her with questions, but that would come later. "Shall we teach this one what happens to those that do not follow the rules?"

"Stop! What does it matter if you freed those four? I now control an entire army. You are all still going to die! Take them!"

The Tark soldiers leapt forward in a wall of death. Amy

felt Reven move beside her. Somehow, her sword leapt out of the scabbard and into her hand, but her body went numb as time slowed down. Her eyes saw a Tark soldier coming for her, his eyes blazing red, his teeth flashing in the light, could feel the hunger and drive rolling off of him, the need to kill and slash and destroy. She was going to die, and this was the last thing she was going to see. Alia was right. What chance did anyone stand against an army like this?

None. Unless you had an elite group of Tallir by your side.

Mira and her brothers raced forward, meeting the rush of Tark. Their blades danced like silver flame, flicking in and out, Tark falling around them like autumn leaves. One brother threw a disc into the air, which exploded, sending dozens of darts whistling a deadly tune to find their targets. Another danced with a whip, the cords ending in sharp blades he whipped back and forth in a deadly dance, a tornado of knives reaching out to slay all they touched. In the center stood Reven and Amy, Reven's blade lashing out to get any who got past the deadly circle. As one, the circle moved through the Tark horde, which rushed forward as Alia screamed her defiance.

Soon, they were at the door, and Mira turned to them. "Go! Quickly!"

"We're not leaving you." Reven cried.

"We will be right behind. When I say three." She turned to her brothers. "Ready?"

The brothers nodded, their hands still moving and blocking the Tark's advance.

Mira grinned. "One. Two. Three!"

The world exploded in a flash of orange flame and smoke. Amy doubled over in a coughing fit. Reven grabbed her and half-carried, half-dragged her towards the hall. Slowly, she got to her feet and was soon running beside him, blind terror driving them forward. She could hear the screams and outrage of the Tark, feel it through the entire city.

Alia had let the Tark loose on the hunt, and they were out for blood.

The group raced through the halls, slashing and dodging at other Tark who were coming to the fight. At one point, Mira was running beside Amy, tossing more flash bombs down hallways as they passed. The explosions echoed in Amy's ear, deafening her. But she kept running, forcing her tired legs onward, even though her muscles quivered and trembled, threatening to collapse on every step. *One more hallway. One more foot. Keep going!*

The group raced down through the castle.

Amy shouted, "Where are we going?"

"This way!" cried Mira, peeling off towards what smelled like the kitchens. "We have a friend."

They crashed through the kitchen, human servants screaming in surprise as they cowered in terror under tables as alarm bells blared through the castle. Amy wanted to stop, to help them, to convince them to escape, but her own drive to survive pushed her forward. There was no more thinking, no more maybes, just pure blind terror pushing her to live. She would do whatever she needed to get out of this hellhole.

The group burst out of the back of the kitchens into the bright sunlight to find a cart standing nearby with two of those strange horse-like creatures already hitched.

"Get in!" Mira yelled.

Reven grabbed Amy, tossing her up into the back before he leapt up. The three other Tallir followed suit, one going to the front to help guard Mira as she drove while the other two sat back with Reven and Amy.

"Ha!" Mira yelled as she slapped the reins and cracked the whip.

The two creatures yowled, their bellowing voices adding to the cacophony and chaos, but they burst into a run. The cart bounced and jostled beneath them, but it held together as Mira sent it hurtling down the narrow alleyways.

"Where are we going to go? She destroyed the Refuge." Amy yelled.

"We have a place, if we can get out of the city." One brother replied.

"How are we going to do that? She has every guard on alarm and we're not all that inconspicuous!" Reven added.

"She is not the only one who can have surprises!" Mira grinned.

Suddenly, more explosions rocked the city, only this time it was above ground. As Amy watched, the towers on the wall that ringed the city exploded in furnaces of fire, flames licking out of the tops reaching into the sky. More screams echoed like thunder, this time from the many Tark who rushed to take care of this new emergency.

Mira urged the steeds to go even faster as she drove them toward one tower.

"What are you doing?" Reven cried.

"Trust." Mira said, concentrating on the wall before her. She forced the horse creatures to go even faster. Suddenly, the smoke and fire cleared, and she drove through a gap in the broken wall. The cart bounced and jostled over the debris, threatening to bounce all of them out, then slamming them to the floor. Just when Amy thought every bone in her body would crack, the cart quieted.

They were out in the open desert, leaving the chaos of the city farther and farther behind, as the horse creatures found even more speed on the flat ground.

24

***

They had been traveling for a few hours when Mira slowed the cart near some spires of red rock that jutted out of the landscape. The group got out, then she slapped the rears of the animals, sending them onward into the landscape. "In case someone tries to follow our tracks."

They set off toward the spires, Mira in the lead, one brother staying behind to cover their trail. They had switched to light colored cloaks to better hide in the sand. Amy felt dead as she trudged behind Reven, but kept pushing herself forward. A dark weight had settled in her mind. Alia had complete control of the Tark and the gateways. All of those people in the Refuge were dead. For what? Power?

Mira led them through the sweltering desert air for a half an hour, up into the spires. Amy was about to ask where they could go when she saw it, half hidden behind a jumble of fallen rock. The entrance to what was probably a cave.

"My brothers and I discovered this place on one of our many reconnaissance trips, although it was something we never told the One about. They taught us growing up to always have a safe place that none knew about, in case things ever go wrong." A weary look crossed her eyes, the look of one who is seeing trouble again after a lifetime of troubles.

"They wouldn't have told her when they were under her control? Maybe she saw it in their minds?" Reven asked anxiously. "You don't know how powerful the abilities of the

Ra'shek are."

Mira shook her head. "My brothers might not have been able to stop her from controlling them, but they know how to block memories. Your kind are not the first our warriors have met, just the first that was powerful enough to push past our blocks. Besides, she was too busy with her plan to think of asking them things like that. They knew what she was doing in their minds, what she searched for. This wasn't a memory she tried to touch."

"Because there would not be any survivors, so why bother asking about hiding places." Reven grimly added. "Thank goodness for inflated egos, I guess."

They reached the mouth of the cave, ducking through the small entrance. After the small opening, the space expanded into an enormous cavern. Amy blinked as her eyes got used to the darkened interior, lit only by a small fire, the smoke drifting up through a hole in the ceiling. She noticed several other people standing or sitting by the fire, all covered in dirt and blood. They looked up as the group entered, hands on weapons, but relaxed as they caught sight of Mira.

One figure locked eyes with her, and Amy's heart jumped into her throat. "Jess!"

Amy leapt forward as Jess stood, the two colliding into a hug.

Amy's breath caught in her throat as tears formed in her

eyes. "How? I thought you were dead!"

Jess laughed, the staccato sound laced with her own tears of joy. "I know. I had resigned myself to that thought ever since Alia's secret guard came for me and took me prisoner. Then she took the elite patrol out on some mission. Next thing I know, Tam and a few others came for me in the cells. We left through an elite tunnel, just as the explosion happened."

She stepped back, her head hanging, tears running down her cheek. Reven stepped up as the other survivors gathered around them. "What happened exactly? All we saw was—"

"The explosion?" Drail supplied, shaking her head. She had a nasty cut on the top of her head that Sephora was trying to bandage. "That was just part of the madness. Thankfully, Sephora and I were out on a scavenging run and were just coming back."

"They sent out scavengers last night? I thought they locked everything down." Reven asked skeptically.

"We weren't supposed to go, but a gear broke on the water wheel that supplies power to the underground gardens. Without that, the plants will wither and die quickly and we need those to survive. Although, I guess needed is the correct word now." Drail grimaced.

"She and I slipped to the surface. We figured we could go out and back before anyone noticed." Sephora supplied. "We were at the tunnels when the explosion happened and we got blasted down the tunnel. The blow disoriented us for a while but when we got our senses back, we tried to get back to the Refuge, but debris blocked the tunnel. We made it to the surface and found a few of the others running for cover. That's when Ausha found us."

"So the entire city is gone?" Amy sunk to the ground. She realized that until this moment she had been holding onto a thread of hope, that perhaps things weren't that bad. Seeing Jess and the others had fed that hope. But hearing about the explosion somehow made the loss more concrete in her mind. Her hope wavered.

Jess nodded somberly. "Whomever planned this did it well. They set off bombs in all the armories. We had them throughout the city, in case the Tark attacked, so that there would be stores everywhere."

A young man stepped forward, his sharp eyes and features reminding Amy of a hawk. A smudge of ash covered one cheek, but his bright blue eyes blazed with anger. "Not to mention someone filled the tower with explosives. They all went off at the same time. The force was enough to break the top of the cavern. Those that weren't killed by the explosion then had to face huge falling boulders."

Jess reached up, placing a calming hand on his arm. "Aden was with Tam when they sniffed out the bombs. They are the ones who came for me. We tried to warn the city, but it all happened too fast."

Aden glared at the fire, anger boiling off of him. His head snapped up as Mira's three brothers stepped inside the entrance. He growled, hand going to his sword. "What are they doing here? They are the ones who set the explosives!"

His words alerted the others, hands flying to weapons as they realized the three brothers were there, standing by the entrance.

Mira raised her hands. "Calm. They were under the One's control. But no more."

"Why would we believe that?" Aden cried. "They were working for the Tark and betrayed the city! They betrayed the One!"

"The One deceived us and sold us out to the Tark." Amy spat out.

The others looked incredulous; the room filling with shouts of confusion and demands for the story.

Reven said, "It's true. We saw it with our own eyes. Alia wanted to regain her royal heritage and rule the planet. To do that, she needed to control the queen. My people can control minds, but to use it, she needed to be near the queen. The only way she could do that was to double-cross us. She planned the 'invasion' so that she could warn the Tark queen and make her an ally. Only she then took control of her mind, and through that, the entire population of the Tark."

A stunned silence greeted him as the weight of the deception filtered through their minds.

Aden shook his head. "And these fools helped them?"

He shifted his weight, baring his sword, but Reven stepped forward, pushing him back.

"Enough! They are friends. Alia can't control their minds anymore, alright?" Reven ordered.

Aden and the others looking like they wanted to argue and fight, but settled into a nervous stance.

Reven said, "Alia doesn't know we are here. We are safe. Now, what happened after the explosion?"

"The Tark came into the cavern." Another woman spoke up from where she sat along the wall, cradling a broken arm. "They came pouring in the main tunnel and from the ceiling. Apparently, a forty-foot drop is not a big deal to them. Or they had ropes. I don't really know. Everything was happening so fast. There were a few who had somehow lived through the explosion and the falling debris. We fought our way out as best we could, but only a couple of us made it out of the city."

"We ran." Jess continued somberly. "There was no fighting, not against all of that. The three of us tried to gather people as we ran, but it was all smoke and blood and Tark everywhere emerging from the smoke. We found a tunnel that hadn't collapsed and ran for street level."

"What happened next? Where is Tam? You said he rescued you." Reven prodded when she paused.

Jess' eyes filled with tears. "There were soldiers waiting on the street level, waiting for the explosion to flush us out like rats. We ran right into a patrol. Tam tried to hold them. He . . . He . . ."

Amy went to her, holding her as she cried, fighting her own tears back. Jess swallowed, struggling to get herself under control. "We ran blindly. That's when we found Ausha and she got us out of the city."

"Who is this Ausha?" Reven asked. He looked at Sephora. "You mentioned her as well."

Mira stepped forward. "Ausha is a friend. She is part of a small group of Tark who remember the days before, where their planet was not dying and they could take care of themselves. Before the gates came and they turned to violence and war. They help us with the chance that their people could return to that."

"She's a Tark? She knows we're here. If Alia—" Reven started saying.

"Calm." Mira held up a hand. "We are safe. For now. By the time Alia would think to ask, we should be gone. Our supplies will not hold out indefinitely."

During all of this, Amy had slumped against the wall,

exhausted. It was too much. Too much pain and death. Too much. "There was a time before all of this?"

Reven noticed she had collapsed and came to sit by her. As if by a signal, the others relaxed as well. At a nod from Mira, the brothers went back outside, probably to stand guard but also to lessen the tension in the room. Jess and the others returned to treating wounds by the fire, and Mira sat down against the wall as well.

She said, "Yes, there was a time before. Ausha told me the tale. It happened before her time, but the tale persists and some within the culture still believe. I met her on one of my scouting trips. We tried to kill each other, of course, but somehow we didn't. We talked and found we had a common interest."

Mira continued, "Before the gates appeared, this planet was lush and provided much food. The bands were warriors and strong, but there were many tribes spread out all over the planet. Then one day, there was an explosion in the sky. A meteorite came hurling down and crashed into the planet, creating a huge plume of rock and dust that covered the sky and blocked out the sun. This disturbance opened the cavern that contained the gates. If they were there before, or if the explosion activated them, no one knows. But once the cavern opened, the energy the gates released changed the land and the Tark."

"How is that?" Reven asked. "I know the gate energy can change those beings that move through it, but I've never heard of it affecting anything outside of them."

"You would have to ask one wiser than I about that. But change this world, it did. Between the dust in the air and the gate energy, the clouds dried up and there was no rain. All the land slowly turned into desert. It forced the tribes into one central place, this city, in order to survive. As for the Tark, it destroyed their ability to procreate. They became more vicious and bloodthirsty. They would have consumed themselves if not for an accident."

"What was that?" Jess asked, enraptured by the story.

"A young female was exploring the cavern with some other young Tark. They were the first to find the gates. Like all kids, they didn't stop at danger but approached the glowing vortices. She got too close and fell through. That should have been the end, but some time later she returned, changed. The girl spoke of another world full of all the lush plants and food that they had before. She also had changed physically. She could now give birth, the only female on the planet who could, and so became the first queen. It was she who devised a plan for the people to survive."

"By going to other planets and conquering them." Amy supplied.

"Yes. One can understand it. I mean, would we not all do

the same to survive? Yet there are those who believe that the Tark should have found another way than living on the misery of others."

Amy thought to the markets, to the Pits, to the pieces of meat, to the babies hanging in the stalls waiting to be someone's dinner and shivered. "They became parasites."

Mira nodded. "Exactly. They don't know how to survive on their own, only by conquering and destroying another. Because of that, they are now nothing but perfect killing machines, scavenging amongst the other worlds."

Silence fell on the cavern as everyone thought the same thought, but only Reven had the courage to state it out loud. "Now they are being led by a megalomaniac with a narcissistic god complex."

"So, what are we going to do?" Jess spoke up after the silence had drowned them for a moment more. "How do we take on an entire bloodthirsty army and a ruler who can read minds? It was incomprehensible before, but now there's what? Ten of us?"

"We can't give up." Aden spoke up. "All those people she killed. All the ones she betrayed. She has to pay!"

Reven shook his head. "I honestly don't know what happened to her, that she would do this. Perhaps her trip through the gates twisted her somehow. Or the grief of losing our planet."

"You knew her back then. Do you know what she'll do?" Drail asked.

"No. I mean, I didn't really know her back then and I definitely can say I don't know her now. She was part of the royal families on my planet, the ones who ruled our tribes and decided on matters. But part of that was that they were bound to take care of the people. The ruling families never allowed one to grow up with an ego like hers. To think I was so excited to know that another had survived. All these years of passing messages, of trying to stop the Tark, I thought she was an ally. But now, I don't even recognize her as someone from my world. Nothing like this ever happened. It just didn't. "

"Then we don't think of her as a Ra'Shek." Sephora spoke up. "We think of her like any other ruler. What do rulers want? Power. What do they want more than power? More power. She obviously doesn't care who she has to step on or kill to get it, as long as all the power and glory and accolades come to her."

"You forgot the whole mind control thing. That's a little hard to get past." Aden sniped.

Sephora nodded. "Reven, how does that work? How much control does she have?"

"There's no way to really know. Even among members of the Ra'shek who all had some level of the gift somewhere stronger than others. I would say she is powerful, though. Mira's brothers have some resistance to that. Alia tried to bash her way into my head, which is difficult between members of my race. She's controlling the queen now as well, and that can't be easy."

Mira spoke up. "I am curious about one thing. My people know how to block minds from reading our thoughts, memories. On our own planet there were many tribes, many species of life, and some had this ability. But when Alia tried to control us, my brothers had no resistance."

Reven nodded. "It's a different technique. Mind reading is more subtle and takes more energy because you have to be more fragile and open to receive the other person's thoughts or speak to them within their mind. It's like shaking someone's hand or giving them a hug. The other person has to be amenable, or it's like running into a brick wall. Mind control is merely blasting a thought at a person and willing them to obey. She probably inflicted pain on them when they didn't obey, which allowed her more control as she whittled away their stamina."

Mira's eyes grew hard, but she stayed silent.

"So, it wouldn't be that hard for her to control the queen." Sephora sighed.

Reven quirked a little smile for the first time as a thought dawned in his head. "It may be harder than we think. I mean, the queen herself has psychic abilities, able to hive speak with the Tark horde. It's why Alia focused on her. By controlling one, you control thousands. But the queen's mind must be formidable to handle the stresses of that. For Alia to conquer and control that kind of mind might take all her power and concentration."

"Meaning she can either control the queen or she can deal with other attacks."

"Exactly. Although I'm not really sure how we use that."

"At the very least we don't have to worry about her using mind control on us." Amy spoke. "Brains are just like computers in that they only have so much power. Even if a brain is extraordinary and able to do amazing things, it still only has so much energy and ability to do fairly simultaneous processes. If she's having to spend so much energy on the queen, it would overload her to do anything else. If the queen is as powerful as you think, she can't take her concentration off her for a second or the bond would break."

"So it compromises her ability to read us." Aden noted. "Which bodes well for slipping into the city and enacting a plan."

"What plan?" Sephora called out. "What could the ten of us do?"

"Fourteen of us." Mira spoke up. "You forget about my

brothers and I."

"We didn't forget." The older man growled. "I remember exactly what they did."

Reven stood up as the negative energy started charging up between the Resistance members and Mira. The older man advanced on Mira, both readying their weapons to pull into their hands, when Reven stepped between them. "Enough. We will not do Alia's work for her."

He turned to the older man. "What's your name?"

"Griff." The man glared at Reven as if he wasn't too happy to be following his lead, either. "Been here longer than almost anyone."

"Look, I get it. It looks like we all just swooped in here. I get they killed people, our friends, doing Alia's bidding. The fact is that we are all that's left to deal with this and we need to work together, not tear each other apart. I don't know about you, but I say Alia's reign ends now." Reven said.

"What are you talking about?" Drail asked.

"We can either start over, building our forces up again a rescued person at a time like we did before. Only this time without the safety of the refuge or access to resources. Or we can take this moment of chaos and make it stop. Alia is certainly not going to wait to assert her dominance and rule. If you think she'll be happy just to have this one little desert planet, you are nuts."

"I say we attack now." Mira spoke up. "We will only grow weaker while she grows stronger."

While some of the more severely injured members of the crew were reluctant, all nodded agreement.

"But what do we do?" The woman with the broken arm, Mary, asked. "There's no way we can sneak into the palace and kill Alia. Even if we could, it would just free the queen. There's no way we can take on the horde by ourselves. Not all of us are even in any shape to fight."

Reven turned to Mira. "Could Ausha give us any help?"

Mira shook her head. "Not a lot. Maybe some food and shelter. A few weapons. But the Tark soldiers watch her group as close as they watched us. It was hard enough for her to come to our aid when Alia and the horde attacked this morning."

"Which means they may not help us at all and may be under surveillance to see if we come to them for aid. I'm sure Alia has everything locked down now."

"Getting in shouldn't be hard." Drail piped up. "The city is probably still in chaos. The Tark are not going to react well to having Alia as a leader, which means she'll probably have to keep them in the hive mind to keep control. In that state, they are not as perceptive or aware, not as able to react to individual things because every thought and decision has to be routed through Alia. It will let her know the second they see any of us, though."

"Yeah, and if they are in hive mind, that means even if Ausha and her crew want to help us, they won't be able to, with Alia controlling everyone. So, we do this ourselves, and we do it quick. Jess, how are we for weapons?" Reven asked.

"All of us have our swords and other personal weapons. I have my bow. We have one small bag of explosives, but it won't be a lot."

"Enough to blow some rocks up?"

She nodded. "Maybe, depending on the setting. What do you have in mind?"

Reven turned to the gathered crew. "The only thing we can do to make sure the Tark and Alia don't hurt anyone else on any other planet. We are going to destroy their access to the gates."

25

***

Amy leaned against the wall, watching the flames dance in the darkness. The others sat around the fire as much for warmth against the night cold as for companionship after the horrors of the day. Reven talked with Griff, Drail and Mira about plans for tomorrow. Mira's brothers were taking turns at watch, the other brothers sleeping near the entrance. Sephora and Aden were tending to the other wounded members of the group, watching over them as they slept.

Jess came over to sit by Amy. "You ok?"

"Are you?"

"Fair question. No, I'm not. Nothing about today or any of this is ok. But at least we're alive, and together."

"For now."

Jess sighed and stared at the fire for a moment before speaking. "You're right. There's no guarantee any of us are walking out of tomorrow alive, or that we can accomplish our mission. But I don't think that's why you're angry. What's really on your mind?"

Amy shifted, wrapping her arms around her knees, resting her head on her arms, her eyes still locked on the fire. "Just trying to process this is breaking my mind. I mean, three days ago, three days, I was a simple hacker. The most I had to worry about was what was for dinner. The closest I got to violence was playing an online video game. And now..."

She let the thought trail off. Jess wrapped her arms

around Amy, resting her head on her shoulder. "I know. War has a way of making people grow up in a way they don't want to."

Amy rested her head on Jess's. "How long has it been for you?"

"A couple of years. Feels like forever."

They sat in the silence, holding on to each other, trying to prop themselves up on the other's strength. Amy finally spoke again. "That night in the Pits. Those women. Even when I was living out of my van, living on my wits and my keyboard, I never knew fear like that. I'm not sure what was worse, going to the slaughter and facing my true death or seeing the shadows that haunted those women's eyes. It was like they would have welcomed death over what they faced. In fact, I know they did. I had the same thoughts."

Jess hugged her close. "You descended into hell. Knowing what goes on there, that they rape those women repeatedly so they can produce children for the Tark to eat, it makes me want to retch. That night we rescued you, there was a part of me that wanted to free all of them. The rational part of me knew we couldn't, but my heart ached. When we were running out, one woman reached out to me. Pleading with me for the knife on my belt. Pleading with me to help her."

Amy swallowed, understanding. "She wanted to die,

rather than stay there."

"I froze. I couldn't give it to her. To see her eyes, to understand that she lives in a world where you would rather die than be a victim over and over. I had never realized until that point how easy we had it in the Refuge. I mean, of course, it was hard finding food and never really seeing sunlight and things. But no matter how hard it was below, I never once was so desperate that I would rather end my own life than not live in it anymore."

Amy grimaced. "For a while that night I couldn't forgive you and Reven for leaving them. But I understood it, once we were on the street, once we got back to the Refuge. This world twists what you think you know. Whatever we thought we stood for, we stand for different things here, good or bad."

"What do you mean?"

Amy nodded at the group. "Look at us. Back on earth, none of us would be together. Most of us would freak out about having living aliens in our midst, not to mention the whole brain-shattering realization that *we are not alone.* But think about all the weird 'I hate you' issues we have on earth. You talk too loud, you believe in this god, you don't believe in god, you voted for this president, on and on. Back on earth, people kill over that shit, but here it is suddenly incredibly petty. Here, all we have is survival, which means all we have is each other. All those other things just don't matter."

"Maybe that's how we get peace on earth. Let everyone live here for a week."

Amy managed a weak laugh. "Yeah, except I'm sure someone would turn into an Alia and figure out how to use it to their advantage and we'll have a whole new mess on our hands."

"I give the politicians two days."

They both laughed, the sound bouncing off the walls. A few of the others looked up and smiled weakly. It felt good to hear laughter, even if it was strained. Amy smiled and returned her gaze to the fire, her body feeling drained and raw. "I kind of keep thinking that tomorrow, we're going to stop the Tarks. But are we really any better than the Tarks? Any of us? I mean, we all use shit for our own advantage. We tear up the earth because we can. People and nations go to war because 'we are better than you and must own what you have'. I'm not just talking Americans and Indians and black people and all the things that we hear about in the news. I'm talking history. Since the first man discovered you could make sticks pointy, we've been killing each other over food, territory or just because we can. Just like the Tarks."

Jess was silent for a moment before responding. "I think you're trying to make a black and white assessment in a gray world. This isn't your computer."

"What do you mean?"

"You're a hacker. Never happier than when you're behind a screen, right? Happy with your zeros and ones because they never lie. You tell them to do something, they do it. You get a result, it's concrete. Something you type either does a thing, or it doesn't."

"Yeah, but what does that have to do with humans being horrible?"

"You're like my little brother. He loved video games, math, and computers. Why? Because it was an equation. A plus B equals C. Do this thing, you get this result. Do this thing wrong, you get that consequence. But that's not how life is. Life is messy and horrible and wonderful all at the same time. You have terrible people who want to watch the world burn, and great people that just want to be happy. Look at the Tark, at Ausha and the others. We condemn the Tark, but they are trying to make things better."

"But that just throws more doubt into the mix. If there are good Tark, how can we condemn an entire race?"

"Because it's what they want. Like Mira said, they believe the Tarks should live or die on their own, without having to rape and pillage other planets. With closing the gates, that's exactly what they'll have to do."

"I guess." Amy looked up at the ceiling, the shadows

dancing on the stone. "Things were all easier behind the screen."

Jess squeezed her arm. "Everything's easier when you're not actually dealing with it."

She stared at her hands. "You know, I used to dream about going back. About sneaking through the gates and finding a way home."

"Used to? Not anymore?"

She sighed. "Maybe. But now I wonder how I could go back. After all the things I've seen and done. The blood that my hands have spilled. How could I go back to a normal life? Go to college, get a job, settle down in a house in the suburbs with the white picket fence? I just don't see it anymore."

"I guess we do what every other soldier does. We deal with it."

Jess smiled and hugged her. "Just promise me you'll make it out, ok?"

"Only if you promise the same thing."

They hugged for a moment more before Jess got up and went over to the fire. Reven came and sat beside Amy. "Have a good chat?"

"Like you didn't hear every word."

He shrugged. "It's a small cave. You going to be okay tomorrow?"

"Well, let's see. I have zero training, zero endurance or

muscle tone. We're outnumbered, outweaponed, and basically out-everything. Yeah, I'll be great."

Reven barked a little laugh. "Well, when you put it that way, what could go wrong?"

His sad smile came to his eyes. "Do you still regret coming to rescue me? Getting caught up in all of this?"

Amy sat there for a second, contemplating the question. Finally, she shook her head. "No. I'm not."

"Really?"

"Trust me, this place will never be first on my hit list for vacation spots. I definitely could have lived without seeing the whole human meat market and the Pits. But I got the chance to meet you and Jess and everyone else. There is more to this universe than the little piece of dirt I called home. I feel like I've had my eyes opened. I'm stronger. Better. I'm not that hacker blindly turning the other way. I'm helping."

Without thinking about it, their hands found each other. Amy looked over at Reven. "Are you scared? For tomorrow?"

He took a deep breath. "I probably should tell you no. Bolster your confidence. Be the take charge, damn the torpedoes type of leader. But I'm not. I'm scared. All of you have to be protected. I'm just one person. How do I do that in the hellstorm we're going to be walking into?"

"I think it's better that you're scared. You're real. None of us would believe you weren't. None of us would trust it. But knowing that you're scared and still walking into tomorrow because you believe in what we are going to do? That people can follow."

"You think?"

She smiled at him. "I know. Look at me. I have zero combat experience other than running. Even that I'm not apparently very good at because I keep getting caught. But I'm willing to face it all head on. Because I know you'll get us through, somehow."

"No pressure or anything."

She laughed again. He smiled. "It's good to hear you laugh."

"For a while there, I wasn't sure I remembered how." Amy admitted. "But it's like my Nonna always told me. Find the good in everything or you lose yourself. There is some good here."

"What is that?"

"Aliens are real, and the ones that don't want to eat me are pretty cool. I made some new friends, even if it is in odd circumstances. I'm still alive. And I'm basically living out the coolest video game ever invented."

"Well, I think I'm sticking to Pac-man if we ever get back to Earth." Reven quipped. "I hope someday we get back there."

There really wasn't much more to say. Amy let her head sink to his shoulder, and they both stared at the flickering fire.

"To tomorrow." She whispered.

"Tomorrow."

26

* * *

Just before daybreak, Vassen, one of Mira's brothers, came back with news of a hunting party searching their trail on the road. He reported the patrol kept going, but Reven had decided it was too risky to stay longer in case the hunters found the animals and wagons that the first group had down in a shelter near the cave. After a meager breakfast of some dried meat that had been in the cave's stores, the group loaded up into the wagon, Mira driving. She clicked to the team and directed them on a path away from the road and across the desert.

Amy gritted her teeth as the cart bounced over the rough terrain. "Why aren't we going on the road?"

Reven didn't look at her, but kept staring ahead. "One, that would be obvious. All the Tark population lives in the city. There isn't a lot of traffic coming off the roads other than occasional hunting parties that go into the mountains. The walls are there more to keep things in than out. They would spot us in a second."

"That's comforting." Amy mumbled.

"Second," Mira supplied from the driver's seat. "The gateways are in a cavern at the base of the mountains that abut the city. It will be easier to find a way in, as the builders of the city did not encircle the mountain within the Great Wall. That way, we will not have to traverse the entire city to get to our target."

Amy opened her mouth to let out the dark retort that sprang to mind, but she bit her tongue and chided herself for being soft. She was in this just like the others, a warrior now. She thought back to what Jess had said. It was time for her to grow up. A hand reached over and squeezed her leg, and she looked up to see Jess give her a sympathetic smile. Amy took a deep breath, steeling herself.

The temperature was sweltering under the heavy sand-colored cloth that Mira had thrown over the top. There was nothing she could do about the dust trail, but hoped that anyone who looked in their direction would merely think it was a trick of the sun or a gust of wind bringing a dust devil to life. For many hours, there was nothing but a flat, barren desert. Slowly, mountains grew in the distance, at first nothing but a purple haze on the horizon but over the hours growing into enormous sharp peaks that towered above the land.

Mira pulled the team to a stop within the rolling foothills at the base of the range. "We are here."

The butterflies took flight in Amy's stomach, but she swallowed them down. She descended from the cart with the others, looking around. Off in the distance, she could just make out the wall of the Tark city and a shiver of fear ran through her. "Can they see us?"

"Perhaps if they are looking directly at us, but the

foothills should hide us," Mira said. "Plus, generations of non-hunting and the twin suns have destroyed the Tarks' long distance sight. They rely on their ability to go onto a planet and destroy or scare the native populace into compliance."

"So, what now?" Jess asked.

"We walk." Mira said. "There are trails through the mountains that the Tark used to get minerals and other elements out of the mountains."

"What about patrols?" Reven asked. "Why would the Tark just leave a huge blindside to their back?"

Mira laughed. "Because they are apex predators. The only attack they ever expected was from the Resistance, coming from inside."

"So no need to watch the yard when the fox is in the henhouse." Griff said.

"Exactly." Mira turned to her brothers. "Scout the trail."

The trio nodded and, without another word, disappeared into the barren landscape. No life lived on these hills except for a forest of skeletal tree trunks that hadn't figured out that they could fall down. Mira turned to the group again. "Reven, you will take point with me. Jess and Draile, you take the rear guard. The rest keep your wits and weapons about you and wait for our signals."

The group silently started walking the trail, with only

their breathing to mark their passage. Amy startled at the slightest sound of a pebble rolling or a dry stick cracking underneath a foot. Any moment she expected the Tark to come rolling down the hills, for a sword or arrow to suddenly pierce her heart. She fought for control of her anxiety, pushing down the terror bubbling in her chest, her mind sending her horrendous visions of her torture and death. A sharp cry resounded above her and she startled, looking upward only to see a black speck circling far above in the sky. She sighed for a moment. This place was so barren and dead she struggled to imagine that any life survived here except for the Tark. Yet somehow it felt better to know that even in this dead world, birds still survived. They weren't completely alone.

Was it her imagination or was the speck getting larger? No, it had to be an illusion. She stopped walking and stared upward, the others behind her stopping in confusion as well, raising their eyes to the sky. It was only when she heard their collective gasp that her over-stressed mind contemplated what her eyes were seeing. The speck was getting closer, and a lot bigger! "Mira!"

It was the only word she could get out before her world exploded in a collision of black feathers and dust. She threw herself blindly away from the explosion, feeling something hiss close to her skin, the wind of its passing pulling at her clothes. Instinctively, she rolled as she landed, watching as a huge shining metallic beak drove itself forcefully into the dirt in the spot she had been. The creature squealed a battle cry, bursting her eardrums with the closeness, and focused to strike at her again.

Amy heard the twin bow shots being released, heard the thump as the arrows buried themselves in the creature's thick skin. The creature reared its head and beat its wings, roaring its fury at being hit. But the arrows were little more than a minor annoyance.

Amy could see it now. It was a huge, mutated raven the size of a small tank. The claws on its feet were like sickle blades, its eyes red, its toothed black beak flashing in the sun. The creature had a scaled hide covered in black feathers, ending in a long, heavily muscled scaled tail like a crocodile's. It flapped its wings, the stench of death and decay rolling over Amy, making her want to retch.

Before a second had passed, the creature had recovered, refocusing on her. With a cry, it launched itself at her, its beak heading for her heart like a missile. Amy tried to roll, tried to pull out her sword, her brain screaming at her to do something, but her fear frozen body refused to respond. Time slowed down as she watched her death approach.

A rope lasso looped out of nowhere to catch the bird's beak, hauling it to the side. The bird blinked at the new intrusion and growled. Mira held the other end of the rope, hauling against it with all her might. The bird huffed and, with a mighty flap of its wings, lifted off the ground, taking Mira with her.

Two more ropes looped out of nowhere, one catching a wing and the other a foot. Mira's brothers gave a quick jerk to disrupt the creature's takeoff and as it crashed to the ground, they quickly tied their ropes to heavy rocks that the bird could not move. They took out more rope, quickly fashioning more nooses.

"Reven!" Mira cried, still bracing herself against the bird's thrashing movements. "Control it!"

"What?" Reven cried in confusion, his sword drawn as he raced to Amy's side. "I can't do that!"   "You must or we will die!" Mira cried. "Believe in who you are. Who your people are. You must become Ra'shek again!"

"I. . .I. . ." Sweat poured down his face. "I don't know —"

"You must!"

"Reven, hurry." Amy cried, taking his hand in hers. "You can do this. I believe in you."

Just then the bird, as if sensing the conversation, roared and whirled its head, dragging Mira off her feet. It lunged for Amy and Reven, anger and hunger radiating off of it. Amy heard a scream, only seconds later realizing it was tearing from her own throat. As if in slow motion she saw Reven stand up, putting himself between her and the bird.

STOP!

Amy winced as the command tore through her brain, as did the others in their group. But amazingly, the bird stopped, its quivering beak inches from Reven's outstretched hand. It twitched and twisted under the control, but remained frozen in an outstretched position. Reven stared at it, sweat beading off his face, his body shaking with the effort to fight the bird's strength. Amy stood up, placing a tentative hand on his arm, willing her strength into him.

"I can't. . .I can't hold it long." His strained voice whispered.

Suddenly an idea came to Amy. "Talk to it."

"What? Are you crazy?"

"You talked to me before. Talk to it. Maybe we can persuade it to not, you know, eat us."

"I can try."

Hello? His mind voice wavered through her mind. He didn't have the control to speak just to the bird. She didn't fight the intrusion, knowing that it could take away from what little control he had. Instead, she tried to focus on the bird, pushing it back out to him.

Eat. Hungry. Food. The bird growled and snapped its beak, but did not move.

Waves of images rolled through Amy's mind, the power driving her back. The onslaught must have gone through the group as well as they all fell to their knees at the power of the images, Reven gasping with maintaining control.

A streak coming out of the sky, striking the land. Dust and sand flying everywhere, the sun blotted out for a hundred years. The land turning cold and barren. Animals dying, skeletons and carcasses rotting everywhere. The sun returning, but to a barren desert land. No food, no hope for the animals left. Starving young ones, dying in the nest. Only the strongest survive, preying on each other when food is scarce. Tarks hunting them, killing their young in the nest. Hungry. Starving. Revenge. Anger. Hate. Fear. Kill!

"Stop" Jess cried, tears falling down her face. "No more."

But the images kept coming, Reven unable to stop the flood from broadcasting through his mind without losing control of the bird. Tears flowed down his eyes, his body collapsing against Amy. Suddenly, the images stopped. The bird stopped struggling and blinked at Reven.

You hate Tark? Tark hunt you?

"Yes." Reven gasped.

The bird shook its head. Amy could sense two thoughts now struggling within its brain. Its empty stomach drove it to eat, to tear, to kill. But it also wanted to know more about Reven, about how he hated the Tark.

Hurt you. Pain you. I know.

A nest. Two young birds, opening their mouths as they asked for food. A beautiful bird, smaller than the one before them with rainbow colored feathers and bright blue eyes, preening in the sunlight, caring for her brood. The male flying off for food. Coming back to fear, pain, death. His mate. His children. Dead by Tark claws. His mate stripped for feathers, cut for food.

The bird let out a cry now, not one of anger or hunger but of pain. It warbled through the barren trees, raising into a heart rendering screech. The bird looked at Reven; the fight gone out of it. It settled to the ground, lowering its beak, trying to show its submission.

I no eat. Release.

Mira argued, but Reven held up a hand. "It's okay. He speaks the truth."

Carefully, distrustfully, Mira and the brothers walked up and untied the ropes. The bird's body quivered with their closeness and his need for food, but he kept his word and did not strike out. Once they released him, the bird sat up, staring at the group.

I called Blackwing.

Reven stood up, facing the bird. He placed a hand on his chest. "Reven. Do you understand my words?"

I understand thoughts. We talk. Revenge.

"Is it really speaking to you?" Amy whispered incredulously.

"I think it is my brain translating its thoughts more than anything else. But it is smart. It read my thoughts just as its thoughts flowed through my link. I think it doesn't want to eat us because it knows we are trying to destroy the Tark. It wants to help."

The bird nodded, chirping a little in pleasure at being understood and understanding Reven's thoughts.

The others walked up cautiously, unsure what to make of their new ally, who, not even a second ago, wanted to rip them all to shreds. Jess crept up to Reven and Amy. "How does he want to help us?"

My brothers and I. Fight.

Images of other birds like him, all different colors. All were strong. Beating wings. Ripping beaks.

Mira walked up, her voice calm. "I have heard tales of these creatures, but thought they were all gone. They are called Torak by the Tark. Fierce warrior birds who populated the mountains, prized for their feathers and flesh."

Blackwing glared at her, and she held her hands up in apology. "I am sorry. Just repeating the tale."

Tarks no hunters. Hunters kill for feed. To protect. They destroy.

"How have you survived?" Amy asked, "If the Tarks

hunted you?"

Hide. Far away. Found food. Water. High in mountains. But gone now. I come back. Find nothing but Tark destruction. Find you.

Amy felt his stomach rumble, the drive warring for a moment against the newfound peace. She dug in her pack, pulling out some dried beef. "It is not much, but we have food to share."

She tossed it in the air, and Blackwing caught it in his beak. He swallowed it whole. It had to be nothing but a small drop in his belly, but he nodded his head in thanks. *Good others share. We fight for good others.*

Amy shivered. "But the Tarks are many. If your and your brother's attack, they will kill you."

Blackwing shook his head. *We try before. Many die.*

"Then why fight with us? More will die."

Blackwing tilted his head so he could look at her eye to eye. *You see.*

He strolled to the base of a tree, the dead trunk reaching high into the sky. Carefully, gently, he scraped his beak across the ground, clearing away the dirt and debris. There, cradled in between pieces of dead wood, was a very tiny green seedling.

Life. Blackwing gave a little squawk of happiness.

Amy and the others came over. Reven crouched down,

staring at the little seedling. "The land is healing."

Land come back. Plants. Animals. Life for mine. Tarks no destroy.

"You want to fight to make sure the Tarks don't destroy what is growing?" Sephora asked with wonder in her voice.

A wave of sadness washed over the link. *Images of that rainbow bird again, her sky-blue eyes glistening in the sun. A wave of love.*

Lightburst. Amy heard the words, but saw what he meant. It was the way the sun reflected off of water, shining in so many colors. That was the name of his mate.

I die that day. Others die too. Die for nothing. Now we die for something.

Images of the small fledglings, the day they hatched, how they grew, how proud he had been.

"I don't think we can wait for your brothers if they are far away." Mira said. "We must attack soon."

Tomorrow sun rise. Brothers come. You see. We help.

With that, he threw back his head, uttering a cry that was almost a howl, the sound echoing off the mountain valleys.

Mira grumbled. "Well, if the Tark didn't know we were here, they do now."

No worry. Safe place up ahead. Tark never comes. Too scared.

"I really don't want to know what scares a Tark."

Sephora whispered.

"Do we have a choice?" Reven asked. He looked at Mira. "It would even up the odds, having a few of these at our back."

Mira stood still for a moment pondering, then took a deep breath and turned to Blackwing. "We accept your offer of help. Show us your safe place."

27

***

The guard stood atop the wall, listlessly watching the city. The middle still smoldered from where it had collapsed into the cavern below two days before. During the confusion, the queen had taken control of the population, leaving them only to run on instinct and basic commands. The city had quieted, although three patrols had left the city that morning on some errand. The humans, however, were much more agitated and anxious. Several had tried to take advantage of the dulled Tark, grabbing weapons and fighting their owners, but a few quick public executions had taken care of the uprisings. Now the humans just whispered, waited, skulking in corners.

Something made the guard look up. He squinted against the bright sun, trying to see what had bothered him. There, far up in the sky, he saw a black shape, so tiny that he almost missed it among the clouds. *A bird,* he absently thought. Was it his thought? It sounded different. The queen maybe.

Whatever it was, the thought left his mind. Until he saw another dot, then another. All rising from behind the high mountain. More black dots joined them, hundreds more, until a massive black swarm hung above the mountains.

Somewhere in the back of his mind, that other voice started screaming in a panic. Mutely, the guard watched as the black mass descended. Diving straight at him.

* * *

—

Amy gasped as the Torak she rode vaulted into the sky, his mighty wing muscles surging beneath him. She grasped the thick rope that they had fashioned into a sort of harness to keep the riders in place. Her ride, Sunflare, turned a kind eye to her. He squawked a quick word of encouragement before he went back to the business of getting them into the sky.

All around her, hundreds of other Torak took to the skies just as the sun started hinting at its presence over the horizon. All the fighters rode on the backs of the largest Torak, with Reven taking point on Blackwing.

Blackwing had said his brothers would come and Amy had watched in astonishment as they had come by the hundreds the night before, filling the small valley that they had taken shelter in. Blackwing had hummed beside her with pleasure, glad that his brethren had answered the call. He had explained through Reven's mind link they had come from all the flocks up and down the mountainside. These were all the bravest and oldest warriors, those who had felt pain at the hands of the Tark and were ready to exact their revenge. The few mothers that were left had stayed home with their brood, as had some of the youngest warriors and the newly mated, so that the flocks could survive.

Amy's breath caught in her throat as she looked at the Torak in a new light. They were not just creatures. They were warriors, fighting for their homeland, flying into battle knowing that not a one of them might return. But they had answered the call. Because their kind needed a chance to live free of the Tark.

Sunflare climbed higher into the sky, circling with his brethren, waiting for BlackWing to lead them over the mountain. Reven had claimed the mind link was too taxing with this many Torak nearby and the space they had to keep between them when flying, so she did not know what Sunflare was thinking or saying. Instead, she concentrated on feeling the Torak beneath her, trying to gauge when he was going to turn or move. *I can do this. I have to do this. If they can be brave, so can I!*

The ground receded to dizzying heights, but Amy refused to let the fear paralyze her. She focused on deep breaths, clinging to the harness. SunFlare turned his head again, giving her an encouraging trill.

Suddenly, Amy realized the flock had all gained altitude, all her friends now flying around her. Jess, riding a Torak with deep black feathers that shone violet in the sun, pumped her arm encouragingly. Amy mimicked the gesture, hoping it looked more brave than she felt.

Blackwing cried out, the sound echoed by the entire

flock of Torak, and as one entity, they wheeled to the east, over the final mountain peak. Amy's breath caught from the thin, cold air, then suddenly her eyes focused and she saw the Tark city far beneath her. The flock only hung there for a moment before Blackwing gave out another bugle. Amy clung to the harness as Sunflare suddenly folded his wings.

She crouched down on his neck, not wanting to get ripped off by the wind as they arrowed down to the ground below. Her ears picked up the screaming whistle of thousands of Torak as they dove as one through the sky, cutting through the air. The Torak were screaming their battle cry as they entered a blood fury. They could see, could smell their quarry! After centuries of pain and fear that had followed their kind, the memories of seeing their loved ones slain time and time again, they were going to fight! They were going to win! They would keep their kind safe for centuries to come.

The rooftops rushed closer and closer and panic started bubbling in Amy's throat that they could not stop. Just as she was about to scream, Sunflare snapped his wings open, angling his body to decelerate as fast as possible. The force of the abrupt stop threw Amy onto his neck, where she clung for dear life.

Other Toraks employed the same move but kept their forward momentum going, extending their scythe-like claws and crashing forcefully into the Tark soldiers on the walls and rooftops. The battle cries turned into cries of victory, blending with cries of pain and alarm from the Tark as death descended on them from above. Beaks and claws found their targets, strong tails whipping back and forth to sweep Tark off ledges to fall to their deaths below. The smell of blood, both Tark and Torak, filled the air as the lethargic Tarks finally got the message to fight back.

Amy only got quick visions of the carnage as Sunflare peeled off from his rampaging brothers along with the others who carried her friends. That small group swerved, coming to a quick landing at the base of the mountain. Quickly she hopped off, landing on her feet behind Sunflare, who gave her a quick nod, then launched himself into the air to join his brothers.

Blackwing bowed to Reven and squawked. Reven opened up the mind link, letting the others hear. He pointed his beak at the entrance. *You go there. Break gates. We take care of others.*

Amy felt a tear trickle down her eye. Even though he had wanted to eat her at first, even though they had only known him a short time, she couldn't bear the thought of him dying. She walked up and reached out a hand. He put his beak into it, his eyes closing.

Don't be sad. All are together, here or in another world.

We fight now. Find our heart loves. We see each other someday again.

He rose and spied a patrol running at them. A bright gleam grew in his eyes as he threw his head back, coiling his body. With a mighty battle cry, he launched into the Tark, talons and beak ripping and tearing. The Tark didn't stand a chance.

There was a hand gripping her arm. Reven. "Hurry. They won't buy us much time and we need to get moving."

The group rushed for the gates. They had discussed this the night before. From reconnaissance by the Resistance warriors, they knew that there were five gates, each leading to a different planet. Reven had originally wanted to just blow up the entrance, blocking their access to the gates, but Amy had come up with an alternative plan.

"Put the explosives at the bottom of the gates."

"What?" Reven asked. "Why would we do that?"

"When the explosion goes off, it gives off waves of energy. Those waves should theoretically disrupt the waves of energy from the gate. They could cancel them out, send them off into another part of space, or create an even bigger explosion which would only help in keeping the Tark away. We can still place a small charge at the entrance to make sure that the gates are useless, but this way we not only destroy the access, we destroy the source."

"She's right." Jess piped up. "If we block the access, they can just dig it back out. But if we block the access and screw up the gates, they have no way out. We could actually end this instead of just delaying it."

"Do we have enough charges?"

She bit her lip. "It's not a lot, but I think we can stretch it. Mira and her brothers have some as well, which helps. But we'll have to have everything timed right. No second chances, no screwups."

They had divided the explosives and detonators between the five groups, two people each, with Mira and her brothers handling the entrance. They would hold back any who would interfere as well as blow the entrance when the others had gotten clear.

"When the alarms sound, most of the Tark soldiers should clear the gates, attending to the emergency. When in hive mind, Alia won't be able to handle giving out too many directions, so she'll probably focus on the Torak. If there are any Tark left, we'll have to dispatch them quickly before Alia can see us,." Jess said grimly.

Reven noted Amy was quiet during most of this discussion. Later, he found her crouched by a fire. "What's wrong? I know it's a suicide mission but . . ."

"It's not that." She stared off into space, taking in the resting Torak and the others. "I just realized that when we blow the gates, we lose our way home."

Reven sat down beside her. "I know. There's a chance we could slip through the gate, but it would put us right back in the base, and it wouldn't be that much better. At least here we might have a chance at being normal."

"Normal." Amy huffed. "What is that anymore?"

Reven put his arm around her. "Whatever happens, I will take care of you."

"You keep saying that."

"Because I mean it. You've saved me. The least I can do is protect you."

She laughed. "Me save you? That's rich."

"You did. Before you, I was hell bent on revenge and destroying the Tark, no matter the cost. I let myself get caught for that reason. I didn't care about my friends, or who got caught up in it."

"Hopefully you realize now how stupid that was."

He nodded. "I have. But it doesn't change how I felt. The only way into the base was to be captured."

"So you used the knowledge that we were looking for you to lure the army in?"

"Not that hard to figure out that you were searching for me. I'm a threat to the Tark. I've disrupted their plans on a few planets. So, I let myself get caught. Only I didn't stop to think."

"Think about what?"

"About all the people that my failure would hurt. Look at Alia. She was so hell-bent on retaining her royal glory and all the things she thought were due her. She betrayed an entire city of innocent people just trying to survive."

"Well, she is a psycho, so. . ."

"I know she is. But is being ignorant of the consequences of my actions any different? Of acting recklessly no matter who gets caught up in the crossfire?"

"I don't think you do that."

"But I do. All I wanted to do was to defeat the Tark. I didn't care what it took. But then you got captured and got sent to the Pits, this person who I barely knew but had gotten her world turned upside down because of me. They sent my friends for Treatment. Suddenly I realized that defeating the Tark wouldn't mean anything if I had all of your blood on my hands."

He looked out at the Torak, troubled.

Amy reached over and took his hand. "Blackwing told us. They fight because they want a better life. They are ok with dying."

"I know. They chose this. But that's what I mean. They are fighting to avenge their loved ones, but they are also fighting for the little ones left living, so they can have a better future. For the planet that is trying to heal itself from the devastation. They are fighting to build something."

"So, what are you building?" Amy asked.

He sighed. "That's just it. I don't know."

She squeezed his hand. "Well then, it's a good thing I do. You're building hope."

He looked at her. "How do you figure?"

"Look at who we have here. A few humans, most who have never seen battle. Strange bird creatures. All of us have lost friends and family to the Tarks, lost our lives to them. Every day I think of the women left in the Pits and I just want to crumble and cry that we couldn't save them. We still won't save them today, just keep the Tark from getting other innocents to add to their number. We're going up against a parasitic species that is literally born to kill and destroy. It would sap all the energy and hope out of anyone, killing this mission before it even began. Yet, here we are. Preparing to ride into battle, knowing we probably won't make it out."

"Then why do it?"

"Because you give us hope it will make a difference. Blackwing and his flock could have attacked at anytime. But they are choosing now to fight because we can close the gates. We can stop them. This is the end of the war and on the other end is a better life. You've built up this hope that it really can happen."

She looked around at the others, laughing and joking

around the small fire they had built. "Look at them. Even though we are saying our goodbyes, knowing that we might never see each other again, we still laugh and joke around. Our spirits are high. Because we all believe that even if we die, the mission will go well tomorrow. That we can stop this from happening to anyone else."

Amy remembered those words as she raced into the darkness of the tunnel's mouth. *I will be strong. I will have hope!*

28

* * *

Mira and her brothers stopped in the doorway. One started pulling some gray lumps out of backpack and some wires. Mira turned to the others. "Twenty minutes. You must be back and clear or we will blow the charges."

Amy swallowed the lump in her throat. The group had agreed, twenty minutes. Any less and they might not get the other charges laid. Any more and the Tark might wonder what was going on at the gates and come investigate. They had also agreed that if the Tark overran Mira's position before the time limit was up; she was to blow the charges anyway, no matter the cost. Beads of sweat trickled down Amy's forehead, but she nodded her understanding, as did the others. Without another word, they broke up into their assigned pairs and ran down the dark tunnel.

Ahead of them, the tunnel branched into five. Reven and Amy veered into the one on the farthest left. The tunnel widened out into the cavern. Amy stopped to shield her eyes against the bright light of the gate that slashed through the darkness.

Quickly, Reven started pulling out the explosives from his pack. "We need to get these as close to the base of the gate as we can. The timer will give us five minutes to get clear, but hopefully, the explosion won't be so big that we can't get out of the main tunnel."

Amy nodded and took some pieces, running with him

over to the gate. The closer they got, the more the energy hummed through the air. It vibrated her bones and rattled her teeth, an uncomfortable energy that made her skin crawl. Almost like it knew what they were trying to do, and it was trying to fight them. She stopped, gasping for breath a little as she fought the feeling. Reven looked back and gave her an understanding nod. He reached back and took the items from her hand, showing that he would try to get closer.

Amy stood there, looking at the gate, the silver light snapping and sparking with blue, gold and red colors. Like on Earth, the Tark had erected a huge silver ring etched with odd symbols and lines. A small control box stood to one side, and she walked over to it.

This controlled and directed the gate's energy. With this, you could direct the gates to go anywhere. But Reven was right. Even if they could get through the gate and get back before the explosives went off, they would just end up back at the base.

"Feeling homesick, are we?" The voice cut through the air. Amy and Reven whirled around at the sound.

Alia stood at the entrance to the cavern, a smug look on her face. She wore a white shirt and breeches with bright silver armor, although she carried no weapon. Two Tark elite soldiers stood on her left and right. "Now, just what do you think you two are doing?"

"How did you. . .Mira and the others?" Reven called out.

"Oh, there's more than one way into this cavern, although only the queen knows it. Thankfully, I have access to her brain and all the knowledge in it. But don't worry, your little friends will get what's coming to them for betraying me, as will you."

Reven and Amy instinctively moved closer together. Reven eyed her, whispering. "I set the timers."

Which means we have five minutes. We don't have time for Alia and her little games! I know we could take her, but the guards?

"Now, tell me what you all are trying to do? Trying to go home?" Alia snarled. "It won't work. Neither will the attack from your little bird friends outside. I don't know where you found them, but they will all die today."

Amy's heart clenched, but she fought to keep control. She had to help Reven figure out a way out of this. It was just like the video games she played, right? The final boss fight? She'd defeated millions of them before. *But none of those were in real life.* She shook her head. She had to do this. Too many were counting on her.

Suddenly she felt a piercing jolt in her brain, fingers stabbing into her consciousness, the pain driving her to her knees. An alien voice. *Tell me what you know.*

Amy fought against the pain. She tried to do what Reven taught her, thinking of a wall. Faintly she heard Reven's shout, felt him standing protectively over her, but it was all a blur next to the pain. She fought against the fingers raking at her mind. *Tell me what you know!*

Alia's attack was powerful. But Amy had learned a thing or two about mind links. As Alia tried to open Amy's mind, the woman opened her own mind to Amy. Amy felt her, saw her. Alia's barriers were weak from the strain of controlling the queen, the chaos outside, and trying to deal with Reven and the invaders.

Amy closed her eyes and took a deep breath. *Let me in.*

Suddenly, she saw the outside. A thousand voices, all crying, some in pain, some in fear, all wondering what to do. Alia had given the warriors basic commands: fight, attack, defend. To the other Tarks, the civilians she told to run, to hide. Amy could see that the humans, unaffected by the mind control, were taking advantage of the chaos. Some were joining the birds in the fight against the Tark. Others were cowering and hiding. Still others were looting and laughing, some joining the Tark in the fight in a disgusting move that made her stomach turn.

Behind all of it, the queen's mind, locked in a cage in Alia's mind. Amy could feel it pulsing and raging against the bars. She reached out, wondering if she could set her free.

What are you doing? Stop that!

Amy gasped as the link was severed, the act so quick that it felt like falling from the top of the building. She would have completely fallen over if Reven hadn't caught her. Alia stood there, panting, glaring at Amy with hatred in her eyes. "How did you do that?"

"Didn't know the link worked both ways, did ya?" Amy taunted her, still trying to catch her own breath. "Or is it just the fact that a lowly human played you at your own game? Too bad you didn't keep it open longer. I might have been able to do some actual damage."

Reven looked at her with a shocked expression for a moment before realizing what had happened, his face beaming with pride. "You used the link to look into her mind?"

"I got the idea when you were talking to Blackwing and we could all hear it. The act of mind speaking is like a tunnel, emotions and thoughts can move both ways. I think it's safe to say she wasn't expecting that."

"So, now she can't attack you without opening herself up to a counterattack."

"Right. She can't block me because she's distracted by the hive mind and controlling the queen. I felt it. She's extended herself, trying to keep hold of all of them. She won't touch me again for fear that I could get to the queen and direct the soldiers. But that still doesn't help us. How much time do we have left?"

Reven glanced back at the timer, his voice shaking. "Only two minutes."

"You little bitch." Alia snarled, then seemed to compose herself. "It doesn't matter what you're up to. I have had enough of dealing with you. I was going to spare you and your little group, make you my personal slaves. But now I think I'll just kill you here and parade your heads around on sticks as proof of what happens to those that defy me."

"Stop this, Alia!" Reven stood up, his hand on his sword hilt. "You've gone far enough. End this."

She laughed, the sound bouncing off the cavern walls. "You've got to be joking. I gave you a choice to serve me and join me in my glorious ascension to my rightful place as ruler of the universe. But no, you fought me. Now you get a traitor's death."

Amy glanced at the timer. *One minute.*

Alia smiled. "Enough of this. I need to get back and deal with the others outside. Kill them."

One of the Tark soldiers grinned with pleasure as she gave them the command to kill. He picked up a two headed war ax. With a flick of his wrist, he sent it spinning across the cavern. Straight at Reven.

Thirty seconds.

Amy watched in slow motion as it cartwheeled toward Reven, the blades glinting in the silver light of the gate. Without thinking, her body moved.

Reven watched the ax in the same slow motion. His body screamed at him to move, to react, but he stood there frozen. Out of the corner of his eye, he saw Amy move. *Please get away. Save yourself.*

He watched instead as she threw herself in front of him. Intersecting the path of the ax. He watched as it crunched into her body, blood and bone spitting out of the wound. In his head he heard a distant screaming, realizing that it was his own voice, the force of the scream bursting blood vessels in his throat.

Amy's mind went black as her world descended into pain. The impact of the weapon threw her off-balance. She staggered backward, far enough that the energy of the gate caught her. The silver light reached over her, tendrils licking at her skin, drawing her in. As her mind gave out and the world faded to black, she felt herself falling backwards into the gate.

The last thing she saw was Reven coming towards her, his body whole. Safe. She hoped he could still find a way out, that the explosion wouldn't hurt him. *Now I've truly saved you, just as you saved me.*

Her last thought before Death came.

29

***

The darkness was warm, enveloping. It surrounded her like a blanket. Only something kept pulling at it, pulling it away from her. Or pulling her from it, she couldn't tell. Off in the distance, a small blue spark of light pierced the darkness.

"Come back. Come back." A voice called somewhere off in the distance, so faint she had to strain to hear it.

"Let me sleep."

"Come back. Come back."

The light grew as the voices kept repeating the words. The voice latched onto her, pulling her from the darkness.

The voice kept talking, refusing to let her sleep. A warm blue light slowly grew within her mind, a pinprick at first, but growing with each breath until it pushed the darkness from her mind.

Bright white light blazed as she tried to crack open her eyes and she quickly shut them. Pain slammed into her being, her senses suddenly aware of every nerve screaming. She gasped slightly, but clutched at the sheets, shaking as a new thought came into her mind.

I'm alive.

The memory of the cavern, of the ax, of the darkness and the knowledge of Death burst into her mind's eye.

Amy could feel that she was lying on some sort of cot, a blanket over her legs. Slowly, she opened her eyes, blinking against the glare of a single bulb that burned overhead.

Slowly, the blurred vision cleared and she could make out details. She was in a vast room; the rafters soaring far overhead. Everything she could see was concrete and metal. Old rusting machines filled the space, waiting for workers that would never come. There was a chair and a table nearby, remnants of the nursing that she had needed piled on top.

She could make out the outline of a man standing by the window.

He turned as she made a small sound, rushing to her side. "Easy. You've been out for a while."

"What. . ."

Reven helped her slowly sit up, propping her up with some pillows.

The words were a croak, and she stopped to lick her dry lips. Reven quickly filled a glass of water and helped her steady her shaking hand as she drank. Even that bit of activity had wiped out the little energy she had. She laid back, feeling the headache growing behind her temples. "How? Where?"

Reven said, "It's a long story. But you're safe. Thank the goddess."

"So I'm not. . ." The impact of the ax came back into her mind.

Carefully, Amy pulled back the blanket, pulling up the hem of her shirt. A bright red gash, healed but angry, ran between her breasts and down past her navel. She gulped and a wave of nausea hit her. She laid back, closing her eyes.

Reven stroked her head. "No, you're not dead. You worried me, though. You've been asleep for almost a week."

Earth? How in the world did they get back on Earth? Briefly, she remembered falling through the gate. *Dead. I was dead, though. So, even if I made it through...*

She whispered. "We made it through. The base personnel didn't arrest us?"

He shook his head. "The explosives went off just as I went through the gate. I grabbed your hand as you fell through. Just as we started transporting, the gate pulsed. It was this brilliant flash of colors I've never seen before. I thought we were going to end up vaporized or thrown into space. But the next thing I know, I'm lying on a street in this town beside you."

"A street? We didn't end up at the base?"

"No. I think when the gate energy pulsed, it broke the connections, pulling the gate from the base and opening another nearby."

"So, where are we?"

"Nearest I can tell, Santa Fe."

"But...but there weren't any cities anywhere near the base. I remember that much from flying in, even with all they tried to cover up. We're probably a hundred miles away or more."

"I know. But maybe that's good. Whisper and all."

"So the gate?"

He shook his head. "I don't know. I have no way of getting in touch with my old informant right now to find out what's happening inside the base."

"Well, there aren't any rogue Tarks showing up in the street, so maybe the gate energy is gone for good." Amy said. Tentatively, she touched the scar with one hand. It didn't bring up any more sparks of pain, just a tingling sensation. "Speaking of okay, how? I thought. . .I mean. . .that ax. . ."

Reven stood up abruptly, his cheeks reddening, and something tangible coming through the air between them as he started pacing between her and the window. Amy watched him for a moment, aware that there was an odd sensation filling her head. *Shame? Why am I feeling shame? Wait, is it coming from Reven? Why would he feel shame? How am I feeling his feelings?* "Reven?"

"When I saw the ax, what you did, when I saw you fall through the gate. . ."

"What?" Amy yelled. The headache was pounding, but she forced it down. She should have been dead. Had Reven saved her from Death?

He licked his lips, hesitant to speak. "I did something. I shouldn't have done it, but I had to save you. I didn't even know if it would work. I'd only ever heard of it working between my people, never another species."

He looked at her, a wave of fear, guilt, pain, loss and joy at her being alive all flooding into Amy's mind at once. It was the mind link, but a thousand times stronger. She didn't know how, but she knew what he had done. "You used yourself to save me."

"My people called it the *t'kul'sha. The Entwining*. My people used it as a commitment to your soul mate. My people believed souls were energy. When you die, your energy waits to be reborn, then lives a new life, bringing new experiences and adventures into your life's weaving. In the *t'kul'sha,* you entwine your soul energies together with your loved one. That way, no matter how or when you are reborn, you recognize them and fall in love again. In extreme cases, the Entwining can save someone who is dying. You boost their energy with yours, allowing them to heal exceptionally fast. But it must be done with permission! I didn't ask you—"

Quickly, Amy reached for his hand. She could feel his pain and anguish flowing through the link, and wanted to wash all of that away. "I give you permission. I mean, really? You think you had to ask? You saved my life!"

Relief washed over him. But another wave of anguish came, and he started pacing again. "You don't understand! The Entwining is permanent. We'll be bound now for all of eternity."

His heart was bursting with some unknown pain, and she struggled to understand why. It was a lot to take in. *Entwined to him forever?*

"My people said it was a fate worse than death to be soul-paired to someone who does not want to share your soul."

Amy finally understood. He was afraid she wouldn't love him as much as he loved her.

It had all happened so fast; she hadn't really known it had happened. The fear, the need to survive had all driven them just to live. But through it all, she had always looked to Reven to be there. Her rational mind piped up that survival situations could cause feelings and emotions between people that wouldn't exist otherwise. Yet even as that part of her brain tried to dismiss the feelings, she knew. It may not be love in the conventional sense of the word, but she had been bound to Reven the moment she met him. Something, a thing she couldn't quite put her finger on, had joined them. Now, apparently, she had all of eternity to study it.

"You can feel me like I can feel you, right? You should have your answer already."

He came back over and sat beside her. She reached out to him. "Look, I do not even know how to process these last days. Heck, right now I can't even process being awake. But I know one thing. I cannot imagine doing any of it without you. It's why when I saw the ax I didn't even hesitate. Didn't even think. I just knew I couldn't let it hurt you. I would die for you, like I know you would die for me. If that doesn't make us soulmates, I don't know what does."

She laid back, her head splitting in two. "But maybe we can wait to explore our deep psychological and philosophical feeling for each other when I can sit up without wanting to throw up?"

This brought out a smile, and he nodded. "Okay, I think that's enough for now. You should get some sleep. I can feel your headache pounding through you." "Huh?" A confused look crossed her face before remembering the link. Amy sighed.e "This is going to take some getting used to."

"Well, we'll figure it out together."

She wanted to say something else, but the words died on her lips as sleep washed over her like a heavy blanket. The last thought was of Reven, whispering good night to her mind, her conscious self comforted, knowing that he would watch over her. Protect her. Forever.

There are worse ways to spend a future...

30

***

Amy stared out the window, cradling a cup of coffee, silently wishing for the warmth to penetrate the constant cold that made her shiver. The cold was not born of the temperature, or a virus chill, but of the knowledge of what was out there waiting for them. It had been four weeks since they had returned. Four weeks of waiting, cringing at every sound, taking turns watching at night. Four weeks of their senses strained to the limit, sure that at the next breath Whisper would come beating down the door to haul them back to the base.

They had needed money, and Reven had ventured out, finding odd jobs for cash to get food and supplies. The abandoned warehouse had become their home, filled with a few scant pieces of furniture and cookware. Amy was too weak to go beyond their home, her body and mind still broken after the events on the Tark homeworld. The physical wounds were healing slowly, leaving her exhausted. The mental wounds were much worse. Anxiety and panic attacks ruled during the day, making her jump and startle at the slightest sound. At night, demons stalked her dreams, raking and clawing at her mind until she woke up screaming. Reven did his best to comfort her, to hold her until peace settled into her mind again. But he couldn't stop them from stealing her sleep, her sanity.

A noise made her twitch, but a patterned knock settled

her mind. A few seconds later, Reven walked in, a backpack slung over his back. He dropped it by their bed and sunk down on the cots they had pushed together. He looked worn out and wet, his hair slicked to his head. She turned and walked slowly over, draping a blanket over him. "You know they have these things called umbrellas."

He snorted. "You only get your smart ass card when you're well enough to go outside."

"So? Any news today?" The not knowing what happened to Jess and the others gnawed at her soul. She sat down beside him, hope spilling out into her voice even though she tried her best to hold it back. Every day he went out, risking exposing their presence to contact the one who had told Reven about the scouts in the first place, the one who had started this whole thing. Reven didn't know who they were, just how they used to get in touch. But whomever the spy had been, they had been silent since the two had returned.

He shook his head. "Nothing. If the contact is still alive, they're lying low and being quiet. It was risky before getting word through the Gates and out of the base. Now, if we destroyed the Gateway, Whisper will have everything locked down tight."

Amy rubbed his back. She could feel his sorrow and anger. Reven had helped her control the walls of her mind, so the Entwining didn't overwhelm her anymore, but they would always share their emotions. "Sadly, Whisper is pretty good at their job."

He looked away, trying to get his emotions under control. When he turned back, his face was more stoic, but she could still see the tears in his eyes. "You'd think after all of this, losing someone else wouldn't affect me."

Amy grew silent. "One day. One day, we will make them pay for all our friends that they took. But we may lose more before that day finally comes."

Amy turned back to the window, watching the rain. Rain didn't happen often here in the desert, but she threw a grateful wish to the heavens for bringing it. It felt wrong for the sun to be shining with the mood she was in.

Reven sighed, laying down on the bed. "So, what do we do now?"

Amy stood and walked back over to the window. "We do what we can. It's a pipe dream to believe that Alia died, and even if she did, the queen would just come back online. But I've been thinking. The Tark aren't our only problem. It's the humans hiding them. The ones sending all those innocents to the lots. It's going to keep happening. Even if we destroyed the Tark and the gate forever, it doesn't stop the problem. Those same humans still have access to the gates and the knowledge to use them. We can't believe they'd use them for good. We don't know that they can't create more gates, but they may."

Reven nodded and stood to come beside her, but before he could speak, there was a loud bang outside. They both jumped, their hands reaching for the knives they carried. As one, they moved toward the door that led to the alley where the noise came from, Reven covering Amy. Slowly, Reven opened the door, trying to see out into the darkness. Carefully, they exited, eyes scanning the alley like hunted animals.

Another noise, louder, spun them around to see a homeless man stumbling out from behind a pile of old trashcans. He had long matted jet black hair, with an old stained overcoat covering a soiled shirt and jeans. The man hunched over, clutching something in his hands, staring up at them with wild, open eyes. Those eyes darted back and forth between Amy and Reven.

"The green-eyed ones tell tales." He nodded and darted toward them, waving his hands as if his words were the most important things that he needed them to understand. "The green eyes ones tell tales!"

"Stop!" Reven took a fighting stance. The knife pointed at the man.

Amy stared at the man, and her breath caught in her throat as she suddenly saw past the grime. She put a hand on

Reven's upheld arm and whispered. "Stop."

"What?"

"I know him." She stepped around Reven.

"Amy? What are you doing?" Reven hissed. "He's dangerous!"

"No. He's not." She held open her hands. "Chris? Is that you?"

The man looked up, startled, before trying to turn. "Chris. No Chris. Chris. No Chris."

Amy stepped forward, catching his shoulder. "Chris. It's me. Amy."

He turned and looked at her, searching her face before shaking his head. "Angels never sleep."

Tears pricked at Amy's eyes, and Reven rushed forward. "What is it?"

She turned to him, burying her face in his shoulder. "I know him."

"From the base?"

"He helped me get in to see you. He was a doctor, and a friend. They did this to him, even though he had a wife and child!"

"A doctor?" Reven stared at the man before him. "How did he end up like this?"

"The Treatment. It messes with people's minds, makes them sound crazy. That way, the government can release them into the public with no one the wiser about what's going on. If the Treated say anything about aliens or the base, people just call them crazy."

"Why would they release him? They could just send him through the gate."

"Maybe they can't. Maybe the gate really is closed, or unstable. So, they turned him loose. After all, what is another crazy homeless man on the street?"

She looked up. Chris had gone back to rummaging in the trash can. "We have to take care of him. He's like this because of me."

A tsunami of shame and guilt suddenly overwhelmed her, and Reven came to her side. She buried her head in his chest, letting his comfort flow into her. She whispered, tears in her eyes. "You're not the only one who used people to get to an end, not understanding the consequences for them. I lied to him. I promised I would protect him."

Amy could feel Reven's indecision. He understood her need, but the knowledge that Chris in his unstable mental condition could make hiding a hundred times harder warred within his mind. But Amy knew what would win. Not just for her. But she knew Reven's heart. He would do anything for someone in need.

He sighed. "Your promises are my promises. Let's get him inside. I don't like us being this exposed."

Amy smiled and hugged him. "Thank you."

She turned to Chris. "Do you want some food?"

"Food?" His wide childlike eyes turned to her, sparkling. "Stomach hungry."

"Then come over here. I have food." Gently, she guided him to the door. They went inside slowly, Chris shuffling his feet and turning every which way with curiosity. Reven made a quick pallet on the floor with some of their blankets and an extra pillow, which Amy told Chris to sit on. Like a child, he obeyed, watching her as she made him a peanut butter sandwich and Reven got him some water. Sated, he curled up on the blankets and fell into a deep sleep.

Amy collapsed on the cot, throwing an arm over her eyes. Reven sat down beside her, rubbing her temple. "The headaches?"

"Guess I'm still not back yet. The adrenalin helped for a bit." She groaned. "How could they do that to him? He had a family."

"After all they've done, you think they care about any individual person if they stand in the way?"

"I know, it's just. . ." She paused, searching for the words. "I guess its human nature. We'd rather have the sugary lie than the dirty truth. We keep hoping in hope, even in a world where darkness has choked everything out."

"Oh, I don't think it's choked everything out." Reven

nodded over to Chris, who was sleeping soundly, safe, warm and fed. "He found his way to you. The universe knew you would care for him."

"You think?"

"I think there's a lot of things we can't explain. Good and bad. But like a wise someone once told me, we have to have hope that things will get better."

Slowly, she sat up and leaned against him, resting her head on his shoulder. She loved these quiet moments with him, feeling his strength. "It has to stop. The Treatments. The feedlots. All of it. People need to know the truth. Every filthy piece."

"How do we do that? We can't exactly start screaming it on the street corner. They'd laugh at us, just another crazy person. How long before Whisper came for us then?"

Amy sat silently for a moment, then smiled, grabbing his hand. "Then we scream it in the one place where we won't stand out. We find other people to help us. We make the world listen."

"Where do we do that?"

"Online, of course." She laughed. "Get me to a computer."

31

***

Jess stood in the queen's old throne room, staring out over the city through the huge open air windows. It had been a month since the initial attack and much had changed. The force of the Torak had caught the Tarks by surprise. Slowed by Alia's hive mind, many of the Tark soldiers had fallen along with the humans helping them. The soldiers had finally responded and fought back, but by this time the populace, human and Tark alike, had seen what was going on and jumped at the chance to be free of their oppressors. With the extra help, the combined Torak/Resistance army had pushed back the queen's soldiers.

Then the explosion of the gates had rocked the city, a chasm erupting from the Terminal, the cracks criss-crossing the city. Buildings had fallen into the chasm, others had collapsed from the shock wave. Alia's hive mind had broken, creating confusion among the soldiers. Jess and the others had emerged from the Terminal barely in time to avoid both the explosion and the chasm, emerging into chaos. Alia had somehow regained control at some point and the battle had raged most of the rest of the day and into the night. But as the next day dawned, the truth emerged. The Resistance, the few of them that were left, had gotten the victory.

But victory had not been completely theirs. Alia was alive and still had control over the queen. In the battle's confusion, Alia and the queen, along with a thousand soldiers, had slipped off into the desert. While the Resistance struggled to take control and put the city back together, they now dealt with skirmishes from Alia along with pockets of her faithful that lay hidden within the city. The Resistance were finding ways, thanks to Mira and her psychic blocking techniques, to keep the Tark that were faithful to the Resistance from falling back into Alia's hive mind should she get too close. But that still couldn't stop those who honestly believed the psychopath was the better option.

"Something on your mind, human Jess?" A Tark female dressed in leather armor walked up to her side.

Jess smiled. "Just looking at where we are, Ausha. And where we need to go."

Ausha smiled that unsettling Tark smile that showed all of her teeth. "At least we have somewhere to go, thanks to you and your feathered friends."

Jess nodded, looking off into the distance. Just visible beyond the walls were the mass graves. There had been so many dead on both sides that it had forced them to drag the bodies outside of the wall. *When this is done, I will make sure we erect a memorial to all who gave their lives to free the city.*

After the initial attack, and with Reven and Amy missing and presumed dead in the Terminal collapse, they had talked Jess into being the leadership of the Resistance. Mira and her brothers had stepped aside, Mira insisting that they were protectors, not leaders, and had sworn themselves to Jess as her guard. With no one else willing to step up, she had reluctantly agreed. Ausha, as leader of the Tark version of the Resistance, worked as Jess' counter-part so both parties had equal say in the future.

Although unsure of the role of leadership, Jess' first act had been to push to destroy the Pits and the feedlots, freeing the humans. There was to be no more slavery and any Tark who had a problem with the new regime could go outside of the walls. Many had stayed, but Jess knew she would be a fool not to believe that there would not be resistance to the new ways. She had resisted sending Mira and her brothers out as spies for a few weeks, but Mira had been right. If she didn't watch for the dissenters, they could destroy what fragile peace they had found.

A beating of wings announced Blackwing. He now sported a scar across one eye and some of his wing feathers were worse for wear. Many of his kind had died in the attack, and after the dust had settled, many had retreated to the mountains to protect their flocks. But Blackwing and some others had stayed, a steadying force to any who would take advantage of the Resistance army, which sadly was weak compared to what lay out in the desert.

He squawked a greeting, then walked over to a chart scratched into the stone of the throne room. Without Reven, it was impossible to understand the Torak; the Torak were quick to understand human and Tark speech, but Jess and the others could not understand the different squeaks and squawks that made up the Torak language. Jess had come up with a solution, scratching a chart with the alphabet on the floor and teaching Blackwing and some of the other Torak to spell, one letter at a time. It was tedious, but it was all they had.

Blackwing tapped at the chart. "P-E-A-C-E."

He had been on a patrol of the city and the surrounding desert. Peace meant that at least for right now, Alia and her followers were lying low. But they wouldn't for long. Without supplies or the ability to scavenge much out in the desert, their only way to survive was to take over the city again.

Not that we're doing much better without the gates for reinforcements. Jess sighed and rubbed her head, the headache coming back again. "Thank you, Blackwing. We couldn't do this without you and your warriors. Go rest. I believe there is food and fresh water waiting in the rookery."

He squawked and nodded his thanks, touching his beak gently to her chest before walking back over to the ledge and taking off. They had repurposed one of the great stone towers as a rookery for the Torak. Blackwing had communicated that some loved the safety of the stone tower so much they wanted to move their flock there. Jess welcomed the added wing power, but worried about what the extra mouths would do to their dwindling cupboard.

"What is it you humans say?" Ausha spoke up. "Penny for your thoughts?"

Jess sighed. "I'm glad Alia is giving us a free day. They've been attacking a lot lately. We barely have a working anything without the pressure of dealing with her again and again."

Ausha nodded. "But we are getting there. However, I feel like there is something else on your mind."

"I'm not a leader, Ausha." Jess felt herself tremble slightly, whether it was from being scared to say the words out loud or the relief of finally saying them. She wasn't sure. "I don't know what to do with all of this. Without the gates, we can't get supplies. We're living off of what we have for now, but those won't last. There are still dissenters in the city. We don't have enough housing with the collapses, not to mention a huge crater thanks to Alia and the cracks coming from the gate chamber. I'm not sure how to do this."

Ausha came over and put a clawed hand gently on her shoulder. "Neither do I, young Jess. But we do what we must. You are smarter than you know. You have kept us going this long."

Jess wanted the vote of confidence to buoy her spirits, but the weight in her soul was too much. Still, she forced a faint smile to her lips. *What is it Mom always said? Positive thinking produces positive results.* "Thanks. Guess all I can do is just take one minute at a time."

Before Ausha could respond, there was a great commotion out on the ledge as a new Torak landed, a noble beast with red feathers tipped in orange and yellow. *Flamefeather, if I remember right.*

Mira was on his back, and she hopped off lightly. Striding over, she bowed to Jess. Jess had tried to make her stop doing that since Mira had pledged herself, but it had been of no use. But that was a battle for another time.

Their sudden arrival had put Jess' nerves on edge. "What now?"

"Trouble." Mira scowled.

Jess sighed. "Of course. Why can't you ever storm in here with good news?"

A faint smile chipped at Mira's stone features. "Perhaps someday. At least this time it is not Alia or her followers."

"The dissenters?"

Alia shook her head. "No, this is something else. Something puzzling. But dangerous I feel."

"Tell me."

"I was on the wall, watching with Flamefeather when there was something off in the distance that caught my eye. It was a glint of light. I thought perhaps it was shining off metal like armor and worried that Alia might try an attack. Flamefeather and I went to investigate."

"And?" Jess prodded.

"What we discovered was not an army. It was a gate."

Jess's stomach dropped. "A gate? Out in the desert?"

"I know. It should not be. But there it was. I was about to send Flamefeather back to tell you, to get others to come. I did not want to leave it undefended."

"Good. The last thing we need is Alia getting control of a gate. But how did a gate just appear in the desert?" Just then, another thought broke into Jess' mind. "Wait. You said you were going to send just Flamefeather back. Why are you here?"

"Because as I watched, the gate collapsed on itself."

Mira waited for the stunned look to cross Jess' face. "I was standing away and there was this odd humming sound that suddenly filled the air. The hair on my arms stood up, electricity crackling and the pressure increasing. Just when I thought I would break, the light just popped. And was gone. The pressure faded, and the air turned to normal. The gate had disappeared."

"How? We had to use explosives to close the other gates." Jess shook her head in confusion.

"I do not know. But the gate was not the only new thing I found." She reached for her pack, which was filled to bursting. Mira reached into it, struggling with something that didn't want to be removed. Finally, Mira pulled out some sort of creature. A small brown thing with long back legs and a thick tail covered in brown fur.

A wallaby. The memory of the creature, seen on a long-ago zoo trip in elementary school, rose into Jess' brain. "What the hell is a wallaby doing in the middle of the desert?"

"Wallaby?" Ausha asked, tripping over the unfamiliar word.

"A creature from my home world. From Earth." Jess shook her head. "You're telling me that not only did a random gate erupt in the desert, but somehow a wallaby hopped through it unharmed?"

Mira shook for a moment and it alarmed Jess before she realized the warrior was trying not to laugh. The wallaby had struggled free of her arms and was now hopping around and exploring the throne room, looking up at Flamefeather with interest. "The universe has many strange ways, young Jess."

Jess gave her a sour look. Then she sighed and rubbed her head. "I don't even know how to process this. But first things first, if gateways are erupting out in the desert where they have never been before, we have a problem. We can't afford Alia finding one."

"What would you have us do?" Ausha asked.

"Send out Blackwing and the patrols, as many as we can spare. Wait, they just returned and are probably exhausted. See if Bash has finally finished his long-distance viewers. We need to spot these gates and secure them as quickly as possible. Ausha, would the Tark be willing to ride out with some of the Resistance?"

She nodded. "I think we should check with the councils, but that should be fine."

Jess sighed. *The damn councils.* Five people elected each from the humans and Tarks, who oversaw any major decisions. At first, it had been welcome from her standpoint. She wasn't a leader so having other people okay her decisions made it easier on her conscious if something went wrong. But now they were only getting in the way, everybody with their own agenda. *Just like back on earth. I guess it took longer than two days, but I knew it would end up like this. But better to bring them in than be accused of going behind their back. Again.*

"Ausha, you're right. We should get the councils involved. Can you gather them for an emergency meeting?"

She nodded and left the throne room. Flamefeather squawked and tapped out something on the chart. "I-G-E-T-B-L-A-C-K-W-I-N-G."

"Yes, thank you, Flamefeather." Jess nodded her thanks. Blackwing may be tired from the patrol, but he was also part of the council as a representative for the Torak.

Flamefeather turned and went toward the ledge, launching himself out into space. Then it was only her and Mira, along with the wallaby still exploring the space.

"What will you tell the council?" Mira asked.

Jess stared at the wallaby. Even with the other humans around, it was hard to remember Earth. But here was this odd creature that had lived across the globe from her, a creature she had only seen a few times behind a fence. And yet, the sight of it now hopping merrily around as it looked for food somehow pulled her closer to Earth than any since she had come through the gate. A sudden longing for home burned in her chest, a pain that she had thought long extinguished. She wasn't sure if she should be happy it still lived or not. Finally, she spoke up. "I don't really know. But this adds a lot of possibilities. And a lot of fears."

"What do you mean?"

"A working gateway to earth, one independent of the base personnel, might give us the lifeline we need for supplies while we rebuild. Vegetables, fruit, non-human meat, building supplies. You get it. But there are also things that trouble me."

"Which are?"

"One, the gateway disappeared, meaning it's unstable. We do not know where it might go, and how long it might stay. Going through could be suicide, or leave someone stranded somewhere they shouldn't be like this little guy."

"And two?"

"Fighting off Alia. I know she'll jump on any chance to go through a gate. A new world. A new chance to rule. Leave us here to die. Protecting random gates, no matter how long they last, could stretch our already thin forces even further. With the dissenters and Alia, it's just too many attack points."

"We can advance the volunteer's training."

Jess shook her head. "We've already got that running as fast as we can. It takes time to make people warriors. I worry if we just throw them out into danger without training, that would be more dangerous than being stretched thin, both physically and with moral."

"So, what do we do?"

"I'm hoping that's what the council can help me figure out."

Mira studied Jess as she once again focused on the wallaby, her face gaining that far-away look. "What are you thinking? Not Jess the general. Jess the person."

"I was thinking it might be nice to go home."

Home. Mira shuddered at the word. *What we all wouldn't give for that.*

—

The explosion had rocked the base, knocking down beams and rocks from the cavern. It destroyed the feedlot; the prisoners dying under the rubble. Which had been a blessing for Colonel Holloway. Without the gate, there was no reason to keep them alive other than a few for the scouts.

It had been two weeks since the explosion. Captain Smith and himself had managed a cover story for the main base personnel, although it was pretty weak and, from the looks he saw, he knew questions were being asked. But it didn't matter. The base. The spying. All of it was for the gate. And now?

Without the damn gateway, we have nothing! He stewed and stormed through the office, throwing things. Captain Smith stood still in a corner, afraid to impede the tornado. Colonel Holloway fixed her with a stern eye. "You're sure?"

She gulped and nodded. *What I wouldn't give to be anywhere but here.* "Yes sir. The cavern is a complete loss, structurally. We rescued as much of the scientific crew and soldiers as we could without endangering others, but cracks run through the rock for over a hundred feet. Even if we could put up another framework, there would be too many stress points."

"Any structural damage to the rest of the base?"

She shook her head. "No. The feedlot was far enough away that the damage was only to that area of the mountain. The primary structure should be fine, but Dr. Himoto says we'll have to continue to monitor the mountain as the stress fractures could spread."

"The gateway?"

"Completely gone."

Colonel Holloway looked deflated as he slumped down into his chair. "And our guests?"

"Um, it's hard to tell. They keep eating the messengers." Captain Smith tried to straighten up and look solid, even as her insides trembled.

Colonel Holloway sighed. *Damn. Damn them all to hell. Reven must have done this, I know. Somehow, somehow, he destroyed my gateway. My path to power.* "Do we have any good news at all?"

"Perhaps, sir." She stepped forward, handing him a computer printout.

Colonel Holloway scanned the document, his eyebrows raising in surprise. "How sure are we?"

"90 percent without visual confirmation."

"How did we find it?"

"Routine satellite scans from our friends at the CIA. It picked up an odd reading. They weren't sure what it was, so they sent it to us. These are the results."

Colonel Holloway looked at the paper again, focusing on the last sentence. *Results conclude energy signature matches that of dimensional anomaly.*

"Where is this again?"

"Australia sir, deep in the Outback." She handed him another paper. "But since then, we've noticed similar energy occurrences in Russia and one here in the States. Illinois, to be exact. But the energies don't seem to be stable and disappear for a while before emerging again."

He leaned forward, a studious expression on his face. A wide smile started cracking on his lips. "Smith, what are our capabilities in these countries?"

"Limited sir. Even with Whisper, you're talking about international waters. We have some leverage with the CIA and their operational command, but without having the president acknowledge our presence, we're working in black conditions. However, we should be able to secure the site in Illinois easily. Luckily for us, the reading seems to be centered in an area of wilderness. There might be some press who get wind of the movement, but the legalities should be fairly straightforward."

"Good." For the first time since the catastrophe, his mood lightened. "Activate Whisper to search and secure the Illinois site. And get me the Director on the phone. I want to see what he can do about getting eyes on the other sites. If those countries find them, we might have a whole new can of worms in the works."

"Yes, sir."

"Dismissed."

Captain Smith sharply exited, the door closing solidly behind her. Colonel Holloway relaxed into his chair, leaning back and looking up at the ceiling, thinking about how the last few minutes had changed the entire ballgame. For the better.

Rogue gateways popping up all over the world. Outside of the scout's control and influence. Outside of the government's oversight. Yes, this game had just gotten a lot more interesting.

PLANETARY DISRUPTION

Odd creatures are popping up all over the earth. From their refuge in the Nevada desert, Amy, Reven and a group of other believers don't think it's a good thing. They start to investigate the anomalies when they receive a cryptic message: *Gateways*.

Soon enough they realize the truth; the battle on the Tark home world has set off a chain of catastrophic events, not just on earth but throughout the universe. It's up to Amy and Reven to stop it if balance is to be returned. Events that Colonel Holloway wants to use to his advantage.

Amy, Reven and the others are on a race against time and Operation Whisper. Along the way they'll meet old friends, new friends, and understand just how much you can lose in the search for the truth.

ABOUT THE AUTHOR

E.R. Cook grew up in Iowa where she spent her days reading and exploring the countryside. As a young child she developed a life-long love affair with books, mostly fantasy and science fiction. In elementary school, she wrote and illustrated her first fiction book about bugs and how they saw the world. This foray into writing sparked a life-long dream to publish her own works and become a writer.

When she's not writing she's having fun with her boyfriend riding trials motorcycles. She also loves riding horses and exploring her creative outlets of painting and pottery.

9 798993 633602